W9-CXE-011

The Best of MASQUES

"A unique collection . . . not your usual run-of-the-mill anthology."
—*Fantasy Mongers*

"Few true fans of the genre will pass up the chance to purchase these new works . . ."
—*Fantasy Review*

STEPHEN KING'S *POPSY* . . .

"An effective tale . . . told in King's cleanest, most engaging manner."
—*Publishers Weekly*

ROBERT R. McCAMMON'S *NIGHTCRAWLERS* . . .

Nominated for a World Fantasy Award—and adapted for an episode of *The Twilight Zone*

"Spellbinding . . . one of the most gripping post-combat war tales ever!"
—*Chicago Star*

"A beautifully charactered moment of shared, personal horror."
—*Fantasy Review*

"Excellent . . . A new meaning is given to the word 'terror!'"
—*Fantasy Mongers*

F. PAUL WILSON'S *SOFT* . . .

"Vivid and viscerally wrenching!"
—*Publishers Weekly*

"One of the best short stories to appear in 1984!"
—*Fantasy Mongers*

RICHARD CHRISTIAN MATHESON'S
THIRD WIND . . .

"Powerful . . . finely crafted!"
—*Chicago Star*

RAY BRADBURY'S
LONG AFTER ECCLESIASTES . . .

"A fine literary contribution."
—*Chicago Star*

AND MANY OTHERS!

THE BEST OF MASQUES

Edited by J.N. Williamson

BERKLEY BOOKS, NEW YORK

All of the stories in this compilation have been previously published in MASQUES or MASQUES II.

THE BEST OF MASQUES

A Berkley Book/published by arrangement with Maclay & Associates, Inc., Baltimore, originators of the Masques series.

PRINTING HISTORY
Berkley edition/June 1988

All rights reserved.
Copyright © 1988 by Maclay & Associates, Inc.
"Introduction" and "Behind the *Masques*" author bios copyright © 1988 by J. N. Williamson.
"Nightcrawlers" copyright © 1984 by Robert R. McCammon.
"Buried Talents" copyright © 1987 by Richard Matheson.
"Soft" copyright © 1984 by F. Paul Wilson.
"Second Sight" copyright © 1987 by Ramsey Campbell.
"Everybody Needs a Little Love" copyright © 1984 by Robert Bloch.
"The Yard" copyright © 1987 by William F. Nolan.
"The Substitute" copyright © 1984 by Gahan Wilson.
"Maurice and Mog" copyright © 1987 by James Herbert.
"Angel's Exchange" copyright © 1984 by Jessica Amanda Salmonson.
"Hidey Hole" copyright © 1987 by Steve Rasnic Tem.
"Long After Ecclesiastes" copyright © 1984 by Ray Bradbury.
"The Night Is Freezing Fast" copyright © 1987 by Thomas F. Monteleone.
"The Old Men Know" copyright © 1984 by Charles L. Grant.
"Splatter" copyright © 1987 by Douglas E. Winter.
"Czadek" copyright © 1984 by Ray Russell.
"Wordsong," copyright © 1987 by J. N. Williamson.
"Down by the Sea Near the Great Big Rock" copyright © 1984 by Joe R. Lansdale.
"Outsteppin' Fetchit" copyright © 1987 by Charles R. Saunders.
"Somebody Like You" copyright © 1984 by Dennis Etchison.
"Third Wind" copyright © 1984 by Richard Christian Matheson.
"The Boy Who Came Back from the Dead" copyright © 1987 by Alan Rodgers.
"Popsy" copyright © 1987 by Stephen King.

This book may not be reproduced in whole or in part, by mimeograph or any other means, without permission. For information address: The Berkley Publishing Group, 200 Madison Avenue, New York, N.Y. 10016

ISBN: 0-425-10693-4

A BERKLEY BOOK ® TM 757,375
Berkley Books are published by The Berkley Publishing Group, 200 Madison Avenue, New York, N.Y. 10016.
The name "BERKLEY" and the "B" logo are trademarks belonging to Berkley Publishing Corporation.

PRINTED IN THE UNITED STATES OF AMERICA

10 9 8 7 6 5 4 3 2 1

Acknowledgments

J. N. Williamson

This list constitutes the names of most of those people without whose cooperation and friendship, imagination, ministration or concurrence, this book wouldn't exist. It must begin with John and Joyce Maclay; Mary, my wife; Ginjer Buchanan of Berkley Books; Michael Congdon; Ray Bradbury and the late Charles Beaumont, for inspiration; and the late Milton L. Hillman, for conjuring the title. It continues, alphabetically, with Paul Dale and Gretta Anderson, *2AM*; Mike Ashley, British Fantasy Society; Balrog 1985 Awards Committee; James H. Bready, Baltimore *Sun*; Francis D. Burke; Mort Castle; Don Congdon; Delores J. Everts; Janet Fox, *Scavenger's Newsletter*; W. Paul Ganley, *Weirdbook*; William Grabowski, *The Horror Show*; Dennis Hamilton; Stacy Hosler; James Kisner; David Knoles; Dean R. Koontz; Allen Koszowski; Stephanie Leonard, *Castle Rock*; *Locus*; Uwe Luserke; David Maclay; John B. Maclay III; Kay McCauley; Kirby McCauley; Ardath Mayhar; Midwest Literary Agency; Harry O. Morris; Stanley Mossman; Nancy Parsegian; Harold Lee Prosser; *Publishers Weekly*; Ray Puechner; James Rooke; Stuart David Schiff, *Whispers*; *Science Fiction Chronicle*; David B. Silva; Eric Slaughter, Waldenbooks; Peter Straub; David W. Taylor, Moravian College; Robert and Phyllis Weinberg; Stan and Iris Wiater, *Fangoria*; Douglas E. Winter; Gene Wolfe; Ron Wolfe; and World Fantasy Convention 1985 Awards Committee.

Contents

The Best of MASQUES: Introduction

J. N. Williamson

A *masque* (if you were wondering) was a drama of horror and revenge enacted during the sixteenth and seventeenth centuries, and it was probably such a production Edgar Allan Poe had in mind when, in 1842, he published "Masque of the Red Death." According to my encyclopedia, playwright Ben (No *H*) Jonson created the first masques with "controlled style" and a "sure sense of structure"—obvious traits in the stories awaiting you now.

*"Blood was its Avatar and its seal—the redness and the horror of blood."**

The best clue to the use of "masques" as a motivational title involves the way old Ben introduced his ideas to admirers at the Devil Tavern. Jonson's tales of terror were chosen and originally published in keeping with the convictions expressed by the late Charles Beaumont, whose yarns were among the finest dramatized by the first "Twilight Zone" television program.

Beaumont wrote in his afterword to the anthology *The Fiend in You* (Ballantine, 1962) that people base nations upon "powers beyond the understanding" of any of us; powers of

*This quote and all italicized quotations in this introduction are taken from "The Masque of the Red Death" by Edgar Allan Poe.

the unknown, supernatural, darkest evil. The common editorial thread running through the stories of *The Best of MASQUES* is therefore Beaumont's belief that "not all things in this world are of this world."

" . . . The musicians looked at each other and smiled as if at their own nervousness and folly . . . "

And sometimes these "things" are frightening entities. Sometimes they are wonderful—in the true sense of that word, filled with wonder—and sometimes they are wise or insightful. At other times they are weird . . . moving . . . hilarious and zany . . . or even precognitive as they illuminate the future in a liberated fashion arguably too free for the constraints of most science fiction and all mainstream fiction.

("There are some who would have thought him mad. His followers felt that he was not.")

Thinking about this book's title, I glanced into my thesaurus under "best" and was promptly referred—a thesaurus is not a dictionary, remember—to the words "good" and "perfect." From Roget's vantage point, the former implies "virtue" and "beneficence," the latter alludes to "paragon, model, and masterpiece." Let me tell you, it took awhile to realize what the anthological gods were up to, but I think I've figured it out. One thing only can you rely upon when you buy anything with "best" in the title: it won't contain "all of" whatever it proves to be! Just the hardcover anthologies from which these fictions were selected by the present publisher represent the *all* of *Masques.*

So what this title suggests, I believe, is twofold: the beneficence of those wordworkers who aren't present, without in the least doubting the virtues of those who are, and the sheer genius of the authors whose model masterpieces of horror and the supernatural you find ahead of you, without in the slightest disparaging the paragons of originality who are not included.

"There were much glare and glitter and piquancy and phantasm . . . There were much of the beautiful, much of the wanton, much of the bizarre, something of the terrible, and not a little of that which might have excited disgust."

The authors of (among many other extraordinary works) *The Martian Chronicles, The Shining, Psycho, Logan's Run, The*

Keep, Hell House, The Fog, Usher's Passing, Sardonicus, Excavation, Imaro, and *The Doll Who Ate His Mother* are part of the assembled company. At least three of the never-before-in-paperback tales you're about to read could be considered mainstream fiction and another six science fiction. When I made the effort to achieve further categorization, I found there were six stories of inexplicable weirdness; five each of overtly horrific, psychological, and occult or fantasy fiction; four each of humor or comics style, techno-horror and ghost story/supernatural yarns. The fact that this brings the total to over forty stories when there are only twenty-two contributions to *The Best of MASQUES* serves to stress the element of fantasy and to underscore the unequaled variety within that genre generally known, simply, as "horror!"

("In truth the masquerade license of the night was nearly unlimited . . .")

Prepare yourself now for suspense and wonder . . . for shocking and strange and illuminating ideas you may never have encountered before . . . for things of this world and things that are not (praise God). I sense your smile, your nervousness, your anticipation of that which is red and piquant, beautiful and wanton. I know you seek the "certain nameless awe" of Poe's dark tale, and the music and drama of the night soul. No one is here who will think you mad.

Let the masque . . . begin.

J. N. Williamson
July 1987

Nightcrawlers

Robert R. McCammon

I

"Hard rain coming down," Cheryl said, and I nodded in agreement.

Through the diner's plate-glass windows, a dense curtain of rain flapped across the Gulf gas pumps and continued across the parking lot. It hit Big Bob's with a force that made the glass rattle like uneasy bones. The red neon sign that said BIG BOB'S! DIESEL FUEL! EATS! sat on top of a high steel pole above the diner so the truckers on the interstate could see it. Out in the night, the red-tinted rain thrashed in torrents across my old pickup truck and Cheryl's baby-blue Volkswagen.

"Well," I said, "I suppose that storm'll either wash some folks in off the interstate or we can just about hang it up." The curtain of rain parted for an instant, and I could see the treetops whipping back and forth in the woods on the other side of Highway 47. Wind whined around the front door like an animal trying to claw its way in. I glanced at the electric clock on the wall behind the counter. Twenty minutes before nine. We usually closed up at ten, but tonight—with tornado warnings in the weather forecast—I was tempted to turn the lock a little early. "Tell you what," I said. "If we're empty at nine, we skedaddle. 'Kay?"

"No argument here," she said. She watched the storm for a

moment longer, then continued putting newly-washed coffee cups, saucers and plates away on the stainless steel shelves.

Lightning flared from west to east like the strike of a burning bullwhip. The diner's lights flickered, then came back to normal. A shudder of thunder seemed to come right up through my shoes. Late March is the beginning of tornado season in south Alabama, and we've had some whoppers spin past here in the last few years. I knew that Alma was at home, and she understood to get into the root cellar right quick if she spotted a twister, like that one we saw in '82 dancing through the woods about two miles from our farm.

"You got any Love-Ins planned this weekend, hippie?" I asked Cheryl, mostly to get my mind off the storm and to rib her, too.

She was in her late-thirties, but I swear that when she grinned she could've passed for a kid. "Wouldn't *you* like to know, redneck?" she answered; she replied the same way to all my digs at her. Cheryl Lovesong—and I *know* that couldn't have been her real name—was a mighty able waitress, and she had hands that were no strangers to hard work. But I didn't care that she wore her long silvery-blond hair in Indian braids with hippie headbands, or came to work in tie-dyed overalls. She was the best waitress who'd ever worked for me, and she got along with everybody just fine—even us rednecks. That's what I am, and proud of it: I drink Rebel Yell whiskey straight, and my favorite songs are about good women gone bad and trains on the long track to nowhere. I keep my wife happy, I've raised my two boys to pray to God and to salute the flag, and if anybody don't like it he can go a few rounds with Big Bob Clayton.

Cheryl would come right out and tell you she used to live in San Francisco in the late 'sixties, and that she went to Love-Ins and peace marches and all that stuff. When I reminded her it was nineteen eighty-four and Ronnie Reagan was president, she'd look at me like I was walking cow-flop. I always figured she'd start thinking straight when all that hippie-dust blew out of her head.

Alma said my tail was going to get burnt if I ever took a shine to Cheryl, but I'm a fifty-five-year-old redneck who stopped sowing his wild seed when he met the woman he married, more than thirty years ago.

Lightning crisscrossed the turbulent sky, followed by a boom of thunder. Cheryl said, "Wow! Look at that light-show!"

"Light-show, my ass," I muttered. The diner was as solid as the Good Book, so I wasn't too worried about the storm. But on a wild night like this, stuck out in the countryside like Big Bob's was, you had a feeling of being a long way off from civilization—though Mobile was only twenty-seven miles south. On a wild night like this, you had a feeling that anything could happen, as quick as a streak of lightning out of the darkness. I picked up a copy of the Mobile *Press-Register* that the last customer—a trucker on his way to Texas—had left on the counter a half-hour before, and I started plowing through the news, most of it bad: those A-rab countries were still squabbling like Hatfields and McCoys in white robes; two men had robbed a Quik-Mart in Mobile and had been killed by the police in a shootout; cops were investigating a massacre at a hotel near Daytona Beach; an infant had been stolen from a maternity ward in Birmingham. The only good things on the front page were stories that said the economy was up and that Reagan swore we'd show the Commies who was boss in El Salvador and Lebanon.

The diner shook under a blast of thunder, and I looked up from the paper as a pair of headlights emerged from the rain into my parking lot.

II

The headlights were attached to an Alabama State Trooper car.

"Half alive, hold the onion, extra brown the buns." Cheryl was already writing on her pad in expectation of the order. I pushed the paper aside and went to the fridge for the hamburger meat.

When the door opened, a windblown spray of rain swept in and stung like buckshot. "Howdy, folks!" Dennis Wells peeled off his gray rainslicker and hung it on the rack next to the door. Over his Smokey the Bear trooper hat was a protective plastic covering, beaded with raindrops. He took off his hat, exposing the thinning blond hair on his pale scalp, as he approached the counter and sat on his usual stool, right next to the cash register. "Cup of black coffee and a rare—" Cheryl was already sliding the coffee in front of him, and the burger sizzled on the griddle.

"Ya'll are on the ball tonight!" Dennis said; he said the same thing when he came in, which was almost every night. Funny the kind of habits you fall into, without realizing it.

"Kinda wild out there, ain't it?" I asked as I flipped the burger over.

"Lordy, yes! Wind just about flipped my car over three, four miles down the interstate. Thought I was gonna be eatin' a little pavement tonight." Dennis was a husky young man in his early thirties, with thick brows over deep-set, light brown eyes. He had a wife and three kids, and he was fast to flash a wallet-full of their pictures. "Don't reckon I'll be chasin' any speeders tonight, but there'll probably be a load of accidents. Cheryl, you sure look pretty this evenin'."

"Still the same old me." Cheryl never wore a speck of makeup, though one day she'd come to work with glitter on her cheeks. She had a place a few miles away, and I guessed she was farming that funny weed up there. "Any trucks moving?"

"Seen a few, but not many. Truckers ain't fools. Gonna get worse before it gets better, the radio says." He sipped at his coffee and grimaced. "Lordy, that's strong enough to jump out of the cup and dance a jig, darlin'!"

I fixed the burger the way Dennis liked it, put it on a platter with some fries and served it. "Bobby, how's the wife treatin' you?" he asked.

"No complaints."

"Good to hear. I'll tell you, a fine woman is worth her weight in gold. Hey, Cheryl! How'd you like a handsome young man for a husband?"

Cheryl smiled, knowing what was coming. "The man I'm looking for hasn't been made yet."

"Yeah, but you ain't met *Cecil* yet, either! He asks me about you every time I see him, and I keep tellin' him I'm doin' everything I can to get you two together." Cecil was Dennis's brother-in-law and owned a Chevy dealership in Bay Minette. Dennis had been ribbing Cheryl about going on a date with Cecil for the past four months. "You'd like him," Dennis promised. "He's got a lot of my qualities."

"Well, that's different. In that case, I'm *certain* I don't want to meet him."

Dennis winced. "Oh, you're a cruel woman! That's what

smokin' banana peels does to you—turns you mean. Anybody readin' this rag?" He reached over for the newspaper.

"Waitin' here just for you," I said. Thunder rumbled, closer to the diner. The lights flickered briefly once . . . then again before they returned to normal. Cheryl busied herself by fixing a fresh pot of coffee, and I watched the rain whipping against the windows. When the lightning flashed, I could see the trees swaying so hard they looked about to snap.

Dennis read and ate his hamburger. "Boy," he said after a few minutes, "the world's in some shape, huh? Those A-rab pig-stickers are itchin' for war. Mobile metro boys had a little gunplay last night. Good for them." He paused and frowned, then tapped the paper with one thick finger. "This I can't figure."

"What's that?"

"Thing in Florida couple of nights ago. Six people killed at the Pines Haven Motor Inn, near Daytona Beach. Motel was set off in the woods. Only a couple of cinderblock houses in the area, and nobody heard any gunshots. Says here one old man saw what he thought was a bright star falling over the motel, and that was it. Funny, huh?"

"A UFO," Cheryl offered. "Maybe he saw a UFO."

"Yeah, and I'm a little green man from Mars," Dennis scoffed. "I'm serious. This is weird. The motel was so blown full of holes it looked like a war had been going on. Everybody was dead—even a dog and a canary that belonged to the manager. The cars out in front of the rooms were blasted to pieces. The sound of one of them explodin' was what woke up the people in those houses, I reckon." He skimmed the story again. "Two bodies were out in the parkin' lot, one was holed up in a bathroom, one had crawled under a bed, and two had dragged every piece of furniture in the room over to block the bed. Didn't seem to help 'em any, though."

I grunted. "Guess not."

"No motive, no witnesses. You better believe those Florida cops are shakin' the bushes for some kind of dangerous maniac—or maybe more than one, it says here." He shoved the paper away and patted the service revolver holstered at his hip. "If I ever got hold of him—or them—he'd find out not to mess with a 'Bama trooper." He glanced quickly over at Cheryl and smiled mischievously. "Probably some crazy hippie who'd been smokin' his tennis shoes."

"Don't knock it," she said sweetly, "until you've tried it." She looked past him, out the window into the storm. "Car's pullin' in, Bobby."

Headlights glared briefly off the wet windows. It was a station wagon with wood-grained panels on the sides; it veered around the gas pumps and parked next to Dennis's trooper car. On the front bumper was a personalized license plate that said: *Ray & Lindy*. The headlights died, and all the doors opened at once. Out of the wagon came a whole family: a man and a woman, a little girl and boy about eight or nine. Dennis got up and opened the diner door as they hurried inside from the rain.

All of them had gotten pretty well soaked between the station wagon and the diner, and they wore the dazed expressions of people who'd been on the road a long time. The man wore glasses and had curly gray hair, the woman was slim and dark haired and pretty. The kids were sleepy-eyed. All of them were well-dressed, the man in a yellow sweater with one of those alligators on the chest. They had vacation tans, and I figured they were tourists heading north from the beach after spring break.

"Come on in and take a seat," I said.

"Thank you," the man said. They squeezed into one of the booths near the windows. "We saw your sign from the interstate."

"Bad night to be on the highway," Dennis told them. "Tornado warnings are out all over the place."

"We heard it on the radio," the woman—Lindy, if the license was right—said. "We're on our way to Birmingham, and we thought we could drive right through the storm. We should've stopped at that Holiday Inn we passed about fifteen miles ago."

"That would've been smart," Dennis agreed. "No sense in pushin' your luck." He returned to his stool.

The new arrivals ordered hamburgers, fries and Cokes. Cheryl and I went to work. Lightning made the diner's lights flicker again, and the sound of thunder caused the kids to jump. When the food was ready and Cheryl served them, Dennis said, "Tell you what. You folks finish your dinners and I'll escort you back to the Holiday Inn. Then you can head out in the morning. How about that?"

"Fine," Ray said gratefully. "I don't think we could've

gotten very much further, anyway." He turned his attention to his food.

"Well," Cheryl said quietly, standing beside me, "I don't guess we get home early, do we?"

"I guess not. Sorry."

She shrugged. "Goes with the job, right? Anyway, I can think of worse places to be stuck."

I figured that Alma might be worried about me, so I went over to the payphone to call her. I dropped a quarter in—and the dial tone sounded like a cat being stepped on. I hung up and tried again. The cat-scream continued. "Damn!" I muttered. "Lines must be screwed up."

"Ought to get yourself a place closer to town, Bobby," Dennis said. "Never could figure out why you wanted a joint in the sticks. At least you'd get better phone service and good lights if you were nearer to Mo—"

He was interrupted by the sound of wet and shrieking brakes, and he swivelled around on his stool.

I looked up as a car hurtled into the parking lot, the tires swerving, throwing up plumes of water. For a few seconds I thought it was going to keep coming, right through the window into the diner—but then the brakes caught and the car almost grazed the side of my pickup as it jerked to a stop. In the neon's red glow I could tell it was a beat-up old Ford Fairlane, either gray or a dingy beige. Steam was rising off the crumpled hood. The headlights stayed on for perhaps a minute before they winked off. A figure got out of the car and walked slowly—with a limp—toward the diner.

We watched the figure approach. Dennis's body looked like a coiled spring, ready to be triggered. "We got us a live one, Bobby boy," he said.

The door opened, and in a stinging gust of wind and rain a man who looked like walking death stepped into my diner.

III

He was so wet he might well have been driving with his windows down. He was a skinny guy, maybe weighed all of a hundred and twenty pounds, even soaking wet. His unruly dark hair was plastered to his head, and he had gone a week or more without a shave. In his gaunt, pallid face his eyes were startlingly blue; his gaze flicked around the diner, lingered for a few seconds on Dennis. Then he limped on down to the far end of the counter and took a seat. He wiped the rain out of his eyes as Cheryl took a menu to him.

Dennis stared at the man. When he spoke, his voice bristled with authority. "Hey, fella." The man didn't look up from the menu. "Hey, I'm talking to *you*."

The man pushed the menu away and pulled a damp packet of Kools out of the breast pocket of his patched Army fatigue jacket. "I can hear you," he said; his voice was deep and husky, and didn't go with his less-than-robust physical appearance.

"Drivin' kinda fast in this weather, don't you think?"

The man flicked a cigarette lighter a few times before he got a flame, then he lit one of his smokes and inhaled deeply. "Yeah," he replied. "I was. Sorry. I saw the sign, and I was in a hurry to get here. Miss? I'd just like a cup of coffee, please. Hot and *real* strong, okay?"

Cheryl nodded and turned away from him, almost bumping into me as I strolled down behind the counter to check him out.

"That kind of hurry'll get you killed," Dennis cautioned.

"Right. Sorry." He shivered and pushed the tangled hair back from his forehead with one hand. Up close, I could see deep cracks around his mouth and the corners of his eyes and I figured him to be in his late thirties or early forties. His wrists were as thin as a woman's; he looked like he hadn't eaten a good meal for more than a month. He stared at his hands through bloodshot eyes. Probably on drugs, I thought. The fella gave me the creeps. Then he looked at me with those eyes—so pale blue they were almost white—and I felt like I'd been nailed to the floor. "Something wrong?" he asked—not rudely, just curiously.

"Nope." I shook my head. Cheryl gave him his coffee and then went over to give Ray and Lindy their check. The man didn't use either cream or sugar. The coffee was steaming, but he drank half of it down like mother's milk. "That's good," he said. "Keep me awake, won't it?"

"More than likely." Over the breast pocket of his jacket was the faint outline of the name that had been sewn there once. I think it was *Price*, but I could've been wrong.

"That's what I want. To stay awake, as long as I can." He finished the coffee. "Can I have another cup, please?"

I poured it for him. He drank that one down just as fast, then he rubbed his eyes wearily.

"Been on the road a long time, huh?"

Price nodded. "Day and night. I don't know which is more tired, my mind or my butt." He lifted his gaze to me again. "Have you got anything else to drink? How about beer?"

"No, sorry. Couldn't get a liquor license."

He sighed. "Just as well. It might make me sleepy. But I sure could go for a beer right now. One sip, to clean my mouth out."

He picked up his coffee cup, and I smiled and started to turn away.

But then he wasn't holding a cup. He was holding a Budweiser can, and for an instant I could smell the tang of a newly-popped beer.

The mirage was only there for maybe two seconds. I blinked, and Price was holding a cup again. "Just as well," he said, and put it down.

I glanced over at Cheryl, then at Dennis. Neither one was paying attention. Damn! I thought. I'm too young to be either losin' my eyesight or my senses! "Uh . . ." I said, or some other stupid noise.

"One more cup?" Price asked. "Then I'd better hit the road again."

My hand was shaking as I picked it up, but if Price noticed he didn't say anything.

"Want anything to eat?" Cheryl asked him. "How about a bowl of beef stew?"

He shook his head. "No, thanks. The sooner I get back on the road, the better it'll be."

Suddenly Dennis swivelled toward him, giving him a cold stare that only cops and drill sergeants can muster. "Back on the *road?*" He snorted. "Fella, you ever been in a tornado before? I'm gonna escort those nice people to the Holiday Inn about fifteen miles back. If you're smart, that's where you'll spend the night, too. No use tryin' to—"

"*No.*" Price's voice was rock-steady. "I'll be spending the night behind the wheel."

Dennis's eyes narrowed. "How come you're in such a hurry? Not runnin' from anybody, are you?"

"Nightcrawlers," Cheryl said.

Price turned toward her like he'd been slapped across the face, and I saw what might've been a spark of fear in his eyes.

Cheryl motioned toward the lighter Price had laid on the counter beside the pack of Kools. It was a beat-up silver Zippo, and inscribed across it was *Nightcrawlers* with the symbol of two crossed rifles beneath it. "Sorry," she said. "I just noticed that, and I wondered what it was."

Price put the lighter away. "I was in 'Nam," he told her. "Everybody in my unit got one."

"Hey." There was suddenly new respect in Dennis's voice. "You a *vet*?"

Price paused so long I didn't think he was going to answer. In the quiet, I heard the little girl tell her mother that the fries were "ucky." Price said, "Yes."

"How about that! Hey, I wanted to go myself, but I got a high number and things were windin' down about that time, anyway. Did you see any action?"

A faint, bitter smile passed over Price's mouth. "Too much."

"What? Infantry? Marines? Rangers?"

Price picked up his third cup of coffee, swallowed some and put it down. He closed his eyes for a few seconds, and when they opened they were vacant and fixed on nothing. "Nightcrawlers," he said quietly. "Special unit. Deployed to recon Charlie positions in questionable villages." He said it like he was reciting from a manual. "We did a lot of crawling through rice paddies and jungles in the dark."

"Bet you laid a few of them Vietcong out, didn't you?" Dennis got up and came over to sit a few places away from the man. "Man, I was behind you guys all the way. I wanted you to stay in there and fight it out!"

Price was silent. Thunder echoed over the diner. The lights weakened for a few seconds; when they came back on, they seemed to have lost some of their wattage. The place was dimmer than before. Price's head slowly turned toward Dennis, with the inexorable motion of a machine. I was thankful I didn't have to take the full force of Price's dead blue eyes, and I saw Dennis wince. "I *should've* stayed," he said. "I should be there right now, buried in the mud of a rice paddy with the eight other men in my patrol."

"Oh," Dennis blinked. "Sorry. I didn't mean to—"

"I came home," Price continued calmly, "by stepping on

the bodies of my friends. Do you want to know what that's like, Mr. Trooper?"

"The war's over," I told him. "No need to bring it back."

Price smiled grimly, but his gaze remained fixed on Dennis. "Some say it's over. I say it came back with the men who were there. Like me. *Especially* like me." Price paused. The wind howled around the door, and the lightning illuminated for an instant the thrashing woods across the highway. "The mud was up to our knees, Mr. Trooper," he said. "We were moving across a rice paddy in the dark, being real careful not to step on the bamboo stakes we figured were planted there. Then the first shots started: *pop pop pop*—like firecrackers going off. One of the Nightcrawlers fired off a flare, and we saw the Cong ringing us. We'd walked right into hell, Mr. Trooper. Some-body shouted, 'Charlie's in the light!' and we started firing, trying to punch a hole through them. But they were every-where. As soon as one went down, three more took his place. Grenades were going off, and more flares, and people were screaming as they got hit. I took a bullet in the thigh and another through the hand. I lost my rifle, and somebody fell on top of me with half his head missing."

"Uh . . . listen," I said. "You don't have to—"

"I *want* to, friend." He glanced quickly at me, then back to Dennis. I think I cringed when his gaze pierced me. "I want to tell it all. They were fighting and screaming and dying all around me, and I felt the bullets tug at my clothes as they passed through. I know I was screaming, too, but what was coming out of my mouth sounded bestial. I ran. The only way I could save my own life was to step on their bodies and drive them down into the mud. I heard some of them choke and blubber as I put my boot on their faces. I knew all those guys like brothers . . . but at that moment they were only pieces of meat. I ran. A gunship chopper came over the paddy and laid down some fire, and that's how I got out. Alone." He bent his face closer toward the other man's. "And you'd better believe I'm in that rice paddy in 'Nam every time I close my eyes. You'd better believe the men I left back there don't rest easy. So you keep your opinions about 'Nam and being 'behind you guys' to yourself, Mr. Trooper. I don't want to hear that bullshit. Got it?"

Dennis sat very still. He wasn't used to being talked to like that, not even from a 'Nam vet, and I saw the shadow of anger pass over his face.

Price's hands were trembling as he brought a little bottle out of his jeans pocket. He shook two blue-and-orange capsules out onto the counter, took them both with a swallow of coffee and then recapped the bottle and put it away. The flesh of his face looked almost ashen in the dim light.

"I know you boys had a rough time," Dennis said, "but that's no call to show disrespect to the law."

"The law," Price repeated. "Yeah. Right. Bull*shit*."

"There are women and children present," I reminded him. "Watch your language."

Price rose from his seat. He looked like a skeleton with just a little extra skin on the bones. "Mister, I haven't slept for more than thirty-six hours. My nerves are shot. I don't mean to cause trouble, but when some fool says he *understands*, I feel like kicking his teeth down his throat—because no one who wasn't there can pretend to understand." He glanced at Ray, Lindy, and the kids. "Sorry, folks. Don't mean to disturb you. Friend, how much do I owe?" He started digging for his wallet.

Dennis slid slowly from his seat and stood with his hands on his hips. "Hold it." He used his trooper's voice again. "If you think I'm lettin' you walk out of here high on pills and needin' sleep, you're crazy. I don't want to be scrapin' you off the highway."

Price paid him no attention. He took a couple of dollars from his wallet and put them on the counter. I didn't touch them. "Those pills will help keep me awake," Price said finally. "Once I get on the road, I'll be fine."

"Fella, I wouldn't let you go if it was high noon and not a cloud in the sky. I sure as hell don't want to clean up after the accident you're gonna have. Now why don't you come along to the Holiday Inn and—"

Price laughed grimly. "Mister Trooper, the last place you want me staying is at a motel." He cocked his head to one side. "I was in a motel in Florida a couple of nights ago, and I think I left my room a little untidy. Step aside and let me pass."

"A motel in Florida?" Dennis nervously licked his lower lip. "What the hell you talkin' about?"

"Nightmares and reality, Mr. Trooper. The point where they cross. A couple of nights ago, they crossed at a motel. I wasn't going to let myself sleep. I was just going to rest for a little

while, but I didn't know they'd come so *fast*." A mocking
smile played at the edges of his mouth, but his eyes were
tortured. "You don't want me staying at that Holiday Inn, Mr.
Trooper. You really don't. Now step aside."

I saw Dennis's hand settled on the butt of his revolver. His
fingers unsnapped the fold of leather that secured the gun in the
holster. I stared at him numbly. My God, I thought. What's
goin' on? My heart had started pounding so hard I was sure
everybody could hear it. Ray and Lindy were watching, and
Cheryl was backing away behind the counter.

Price and Dennis faced each other for a moment, as the rain
whipped against the windows and thunder boomed like
shellfire. Then Price sighed, as if resigning himself to
something. He said, "I think I want a t-bone steak. Extra-rare.
How 'bout it?" He looked at me.

"A steak?" My voice was shaking. "We don't have a t-
bone—"

Price's gaze shifted to the counter right in front of me. I
heard a sizzle. The aroma of cooking meat drifted up to me.

"Oh . . . wow," Cheryl whispered.

A large t-bone steak lay on the countertop, pink and oozing
blood. You could've fanned a menu in my face and I would've
keeled over. Wisps of smoke were rising from the steak.

The steak began to fade, until it was only an outline on the
counter. The lines of oozing blood vanished. After the mirage
was gone, I could still smell the meat—and that's how I knew I
wasn't crazy.

Dennis's mouth hung open. Ray had stood up from the booth
to look, and his wife's face was the color of spoiled milk. The
whole world seemed to be balanced on a point of silence—until
the wail of the wind jarred me back to my senses.

"I'm getting good at it," Price said softly. "I'm getting very,
very good. Didn't start happening to me until about a year ago.
I've found four other 'Nam vets who can do the same thing.
What's in your head comes true—as simple as that. Of course,
the images only last for a few seconds—as long as I'm awake.
I mean, I've found out that those other men were drenched by a
chemical spray we call Howdy Doody—because it made you
stiffen up and jerk like you were hanging on strings. I got hit
with it near Khe Sahn. That shit almost suffocated me. It fell
like black tar, and it burned the land down to a paved parking
lot." He stared at Dennis. "You don't want me around here,

Mr. Trooper. Not with the body count I've still got in *my* head."

"You . . . were at . . . that motel, near Daytona Beach?"

Price closed his eyes. A vein had begun beating at his right temple, royal blue against the pallor of his flesh. "Oh Jesus," he whispered. "I fell asleep, and I couldn't wake myself up. I was having the nightmare. The same one. I was locked in it, and I was trying to scream myself awake." He shuddered, and two tears ran slowly down his cheeks. "*Oh*," he said, and flinched as if remembering something horrible. "They . . . they were coming through the door when I woke up. Tearing the door right off its hinges. I woke up . . . just as one of them was pointing his rifle at me. And I saw his face. I saw his muddy, misshapen face." His eyes suddenly jerked open. "I didn't know they'd come so fast."

"Who?" I asked him. "*Who* came so fast?"

"The Nightcrawlers," Price said, his face void of expression, masklike. "Dear God . . . maybe if I'd stayed asleep a second more. But I ran again, and I left those people dead in that motel."

"You're gonna come with me." Dennis started pulling his gun from the holster. Price's head snapped toward him. "I don't know what kinda fool game you're—"

He stopped, staring at the gun he held.

It wasn't a gun anymore. It was an oozing mass of hot rubber. Dennis cried out and slung the thing from his hand. The molten mess hit the floor with a pulpy *splat*.

"I'm leaving now." Price's voice was calm. "Thank you for the coffee." He walked past Dennis, toward the door.

Dennis grasped a bottle of ketchup from the counter. Cheryl cried out, "*Don't!*" but it was too late. Dennis was already swinging the bottle. It hit the back of Price's skull and burst open, spewing ketchup everywhere. Price staggered forward, his knees buckling. When he went down, his skull hit the floor with a noise like a watermelon being dropped. His body began jerking involuntarily.

"Got him!" Dennis shouted triumphantly. "Got that crazy bastard, didn't I?"

Lindy was holding the little girl in her arms. The boy craned his neck to see. Ray said nervously, "You didn't kill him, did you?"

"He's not dead," I told him. I looked over at the gun; it was solid again. Dennis scooped it up and aimed it at Price, whose body continued to jerk. Just like Howdy Doody, I thought. Then Price stopped moving. "He's dead!" Cheryl's voice was near frantic. "Oh God, you killed him, Dennis!"

Dennis prodded the body with the toe of his boot, then bent down. "Naw. His eyes are movin' back and forth behind the lids." Dennis touched his wrist to check the pulse, then abruptly pulled his own hand away. "Jesus Christ! He's as cold as a meat-locker!" He took Price's pulse and whistled. "Goin' like a racehorse at the Derby."

I touched the place on the counter where the mirage-steak had been. My fingers came away slightly greasy, and I could smell the cooked meat on them. At that instant, Price twitched. Dennis scuttled away from him like a crab. Price made a gasping, choking noise.

"What'd he say?" Cheryl asked. "He said something!"

"No he didn't." Dennis stuck him in the ribs with his pistol. "Come on. Get up."

"Get him out of here," I said. "I don't want him—"

Cheryl shushed me. "Listen. Can you hear that?"

I heard only the roar and crash of the storm.

"Don't you *hear* it?" she asked me. Her eyes were getting scared and glassy.

"Yes!" Ray said. "Yes! Listen!"

Then I did hear something, over the noise of the keening wind. It was a distant *chuk-chuk-chuk,* steadily growing louder and closer. The wind covered the noise for a minute, then it came back: CHUK-CHUK-CHUK, almost overhead.

"It's a helicopter!" Ray peered through the window. "Somebody's got a helicopter out there!"

"Ain't nobody can fly a chopper in a storm!" Dennis told him. The noise of the rotors swelled and faded, swelled and faded . . . and stopped.

On the floor, Price shivered and began to contort into a fetal position. His mouth opened, his face twisted in what appeared to be agony.

Thunder spoke. A red fireball rose up from the woods across the road and hung lazily in the sky for a few seconds before it descended toward the diner. As it fell, the fireball exploded soundlessly into a white, glaring eye of light that almost blinded me.

Price said something in a garbled, panicked voice. His eyes were tightly closed, and he had squeezed up with his arms around his knees.

Dennis rose to his feet; he squinted as the eye of light fell toward the parking lot and winked out in a puddle of water. Another fireball floated up from the woods, and again blossomed into painful glare.

Dennis turned toward me. "I heard him." His voice was raspy. "He said . . . 'Charlie's in the light.'"

As the second flare fell to the ground and illuminated the parking lot, I thought I saw figures crossing the road. They walked stiff-legged, in an eerie cadence. The flare went out.

"Wake him up," I heard myself whisper. "Dennis . . . dear God . . . *wake him up*."

IV

Dennis stared stupidly at me, and I started to jump across the counter to get to Price myself.

A gout of flame leaped in the parking lot. Sparks marched across the concrete. I shouted, "Get down!" and twisted around to push Cheryl back behind the shelter of the counter.

"What the *hell*—" Dennis said.

He didn't finish. There was a metallic thumping of bullets hitting the gas pumps and the cars. I knew if that gas blew we were all dead. My truck shuddered with the impact of slugs, and I saw the whole thing explode as I ducked behind the counter. Then the windows blew inward with a Godawful crash, and the diner was full of flying glass, swirling wind and sheets of rain. I heard Lindy scream, and both the kids were crying and I think I was shouting something myself.

The lights had gone out, and the only illumination was the reflection of red neon off the concrete and the glow of the fluorescents over the gas pumps. Bullets whacked into the wall, and crockery shattered as if it had been hit with a hammer. Napkins and sugar packets were flying everywhere.

Cheryl was holding onto me as if her fingers were nails sunk to my bones. Her eyes were wide and dazed, and she kept trying to speak. Her mouth was working, but nothing came out.

There was another explosion as one of the other cars blew. The whole place shook, and I almost puked with fear.

Another hail of bullets hit the wall. They were tracers, and they jumped and ricocheted like white-hot cigarette butts. One of them sang off the edge of a shelf and fell to the floor about three feet away from me. The glowing slug began to fade, like the beer can and the mirage-steak. I put my hand out to find it, but all I felt was splinters of glass and crockery. A phantom bullet, I thought. Real enough to cause damage and death— and then gone.

You don't want me around here, Mr. Trooper, Price had warned. *Not with the body count I've got in my head.*

The firing stopped. I got free of Cheryl and said, "You stay right *here.*" Then I looked up over the counter and saw my truck and the station-wagon on fire, the flames being whipped by the wind. Rain slapped me across the face as it swept in where the window glass used to be. I saw Price lying still huddled on the floor, with pieces of glass all around him. His hands were contorted, his eyes still closed. The pool of ketchup around his head made him look like his skull had been split open. He was peering into Hell and I averted my eyes before I lost my own mind.

Ray and Lindy and the two children had huddled under the table of their booth. The woman was sobbing brokenly. I looked at Dennis, lying a few feet from Price: he was sprawled on his face, and there were four holes punched through his back. It was not ketchup that ran in rivulets around Dennis's body. His right arm was outflung, and the fingers twitched around the gun he gripped.

Another flare sailed up from the woods like a Fourth-of-July sparkler.

When the light brightened, I saw them: at least five figures, maybe more. They were crouched over, coming across the parking lot—but slowly, the speed of nightmares. Their clothes flapped and hung around them, and the flare's light glanced off their helmets. They were carrying weapons—rifles, I guessed. I couldn't see their faces, and that was for the best.

On the floor, Price moaned. I heard him say "light . . . in the light . . ."

The flare hung right over the diner. And then I knew what was going on. *We* were in the light. We were all caught in Price's nightmare, and the Nightcrawlers that Price had left in the mud were fighting the battle again—the same way it had been fought at the Pines Haven Motor Inn. The Nightcrawlers had come back to life, powered by Price's guilt and whatever that Howdy Doody shit had done to him.

And we were in the light, where Charlie had been out in that rice paddy.

There was a noise like castanets clicking. Dots of fire arced through the broken windows and thudded into the counter. The stools squealed as they were hit and spun. The cash register rang and the drawer popped open, and then the entire register blew apart and bills and coins scattered. I ducked my head, but a wasp of fire—I don't know what, a bit of metal or glass maybe—sliced my left cheek open from ear to upper lip. I fell to the floor behind the counter with blood running down my face.

A blast shook the rest of the cups, saucers, plates and glasses off the shelves. The whole roof buckled inward, throwing loose ceiling tiles, light fixtures and pieces of metal framework.

We were all going to die. I knew it, right then. Those things were going to destroy us. But I thought of the pistol in Dennis's hand, and of Price lying near the door. If we were caught in Price's nightmare and the blow from the ketchup bottle had broken something in his skull, then the only way to stop his dream was to kill him.

I'm no hero. I was about to piss in my pants, but I knew I was the only one who could move. I jumped up and scrambled over the counter, falling beside Dennis and wrenching at that pistol. Even in death, Dennis had a strong grip. Another blast came, along the wall to my right. The heat of it scorched me, and the shockwave skidded me across the floor through glass and rain and blood.

But I had that pistol in my hand.

I heard Ray shout, "Look out!"

In the doorway, silhouetted by flames, was a skeletal thing wearing muddy green rags. It wore a dented-in helmet and carried a corroded, slime-covered rifle. Its face was gaunt and shadowy, the features hidden behind a scum of rice-paddy muck. It began to lift the rifle to fire at me—slowly, slowly . . .

I got the safety off the pistol and fired twice, without aiming. A spark leapt off the helmet as one of the bullets was deflected, but the figure staggered backward and into the conflagration of the station wagon, where it seemed to melt into ooze before it vanished.

More tracers were coming in. Cheryl's Volkswagen shuddered, the tires blowing out almost in unison. The state trooper car was already bullet-riddled and sitting on flats.

Another Nightcrawler, this one without a helmet and with slime covering the skull where the hair had been, rose up beyond the window and fired its rifle. I heard the bullet whine past my ear, and as I took aim I saw its bony finger tightening on the trigger again.

A skillet flew over my head and hit the thing's shoulder, spoiling its aim. For an instant the skillet stuck in the Nightcrawler's body, as if the figure itself was made out of mud. I fired once . . . twice . . . and saw pieces of matter fly from the thing's chest. What might've been a mouth opened in a soundless scream, and the thing slithered out of sight.

I looked around. Cheryl was standing behind the counter, weaving on her feet, her face white with shock. "Get down!" I shouted, and she ducked for cover.

I crawled to Price, shook him hard. His eyes would not open. "Wake up!" I begged him. "Wake up, damn you!" And then I pressed the barrel of the pistol against Price's head. Dear God, I didn't want to kill anybody, but I knew I was going to have to blow the Nightcrawlers right out of his brain. I hesitated—too long.

Something smashed into my left collarbone. I heard the bone snap like a broomstick being broken. The force of the shot slid me back against the counter and jammed me between two bullet-pocked stools. I lost the gun, and there was a roaring in my head that deafened me.

I don't know how long I was out. My left arm felt like dead meat. All the cars in the lot were burning, and there was a hole in the diner's roof that a tractor-trailer truck could've dropped through. Rain was sweeping into my face, and when I wiped my eyes clear I saw them, standing over Price.

There were eight of them. The two I thought I'd killed were back. They trailed weeds, and their boots and ragged clothes were covered in mud. They stood in silence, staring down at their living comrade.

I was too tired to scream. I couldn't even whimper. I just watched.

Price's hands lifted into the air. He reached for the Nightcrawlers, and then his eyes opened. His pupils were dead white, surrounded by scarlet.

"End it," he whispered. "End it . . ."

One of the Nightcrawlers aimed its rifle and fired. Price jerked. Another Nightcrawler fired, and then they were all firing, point-blank, into Price's body. Price thrashed and clutched at his head, but there was no blood; the phantom bullets weren't hitting him.

The Nightcrawlers began to ripple and fade. I saw the flames of the burning cars through their bodies. The figures became transparent, floating in vague outlines. Price had awakened too fast at the Pines Haven Motor Inn, I realized; if he had remained asleep, the creatures of his nightmares would've ended it there, at that Florida motel. They were killing him in front of me—or he was allowing them to end it, and I think that's what he must've wanted for a long, long time.

He shuddered, his mouth releasing a half-moan, half-sigh.

It sounded almost like relief.

I saw his face. His eyes were closed, and I think he must've found peace at last.

V

A trucker hauling lumber from Mobile to Birmingham saw the burning cars. I don't even remember what he looked like.

Ray was cut up by glass, but his wife and the kids were okay. Physically, I mean. Mentally, I couldn't say.

Cheryl went into the hospital for a while. I got a postcard from her with the Golden Gate Bridge on the front. She promised she'd write and let me know how she was doing, but I doubt if I'll ever hear from her. She was the best waitress I ever had, and I wish her luck.

The police asked me a thousand questions, and I told the story the same way every time. I found out later that no bullets or shrapnel were ever dug out of the walls or the cars or Dennis's body—just like in the case of that motel massacre. There was no bullet in me, though my collarbone was snapped clean in two.

Price had died of a massive brain hemorrhage. It looked, the police told me, as if it had exploded in his skull.

I closed the diner. Farm life is fine. Alma understands, and we don't talk about it.

But I never showed the police what I found, and I don't know exactly why not.

I picked up Price's wallet in the mess. Behind a picture of a smiling young woman holding a baby there was a folded piece of paper. On that paper were the names of four men.

Beside one name, Price had written DANGEROUS.

I've found four other 'Nam vets who can do the same thing, Price had said.

I sit up at night a lot, thinking about that and looking at those names. Those men had gotten a dose of that Howdy Doody shit in a foreign place they hadn't wanted to be, fighting a war that turned out to be one of those crossroads of nightmare and reality. I've changed my mind about 'Nam, because I understand now that the worst of the fighting is still going on, in the battlefields of memory.

A Yankee who called himself Tompkins came to my house one May morning and flashed me an ID that said he worked for a veterans' association. He was very soft-spoken and polite, but he had deep-set eyes that were almost black, and he never blinked. He asked me all about Price, seemed real interested in picking my brain of every detail. I told him the police had the story, and I couldn't add any more to it. Then I turned the tables and asked him about Howdy Doody. He smiled in a puzzled kind of way and said he'd never heard of any chemical defoliant called that. No such thing, he said. Like I said, he was very polite.

But I know the shape of a gun tucked into a shoulder-holster. Tompkins was wearing one, under his seersucker coat. I never could find any veterans' association that knew anything about him, either.

Maybe I should give that list of names to the police. Maybe I will. Or maybe I'll try to find those four men myself, and try to make sense out of what's being hidden.

I don't think Price was evil. No. He was just scared, and who can blame a man for running from his own nightmares? I like to believe that, in the end, Price had the courage to face the Nightcrawlers, and in committing suicide he saved our lives.

The newspapers, of course, never got the real story. They called Price a 'Nam vet who'd gone crazy, killed six people in a

Florida motel and then killed a state trooper in a shootout at Big Bob's diner and gas stop.

But I know where Price is buried. They sell little American flags at the five-and-dime in Mobile. I'm alive, and I can spare the change.

And then I've got to find out how much courage *I* have.

Buried Talents

Richard Matheson

A man in a wrinkled, black suit entered the fair grounds. He was tall and lean, his skin the color of drying leather. He wore a faded sport shirt underneath his suit coat, white with yellow stripes. His hair was black and greasy, parted in the middle and brushed back flat on each side. His eyes were pale blue. There was no expression on his face. It was a hundred and two degrees in the sun but he was not perspiring.

He walked to one of the booths and stood there watching people try to toss ping pong balls into dozens of little fish bowls on a table. A fat man wearing a straw hat and waving a bamboo cane in his right hand kept telling everyone how easy it was. "Try your luck!" he told them. "Win a prize! There's nothing to it!" He had an unlit half-smoked cigar between his lips which he shifted from side to side as he spoke.

For awhile, the tall man in the wrinkled, black suit stood watching. Not one person managed to get a ping pong ball into a fish bowl. Some of them tried to throw the balls in. Others tried to bounce them off the table. None of them had any luck.

At the end of seven minutes, the man in the black suit pushed between the people until he was standing by the booth. He took a quarter from his right hand trouser pocket and laid it on the counter. "Yes, sir!" said the fat man. "Try your luck!" He tossed the quarter into a metal box beneath the counter. Reaching down, he picked three grimy ping pong balls from a basket. He clapped them on the counter and the tall man picked them up.

"Toss a ball in the fish bowl!" said the fat man. "Win a prize! There's nothing to it!" Sweat was trickling down his florid face. He took a quarter from a teenage boy and set three ping pong balls in front of him.

The man in the black suit looked at the three ping pong balls on his left palm. He hefted them, his face immobile. The man in the straw hat turned away. He tapped at the fish bowls with his cane. He shifted the stump of cigar in his mouth. "Toss a ball in the fish bowl!" he said. "A prize for everybody! Nothing to it!"

Behind him, a ping pong ball clinked into one of the bowls. He turned and looked at the bowl. He looked at the man in the black suit. "There you are!" he said. "See that? Nothing to it! Easiest game on the fairgrounds!"

The tall man threw another ping pong ball. It arced across the booth and landed in the same bowl. All the other people trying missed.

"Yes, sir!" the fat man said. "A prize for everybody! Nothing to it!" He picked up two quarters and set six ping pong balls before a man and wife.

He turned and saw the third ping pong ball dropping into the fish bowl. It didn't touch the neck of the bowl. It didn't bounce. It landed on the other two balls and lay there.

"See?" the man in the straw hat said, "A prize on his very first turn! Easiest game on the fairgrounds!" Reaching over to a set of wooden shelves, he picked up an ash tray and set it on the counter. "Yes, sir! Nothing to it!" he said. He took a quarter from a man in overalls and set three ping pong balls in front of him.

The man in the black suit pushed away the ash tray. He laid another quarter on the counter. "Three more ping pong balls," he said.

The fat man grinned. "Three more ping pong balls it is!" he said. He reached below the counter, picked up three more balls and set them on the counter in front of the man. "Step right up!" he said. He caught a ping pong ball which someone had bounced off the table. He kept an eye on the tall man while he stooped to retrieve some ping pong balls on the ground.

The man in the black suit raised his right hand, holding one of the ping pong balls. He threw it overhand, his face expressionless. The ball curved through the air and fell into the fish bowl with the other three balls. It didn't bounce.

The man in the straw hat stood with a grunt. He dumped a handful of ping pong balls into the basket underneath the counter. "Try your luck and win a prize!" he said. "Easy as pie!" He set three ping pong balls in front of a boy and took his quarter. His eyes grew narrow as he watched the tall man raise his hand to throw the second ball. "No leaning in," he told the man.

The man in the black suit glanced at him. "I'm not," he said.

The fat man nodded. "Go ahead," he said.

The tall man threw the second ping pong ball. It seemed to float across the booth. It fell through the neck of the bowl and landed on top of the other four balls.

"Wait a second," said the fat man, holding up his hand.

The other people who were throwing stopped. The fat man leaned across the table. Sweat was running down beneath the collar of his long-sleeved shirt. He shifted the soggy cigar in his mouth as he scooped the five balls from the bowl. He straightened up and looked at them. He hooked the bamboo cane over his left forearm and rolled the balls between his palms.

"Okay, folks!" he said. He cleared his throat. "Keep throwing! Win a prize!" He dropped the balls into the basket underneath the counter. Taking another quarter from the man in overalls, he set three ping pong balls in front of him.

The man in the black suit raised his hand and threw the sixth ball. The fat man watched it arc through the air. It fell into the bowl he'd emptied. It didn't roll around inside. It landed on the bottom, bounced once, straight up, then lay motionless.

The fat man grabbed the ash tray, stuck it on its shelf and picked up a fish bowl like the ones on the table. It was filled with pink colored water and had a goldfish fluttering around in it. "There you go!" he said. He turned away and tapped at the empty fish bowls with his cane. "Step right up!" he said. "Toss a ball in the fish bowl! Win a prize! There's nothing to it!"

Turning back, he saw that the man in the wrinkled suit had pushed away the goldfish in the bowl and placed another quarter on the counter. "Three more ping pong balls," he said.

The fat man looked at him. He shifted the damp cigar in his mouth.

"Three more ping pong balls," the tall man said.

The man in the straw hat hesitated. Suddenly, he noticed people looking at him and, without a word, he took the quarter and set three ping pong balls on the counter. He turned around and tapped the fish bowls with his cane. "Step right up and try your luck!" he said. "Easiest game on the fairgrounds!" He removed his straw hat and rubbed the left sleeve of his shirt across his forehead. He was almost bald. The small amount of hair on his head was plastered to his scalp by sweat. He put his straw hat back on and set three ping pong balls in front of a boy. He put the quarter in the metal box underneath the counter.

A number of people were watching the tall man now. When he threw the first of the three ping pong balls into the fish bowl some of them applauded and a small boy cheered. The fat man watched suspiciously. His small eyes shifted as the man in the black suit threw his second ping pong ball into the fish bowl with the other two balls. He scowled and seemed about to speak. The scatter of applause appeared to irritate him.

The man in the wrinkled suit tossed the third ping pong ball. It landed on top of the other three. Several people cheered and all of them clapped.

The fat man's cheeks were redder now. He put the fish bowl with the goldfish back on its shelf. He gestured toward a higher shelf. "What'll it be?" he asked.

The tall man put a quarter on the counter. "Three more ping pong balls," he said. The man in the straw hat stared at him. He chewed on his cigar. A drop of sweat ran down the bridge of his nose.

"Well, give the man his ping pong balls," said one of the men who was watching.

The fat man glanced around. He managed to grin. "All right!" he said in a brisk voice. He picked up three more ping pong balls from the basket and rolled them between his palms.

"Don't give him the bad ones now," someone said in a mocking voice.

"No bad ones!" the fat man said. "They're all the same!" He set the balls on the counter and picked up the quarter. He tossed it into the metal box underneath the counter. The man in the black suit raised his hand.

"Wait a second," the fat man said. He turned and reached across the table. Picking up the fish bowl, he turned it over and dumped the four ping pong balls into the basket. He seemed to hesitate before he put the empty fish bowl back in place.

Nobody else was throwing now. They watched the tall man curiously as he raised his hand and threw the first of his three ping pong balls. It curved through the air and landed in the same fish bowl, dropping straight down through the neck. It bounced once, then was still. The people cheered and applauded. The fat man rubbed his left hand across his eyebrows and flicked the sweat from his fingertips with an angry gesture.

The man in the black suit threw his second ping pong ball. It landed in the same fish bowl.

"*Hold* it," said the fat man.

The tall man looked at him.

"What are you doing?" the fat man asked.

"Throwing ping pong balls," the tall man answered. Everybody laughed. The fat man's face got redder. "I know that!" he said.

"It's done with mirrors," someone said and everybody laughed again.

"*Funny,*" said the fat man. He shifted the wet cigar in his mouth and gestured curtly "Go on," he said.

The tall man in the black suit raised his hand and threw the third ping pong ball. It arced across the booth as though it were being carried by an invisible hand. It landed in the fish bowl on top of the other two balls. Everybody cheered and clapped their hands.

The fat man in the straw hat grabbed a casserole dish and dumped it on the counter. The man in the black suit didn't look at it. He put another quarter down. "Three more ping pong balls," he said.

The fat man turned away from him. "Step right up!" he called. "Toss a ping pong ball—!"

The noise of disapproval everybody made drowned him out. He turned back, bristling. "Four rounds to a customer!" he shouted.

"Where does it say that?" someone asked.

"That's the rule!" the fat man said. He turned his back on the man and tapped the fish bowls with his cane. "Step right up and win a prize!" he said.

"I came here yesterday and played *five* rounds!" a man said loudly.

"That's because you didn't win!" a teenage boy replied. Most of the people laughed and clapped but some of them booed. "Let him play!" a man's voice ordered. Everybody took it up immediately. "Let him play!" they demanded.

The man in the straw hat swallowed nervously. He looked around, a truculent expression on his face. Suddenly, he threw his hands up. "All right!" he said. "Don't get so excited!" He glared at the tall man as he picked up the quarter. Bending over, he grabbed three ping pong balls and slammed them on the counter. He leaned in close to the man and muttered, "If you're pulling something fast, you'd better cut it out. This is an honest game."

The tall man stared at him. His face was blank. His eyes looked very pale in the leathery tan of his face. "What do you mean?" he asked.

"No one can throw that many balls in succession into those bowls," the fat man said.

The man in the black suit looked at him without expression. *"I* can," he said.

The fat man felt a coldness on his body. Stepping back, he watched the tall man throw the ping pong balls. As each of them landed in the same fish bowl, the people cheered and clapped their hands.

The fat man took a set of steak knives from the top prize shelf and set it on the counter. He turned away quickly. "Step right up!" he said. "Toss a ball in the fish bowl! Win a prize!" His voice was trembling.

"He wants to play again," somebody said.

The man in the straw hat turned around. He saw the quarter on the counter in front of the tall man. "No more prizes," he said.

The man in the black suit pointed at the items on top of the wooden shelves—a four-slice electric toaster, a short wave radio, a drill set and a portable typewriter. "What about them?" he asked.

The fat man cleared his throat. "They're only for display," he said. He looked around for help.

"Where does it say *that*?" someone demanded.

"That's what they are, so just take my word for it!" the man in the straw hat said. His face was dripping sweat.

"I'll play for them," the tall man said.

"Now *look!*" The fat man's face was very red. "They're only for display, I said! Now get the hell—!"

He broke off with a wheezing gasp and staggered back against the table, dropping his cane. The faces of the people swam before his eyes. He heard their angry voices as though from a distance. He saw the blurred figure of the man in the black suit turn away and push through the crowd. He straightened up and blinked his eyes. The steak knives were gone.

Almost everybody left the booth. A few of them remained. The fat man tried to ignore their threatening grumbles. He picked a quarter off the counter and set three ping pong balls in front of a boy. "Try your luck," he said. His voice was faint. He tossed the quarter into the metal box underneath the counter. He leaned against a corner post and pressed both hands against his stomach. The cigar fell out of his mouth. "God," he said.

It felt as though he were bleeding inside.

Soft

F. Paul Wilson

I was lying on the floor watching TV and exercising what was left of my legs when the newscaster's jaw collapsed. He was right in the middle of the usual plea for anybody who thought they were immune to come to Rockefeller Center when—*pflumpf!*—the bottom of his face went soft.

I burst out laughing.

"Daddy!" Judy said, shooting me a razor-blade look from her wheelchair.

I shut up.

She was right. Nothing funny about a man's tongue wiggling around in the air snakelike while his lower jaw flopped down in front of his throat like a sack of Jell-O and his bottom teeth jutted at the screen crowns-on, rippling like a line of buoys on a bay. A year ago I would have gagged. But I've changed in ways other than physical since this mess began, and couldn't help feeling good about one of those pretty-boy newsreaders going soft right in front of the camera. I almost wished I had a bigger screen so I could watch twenty-one color inches of the scene. He was barely visible on our five-inch black-and-white.

The room filled with white noise as the screen went blank. Someone must have taken a look at what was going out on the airwaves and pulled the plug. Not that many people were watching anyway.

I flipped the set off to save the batteries. Batteries were as good as gold now. *Better* than gold. Who wanted gold nowadays?

I looked over at Judy and she was crying softly. Tears slid down her cheeks.

"Hey, hon—"

"I can't help it, Daddy. I'm so *scared!*"

"Don't be, Jude. Don't worry. Everything will work out, you'll see. We've got this thing licked, you and me."

"How can you be so sure?"

"Because it hasn't progressed in weeks! It's over for us— we've got immunity."

She glanced down at her legs, then quickly away. "It's already too late for me."

I reached over and patted my dancer on the hand. "Never too late for you, shweetheart," I said in my best Bogart. That got a tiny smile out of her.

We sat there in the silence, each thinking our own thoughts. The newsreader had said the cause of the softness had been discovered: A virus, a freak mutation that disrupted the calcium matrix of bones.

Yeah. Sure. That's what they said last year when the first cases cropped up in Boston. A virus. But they never isolated the virus, and the softness spread all over the world. So they began searching for "a subtle and elusive environmental toxin." They never pinned that one down either.

Now we were back to a virus again. Who cared? It didn't matter. Judy and I had beat it. Whether we had formed the right antibodies or the right antitoxin was just a stupid academic question. The process had been arrested in us. Sure, it had done some damage, but it wasn't doing any more, and that was the important thing. We'd never be the same, but we were going to live!

"But that man," Judy said, nodding toward the TV. "He said they were looking for people in whom the disease had started and then stopped. That's us, Dad. They said they need to examine people like us so they can find out how to fight it, maybe develop a serum against it. We should—"

"Judy-Judy-Judy!" I said in Cary Grantese to hide my annoyance. How many times did I have to go over this? "We've been through all this before. I told you: It's too late for them. Too late for everybody but us immunes."

I didn't want to discuss it—Judy didn't understand about those kind of people, how you can't deal with them.

"I want you to take me down there," she said in the tone she used when she wanted to be stubborn. "If you don't want to help, okay. But *I* do."

"No!" I said that louder than I wanted to and she flinched. More softly: "I know those people. I worked all those years in the Health Department. They'd turn us into lab specimens. They'll suck us dry and use our immunity to try and save themselves."

"But I want to help *some*body! I don't want us to be the last two people on earth!"

She began to cry again.

Judy was frustrated. I could understand that. She was unable to leave the apartment by herself and probably saw me at time as a dictator who had her at his mercy. And she was frightened, probably more frightened than I could imagine. She was only eighteen and everyone she had ever known in her life—including her mother—was dead.

I hoisted myself into the chair next to her and put my arm around her shoulders. She was the only person in the world who mattered to me. That had been true even before the softness began.

"We're not alone. Take George, for example. And I'm sure there are plenty of other immunes around, hiding like us. When the weather warms up, we'll find each other and start everything over new. But until then, we can't allow the bloodsuckers to drain off whatever it is we've got that protects us."

She nodded without saying anything. I wondered if she was agreeing with me or just trying to shut me up.

"Let's eat," I said with a gusto I didn't really feel.

"Not hungry."

"Got to keep up your strength. We'll have soup. How's that sound?"

She smiled weakly. "Okay . . . soup."

I forgot and almost tried to stand up. Old habits die hard. My lower legs were hanging over the edge of the chair like a pair of sand-filled dancer's tights. I could twitch the muscles and see them ripple under the skin, but a muscle is pretty useless unless it's attached to a bone, and the bones down there were gone.

I slipped off my chair to what was left of my knees and

shuffled over to the stove. The feel of those limp and useless leg muscles squishing under me was repulsive but I was getting used to it.

It hit the kids and old people first, supposedly because their bones were a little soft to begin with, then moved on to the rest of us, starting at the bottom and working its way up—sort of like a Horatio Alger success story. At least that's the way it worked in most people. There were exceptions, of course, like that newscaster. I had followed true to form: My left lower leg collapsed at the end of last month; my right went a few days later. It wasn't a terrible shock. My feet had already gone soft so I knew the legs were next. Besides, I'd heard the sound.

The sound comes in the night when all is quiet. It starts a day or two before a bone goes. A soft sound, like someone gently crinkling cellophane inside your head. No one else can hear it. Only you. I think it comes from the bone itself—from millions of tiny fractures slowly interconnecting into a mosaic that eventually causes the bone to dissolve into mush. Like an on-rushing train far far away can be heard if you press your ear to the track, so the sound of each microfracture transmits from bone to bone until it reaches your middle ear.

I haven't heard the sound in almost four weeks. I thought I did a couple of times and broke out in a cold, shaking sweat, but no more of my bones have gone. Neither have Judy's The average case goes from normal person to lump of jelly in three to four weeks. Sometimes it takes longer, but there's always a steady progression. Nothing more has happened to me or Judy since last month.

Somehow, someway, we're immune.

With my lower legs dragging behind me, I got to the counter of the kitchenette and kneed my way up the stepstool to where I could reach things. I filled a pot with water—at least the pressure was still up—and set it on the sterno stove. With gas and electricity long gone, sterno was a lifesaver.

While waiting for the water to boil I went to the window and looked out. The late afternoon March sky was full of dark gray clouds streaking to the east. Nothing moving on West Street one floor below but a few windblown leaves from God-knows-where. I glanced across at the windows of George's apartment, looking for movement but finding none, then back down to the street below.

I hadn't seen anybody but George on the street for ages,

hadn't seen or smelled smoke in well over two months. The last fires must have finally burned themselves out. The riots were one direct result of the viral theory. Half the city went up in the big riot last fall—half the city and an awful lot of people. Seems someone got the bright idea that if all the people going soft were put out of their misery and their bodies burned, the plague could be stopped, at least here in Manhattan. The few cops left couldn't stop the mobs. In fact a lot of the city's ex-cops had been *in* the mobs! Judy and I lost our apartment when our building went up. Luckily we hadn't any signs of softness then. We got away with our lives and little else.

"Water's boiling, Dad," Judy said from across the room.

I turned and went back to the stove, not saying anything, still thinking about how fast our nice rent-stabilized apartment house had burned, taking everything we had with it.

Everything was gone . . . furniture and futures . . . gone. All my plans. Gone. Here I stood—if you could call it that—a man with a college education, a B.S. in biology, a secure city job, and what was left? No job. Hell—no *city!* I'd had it all planned for my dancer. She was going to make it *so* big. I'd hang onto my city job with all those civil service idiots in the Department of Health, putting up with their sniping and their backstabbing and their lousy office politics so I could keep all the fringe benefits and foot the bill while Judy pursued the dance. She was going to have it *all*! Now what? All her talent, all her potential . . . where was it going?

Going soft . . .

I poured the dry contents of the Lipton envelope into the boiling water and soon the odor of chicken noodle soup filled the room.

Which meant we'd have company soon.

I dragged the stepstool over to the door. Already I could hear their claws begin to scrape against the outer surface of the door, their tiny teeth begin to gnaw at its edges. I climbed up and peered through the hole I'd made last month at what had then been eye-level.

There they were. The landing was full of them. Gray and brown and dirty, with glinty little eyes and naked tails. Revulsion rippled down my skin. I watched their growing numbers every day now, every time I cooked something, but still hadn't got used to them.

So I did Cagney for them: "Yooou diirty raaats!" and turned

to wink at Judy on the far side of the fold-out bed. Her expression remained grim.

Rats. They were taking over the city. They seemed to be immune to the softness and were traveling in packs that got bigger and bolder with each passing day. Which was why I'd chosen this building for us: Each apartment was boxed in with pre-stressed concrete block. No rats in the walls here.

I waited for the inevitable. Soon it happened: A number of them squealed, screeched, and thrashed as the crowding pushed them at each other's throats, and then there was bedlam out there. I didn't bother to watch any more. I saw it every day. The pack jumped on the wounded ones. Never failed. They were so hungry they'd eat anything, even each other. And while they were fighting among themselves they'd leave us in peace with our soup.

Soon I had the card table between us and we were sipping the yellow broth and those tiny noodles. I did a lot of *mmm-good*ing but got no response from Judy. Her eyes were fixed on the walkie-talkie on the end table.

"How come we haven't heard from him?"

Good question—one that had been bothering me for a couple of days now. Where *was* George? Usually he stopped by every other day or so to see if there was anything we needed. And if he didn't stop by, he'd call us on the walkie-talkie. We had an arrangement between us that we'd both turn on our headsets every day at six P.M. just in case we needed to be in touch. I'd been calling over to George's place across the street at six o'clock sharp for three days running now with no result.

"He's probably wandering around the city seeing what he can pick up. He's a resourceful guy. Probably came back with something we can really use but haven't thought of."

Judy didn't flash me the anticipated smile. Instead, she frowned. "What if he went down to the research center?"

"I'm sure he didn't," I told her. "He's a trusting soul, but he's not a fool."

I kept my eyes down as I spoke. I'm not a good liar. And that very question had been nagging at my gut. What if George had been stupid enough to present himself to the researchers? If he had, he was through. They'd never let him go and we'd never see him again.

For George wasn't an immune like us. He was different. Judy and I had caught the virus—or toxin—and defeated it. We were left with terrible scars from the battle but we had survived. We *acquired* our immunity through battle with the softness agent. George was special—he had remained untouched. He'd exposed himself to infected people for months as he helped everyone he could, and was still hard all over. Not so much as a little toe had gone soft on him. Which meant—to me at least—that George had been *born* with some sort of immunity to the softness.

Wouldn't those researchers love to get their needles and scalpels into *him*!

I wondered if they had. It was possible George might have been picked up and brought down to the research center against his will. He told me once that he'd seen official-looking vans and cars prowling the streets, driven by guys wearing gas masks or the like. But that had been months ago and he hadn't reported anything like it since. Certainly no cars had been on this street in recent memory. I warned him time and again about roaming around in the daylight but he always laughed good-naturedly and said nobody'd ever catch him—he was too fast.

What if he'd run into someone faster?

There was only one thing to do.

"I'm going to take a stroll over to George's just to see if he's okay."

Judy gasped. "No, Dad! You can't! It's too far!"

"Only across the street."

"But your legs—".

"—are only half gone."

I'd met George shortly after the last riot. I had two hard legs then. I'd come looking for a sturdier building than the one we'd been burned out of. He helped us move in here.

I was suspicious at first, I admit that. I mean, I kept asking myself, *What does this guy want?* Turned out he only wanted to be friends. And so friends we became. He was soon the only other man I trusted in this whole world. And that being the case, I wanted a gun—for protection against all those other men I didn't trust. George told me he had stolen a bunch during the early lootings. I traded him some sterno and batteries for a .38 and a pump-action 12-gauge shotgun with ammo for both. I promptly sawed off the barrel of the shotgun. If the need arose, I could clear a room real fast with that baby.

So it was the shotgun I reached for now. No need to fool with it—I kept its chamber empty and its magazine loaded with #5

shells. I laid it on the floor and reached into the rag bag by the
door and began tying old undershirts around my knees. Maybe
I shouldn't call them knees; with the lower legs and caps gone,
"knee" hardly seems appropriate, but it'll have to serve.

From there it was a look through the peep hole to make sure
the hall was clear, a blown kiss to Judy, then a shuffle into the
hall. I was extra wary at first, ranging the landing up and
down, looking for rats. But there weren't any in sight. I slung
the shotgun around my neck, letting it hang in front as I started
down the stairs one by one on hands and butt, knees first, each
flabby lower leg dragging alongside its respective thigh.

Two flights down to the lobby, then up on my padded knees
to the swinging door, a hard push through and I was out on the
street.

Silence.

We kept our windows tightly closed against the cold and so I
hadn't noticed the change. Now it hit me like a slap in the face.
As a lifelong New Yorker I'd never heard—or *not* heard—the
city like this. Even when there'd been nothing doing on your
street, you could always hear that dull roar pulsing from the
sky and the pavement and the walls of the buildings. It was the
life sound of the city, the beating of its heart, the whisper of its
breath, the susurrant rush of blood through its capillaries.

It had stopped.

The shiver that ran over me was not just the result of the
sharp edge of the March wind. The street was deserted. A
plague had been through here, but there were no contorted
bodies strewn about. You didn't fall down and die on the spot
with the softness. No, that would be too kind. You died by
inches, by bone lengths, in back rooms, trapped, unable to
make it to the street. No public displays of morbidity. Just
solitary deaths of quiet desperation.

In a secret way I was glad everyone was gone—nobody
around to see me tooling across the sidewalk on my rag-
wrapped knees like some skid row geek.

The city looked different from down here. You never realize
how cracked the sidewalks are, how *dirty*, when you have legs
to stand on. The buildings, their windows glaring red with the
setting sun that had poked through the clouds over New Jersey,
looked half again as tall as they had when I was a taller man.

I shuffled to the street and caught myself looking both ways
before sliding off the curb. I smiled at the thought of getting

run down by a truck on my first trip in over a month across a street that probably hadn't seen the underside of a car since December.

Despite the absurdity of it, I hurried across, and felt relief when I finally reached the far curb. Pulling open the damn doors to George's apartment building was a chore, but I slipped through both of them and into the lobby. George's bike—a light frame Italian model ten-speeder—was there. I didn't like that. George took that bike everywhere. Of course he could have found a car and some gas and gone sightseeing and not told me, but still the sight of that bike standing there made me uneasy.

I shuffled by the silent bank of elevators, watching my longing expression reflected in their silent, immobile chrome doors as I passed. The fire door to the stairwell was a heavy one, but I squeezed through and started up the steps—backwards. Maybe there was a better way, but I hadn't found it. It was all in the arms: Sit on the bottom step, get your arms back, palms down on the step above, lever yourself up. Repeat this ten times and you've done a flight of stairs. Two flights per floor. Thank the Lord or Whatever that George had decided he preferred a second floor apartment to a penthouse after the final power failure.

It was a good thing I was going up backwards. I might never have seen the rats if I'd been faced around the other way.

Just one appeared at first. Alone, it was almost cute with its twitching whiskers and its head bobbing up and down as it sniffed the air at the bottom of the flight. Then two more joined it, then another half dozen. Soon they were a brown wave, undulating up the steps toward me. I hesitated for an instant, horrified and fascinated by their numbers and all their little black eyes sweeping toward me, then I jolted myself into action. I swung the scatter gun around, pumped a shell into the chamber, and let them have a blast. Dimly through the reverberating roar of the shotgun I heard a chorus of squeals and saw flashes of flying crimson blossoms, then I was ducking my face into my arms to protect my eyes from the ricocheting shot. I should have realized the danger of shooting in a cinderblock stairwell like this. Not that it would have changed things—I still had to protect myself—but I should have anticipated the ricochets.

The rats did what I'd hoped they'd do—jumped on the dead

and near-dead of their number and forgot about me. I let the
gun hang in front of me again and continued up the stairs to
George's floor.

He didn't answer his bell but the door was unlocked. I'd
warned him about that in the past but he'd only laughed in that
carefree way of his. "Who's gonna pop in?" he'd say.
Probably no one. But that didn't keep me from locking mine,
even though George was the only one who knew where I lived.
I wondered if that meant I didn't really trust George.

I put the question aside and pushed the door open.

It stank inside. And it was empty as far as I could see. But
there was this sound, this wheezing, coming from one of the
bedrooms. Calling his name and announcing my own so I
wouldn't get my head blown off, I closed the door behind me—
locked it—and followed the sound. I found George.

And retched.

George was a blob of flesh in the middle of his bed. Everything but some ribs, some of his facial bones, and the back of
his skull had gone soft on him.

I stood there on my knees in shock, wondering how this
could have happened. George was *immune*! He'd laughed at
the softness! He'd been walking around as good as new just
last week. And now . . .

His lips were dry and cracked and blue—he couldn't speak,
couldn't swallow, could barely breathe. And his eyes . . .
they seemed to be just floating there in a quivering pool
of flesh, begging me . . . darting to his left again and
again . . . begging me . . .

For what?

I looked to his left and saw the guns. He had a suitcase full
of them by the bedroom door. All kinds. I picked up a heavy-
looking revolver—an S&W .357—and glanced at him. He
closed his eyes and I thought he smiled.

I almost dropped the pistol when I realized what he wanted.

"No, George!"

He opened his eyes again. They began to fill with tears.

"George—I can't!"

Something like a sob bubbled past his lips. And his
eyes . . . his pleading eyes . . .

I stood there a long time in the stink of his bedroom,
listening to him wheeze, feeling the sweat collect between my

palm and the pistol grip. I knew I couldn't do it. Not George, the big, friendly, good-natured slob I'd been depending on.

Suddenly, I felt my pity begin to evaporate as a flare of irrational anger began to rise. I *had* been depending on George now that my legs were half gone, and here he'd gone soft on me. The bitter disappointment fueled the anger. I knew it wasn't right, but I couldn't help hating George just then for letting me down.

"Damn you, George!"

I raised the pistol and pointed it where I thought his brain should be. I turned my head away and pulled the trigger. Twice. The pistol jumped in my hand. The sound was deafening in the confines of the bedroom.

Then all was quiet except for the ringing in my ears. George wasn't wheezing anymore. I didn't look around. I didn't have to see. I have a good imagination.

I fled that apartment as fast as my ruined legs would carry me.

But I couldn't escape the vision of George and how he looked before I shot him. It haunted me every inch of the way home, down the now empty stairs where only a few tufts of dirty brown fur were left to indicate that rats had been swarming there, out into the dusk and across the street and up more stairs to home.

George . . . how could it be? He was immune!

Or was he? Maybe the softness had followed a different course in George, slowly building up in his system until every bone in his body was riddled with it and he went soft all at once. *God*, what a noise he must have heard when all those bones went in one shot! That was why he hadn't been able to call or answer the walkie-talkie.

But what if it had been something else? What if the virus theory was right and George was the victim of a more virulent mutation? The thought made me sick with dread. Because if that were true, it meant Judy would eventually end up like George. And I was going to have to do for her what I'd done for George.

But what of me, then? Who was going to end it for *me*? I didn't know if I had the guts to shoot myself. And what if my hands went soft before I had the chance?

I didn't want to think about it, but it wouldn't go away. I couldn't remember ever being so frightened. I almost considered going down to Rockefeller Center and presenting Judy and myself to the leechers, but killed that idea real quick. Never. I'm no jerk. I'm college educated. A degree in biology! I know what they'd do to us!

Inside, Judy had wheeled her chair over to the door and was waiting for me. I couldn't let her know.

"Not there," I told her before she could ask, and I busied myself with putting the shotgun away so I wouldn't have to look her straight in the eyes.

"Where could he be?" Her voice was tight.

"I wish I knew. Maybe he went down to Rockefeller Center. If he did, it's the last we'll ever see of him."

"I can't believe that."

"Then tell me where else he can be."

She was silent.

I did Warner Oland's Chan: "Numbah One Dawtah is finally at loss for words. Peace reigns at last."

I could see that I failed to amuse, so I decided a change of subject was in order.

"I'm tired," I said. It was the truth. The trip across the street had been exhausting.

"Me, too." She yawned.

"Want to get some sleep?" I knew she did. I was just staying a step or two ahead of her so she wouldn't have to ask to be put to bed. She was a dancer, a fine, proud artist. Judy would never have to ask anyone to put her to bed. Not while I was around. As long as I was able I would spare her the indignity of dragging herself along the floor.

I gathered Judy up in my arms. The whole lower half of her body was soft; her legs hung over my left arm like weighted drapes. It was all I could do to keep from crying when I felt them so limp and formless. My dancer . . . you should have seen her in *Swan Lake*. Her legs had been so strong, so sleekly muscular, like her mother's . . .

I took her to the bathroom and left her in there. Which left me alone with my daymares. What if there really was a mutation of the softness and my dancer began leaving me again, slowly, inch by inch. What was I going to do when she was gone? My wife was gone. My folks were gone. What few friends I'd ever had were gone. Judy was the only attachment I had left. Without her I'd break loose from everything and just float off into space. I needed her . . .

When she was finished in the bathroom I carried her out and arranged her on the bed. I tucked her in and kissed her goodnight.

Out in the living room I slipped under the covers of the fold-out bed and tried to sleep. It was useless. The fear wouldn't leave me alone. I fought it, telling myself that George was a freak case, that Judy and I had licked the softness. We were *immune* and we'd *stay* immune. Let everyone else turn into puddles of Jell-O, I wasn't going to let them suck us dry to save themselves. We were on our way to inheriting the earth, Judy and I, and we didn't even have to be meek about it.

But still sleep refused to come. So I lay there in the growing darkness in the center of the silent city and listened . . . listened as I did every night . . . as I knew I would listen for the rest of my life . . . listened for that sound . . . that cellophane crinkling sound . . .

Second Sight

Ramsey Campbell

Key was waiting for Hester when his new flat first began to sound like home. The couple upstairs had gone out for a while, and they'd remembered to turn their television off. He paced through his rooms in the welcome silence, floorboards creaking faintly underfoot, and as the kitchen door swung shut behind him, he recognized the sound. For the first time the flat seemed genuinely warm, not just with central heating. But he was in the midst of making coffee when he wondered which home the flat sounded like.

The doorbell rang, softly since he'd muffled the sounding bowl. He went back through the living room, past the bookcases and shelves of records, and down the short hall to admit Hester. Her full lips brushed his cheek, her long eyelashes touched his eyelid like the promise of another kiss. "Sorry I'm late. Had to record the mayor," she murmured. "Are you about ready to roll?"

"I've just made coffee," he said, meaning yes.

"I'll get the tray."

"I can do it," he protested, immediately regretting his petulance. So this peevishness was what growing old was like. He felt both dismayed and amused by himself for snapping at Hester after she'd taken the trouble to come to his home to record him. "Take no notice of the old grouch," he muttered,

43

and was rewarded with a touch of her long cool fingers on his lips.

He sat in the March sunlight that welled and clouded and welled again through the window, and reviewed the records he'd listened to this month, deplored the acoustic of the Brahms recordings, praised the clarity of the Tallis. Back at the radio station, Hester would illustrate his reviews with extracts from the records. "Another impeccable unscripted monologue," she said. "Are we going to the film theater this week?"

"If you like. Yes, of course. Forgive me for not being more sociable," he said, reaching for an excuse. "Must be my second childhood creeping up on me."

"So long as it keeps you young."

He laughed at that and patted her hand, yet suddenly he was anxious for her to leave, so that he could think. Had he told himself the truth without meaning to? Surely that should gladden him: he'd had a happy childhood, he didn't need to think of the aftermath in that house. As soon as Hester drove away he hurried to the kitchen, closed the door again and again, listening intently. The more he listened, the less sure he was how much it sounded like a door in the house where he'd spent his childhood.

He crossed the kitchen, which he'd scrubbed and polished that morning, to the back door. As he unlocked it he thought he heard a dog scratching at it, but there was no dog outside. Wind swept across the muddy fields and through the creaking trees at the end of the short garden, bringing him scents of early spring and a faceful of rain. From the back door of his childhood home he'd been able to see the graveyard, but it hadn't bothered him then; he'd made up stories to scare his friends. Now the open fields were reassuring. The smell of damp wood that seeped into the kitchen must have to do with the weather. He locked the door and read Sherlock Holmes for a while, until his hands began to shake. Just tired, he told himself.

Soon the couple upstairs came home. Key heard them dump their purchases in their kitchen, then footsteps hurried to the television. In a minute they were chattering above the sounds of a gunfight in Abilene or Dodge City or at some corral, as if they weren't aware that spectators were expected to stay off the street or at least keep their voices down. At dinnertime they sat

down overhead to eat almost when Key did, and the double
image of the sounds of cutlery made him feel as if he were in
their kitchen as well as in his own. Perhaps theirs wouldn't
smell furtively of damp wood under the linoleum.

After dinner he donned headphones and put a Bruckner
symphony on the compact disc player. Mountainous shapes of
music rose out of the dark. At the end he was ready for bed,
and yet once there he couldn't sleep. The bedroom door had
sounded suddenly very much more familiar. If it reminded him
of the door of his old bedroom, what was wrong with that? The
revival of memories was part of growing old. But his eyes
opened reluctantly and stared at the murk, for he'd realized that
the layout of his rooms was the same as the ground floor of his
childhood home.

It might have been odder if they were laid out differently. No
wonder he'd felt vulnerable for years as a young man after he'd
been so close to death. All the same, he found he was listening
for sounds he would rather not hear, and so when he slept at
last he dreamed of the day the war had come to him.

It had been early in the blitz, which had almost passed the
town by. He'd been growing impatient with hiding under the
stairs whenever the siren howled, with waiting for his call-up
papers so that he could help fight the Nazis. That day he'd
emerged from shelter as soon as the All Clear had begun to
sound. He'd gone out of the back of the house and gazed at the
clear blue sky, and he'd been engrossed in that peaceful clarity
when the stray bomber had droned overhead and dropped a
bomb that must have been meant for the shipyard up the river.

He'd seemed unable to move until the siren had shrieked
belatedly. At the last moment he'd thrown himself flat,
crushing his father's flowerbed, regretting that even in the
midst of his panic. The bomb had struck the graveyard. Key
saw the graves heave up, heard the kitchen window shatter
behind him. A tidal wave composed of earth and headstones
and fragments of a coffin and whatever else had been upheaved
rushed at him, blotting out the sky, the searing light. It took
him a long time to struggle awake in his flat, longer to persuade
himself that he wasn't still buried in the dream.

He spent the day appraising and waiting for Hester. He kept
thinking he heard scratching at the back door, but perhaps that
was static from the television upstairs, which sounded more
distant today. Hester said she'd seen no animals near the flats,

but she sniffed sharply as Key put on his coat. "I should tackle your landlord about the damp."

The film theater, a converted warehouse near the shipyard, was showing *Citizen Kane*. The film had been made the year the bomb had fallen, and he'd been looking forward to seeing it then. Now, for the first time in his life, he felt that a film contained too much talk. He kept remembering the upheaval of the graveyard, eager to engulf him.

Then there was the aftermath. While his parents had been taking him to the hospital, a neighbor had boarded up the smashed window. Home again, Key had overheard his parents arguing about the window. Lying there almost helplessly in bed, he'd realized they weren't sure where the wood that was nailed across the frame had come from.

Their neighbor had sworn it was left over from work he'd been doing in his house. The wood seemed new enough; the faint smell might be trickling in from the graveyard. All the same, Key had given a piano recital as soon as he could, so as to have money to buy a new pane. But even after the glass had been replaced the kitchen had persisted in smelling slyly of rotten wood.

Perhaps that had had to do with the upheaval of the graveyard, though that had been tidied up by then, but weren't there too many perhapses? The loquacity of *Citizen Kane* gave way at last to music. Key drank with Hester in the bar until closing time, and then he realized that he didn't want to be alone with his gathering memories. Inviting Hester into his flat for coffee only postponed them, but he couldn't expect more of her, not at his age.

"Look after yourself," she said at the door, holding his face in her cool hands and gazing at him. He could still taste her lips as she drove away. He didn't feel like going to bed until he was calmer. He poured himself a large scotch.

The Debussy preludes might have calmed him, except that the headphones couldn't keep out the noise from upstairs. Planes zoomed, guns chattered, and then someone dropped a bomb. The explosion made Key shudder. He pulled off the headphones and threw away their tiny piano, and was about to storm upstairs to complain when he heard another sound. The kitchen door was opening.

Perhaps the impact of the bomb had jarred it, he thought distractedly. He went quickly to the door. He was reaching for the doorknob when the stench of rotten wood welled out at him, and he glimpsed the kitchen—his parents' kitchen, the replaced pane above the old stone sink, the cracked back door at which he thought he heard a scratching. He slammed the kitchen door, whose sound was inescapably familiar, and stumbled to his bed, the only refuge he could think of.

He lay trying to stop himself and his sense of reality from trembling. Now, when the television might have helped convince him where he was, someone upstairs had switched it off. He couldn't have seen what he'd thought he'd seen, he told himself. The smell and the scratching might be there, but what of it? Was he going to let himself slip back into the way he'd felt after his return from hospital, terrified of venturing into a room in his own home, terrified of what might be waiting there for him? He needn't get up to prove that he wasn't, so long as he felt that he could. Nothing would happen while he lay there. That growing conviction allowed him eventually to fall asleep.

The sound of scratching woke him. He hadn't closed his bedroom door, he realized blurrily, and the kitchen door must have opened again, otherwise he wouldn't be able to hear the impatient clawing. He shoved himself angrily into a sitting position, as if his anger might send him to slam the doors before he had time to feel uneasy. Then his eyes opened gummily, and he froze, his breath sticking in his throat. He was in his bedroom—the one he hadn't seen for almost fifty years.

He gazed at it—at the low slanted ceiling, the unequal lengths of flowered curtains, the corner where the new wallpaper didn't quite cover the old—with a kind of paralyzed awe, as if to breathe would make it vanish. The breathless silence was broken by the scratching, growing louder, more urgent. The thought of seeing whatever was making the sound terrified him, and he grabbed for the phone next to his bed. If he had company—Hester—surely the sight of the wrong room would go away. But there had been no phone in his old room, and there wasn't one now.

He shrank against the pillow, smothering with panic, then he threw himself forward. He'd refused to let himself be cowed all those years ago and by God, he wouldn't let himself be now. He strode across the bedroom, into the main room.

It was still his parent's house. Sagging chairs huddled around the fireplace. The crinkling ashes flared, and he glimpsed his face in the mirror above the mantel. He'd never

seen himself so old. "Life in the old dog yet," he snarled, and
flung open the kitchen door, stalked past the blackened range
and the stone sink to confront the scratching.

The key that had always been in the back door seared his
palm with its chill. He twisted it, and then his fingers stiffened,
grew clumsy with fear. His awe had blotted out his memory,
but now he remembered what he'd had to ignore until he and
his parents had moved away after the war. The scratching
wasn't at the door at all. It was behind him, under the floor.

He twisted the key so violently that the shaft snapped in half.
He was trapped. He'd only heard the scratching all those years
ago, but now he would see what it was. The urgent clawing
gave way to the sound of splintering wood. He made himself
turn on his shivering legs, so that at least he wouldn't be seized
from behind.

The worn linoleum had split like rotten fruit, a split as long
as he was tall, from which broken planks bulged jaggedly. The
stench of earth and rot rose toward him, and so did a dim
shape—a hand, or just enough of one to hold together and
beckon jerkily. "Come to us," whispered a voice from a mouth
that sounded clogged with mud. "We've been waiting for
you."

Key staggered forward, in the grip of the trance that had held
him ever since he'd wakened. Then he flung himself aside,
away from the yawning pit. If he had to die, it wouldn't be like
this. He fled through the main room, almost tripping over a
Braille novel, and dragged at the front door, lurched into the
open. The night air seemed to shatter like ice into his face. A
high sound filled his ears, speeding closer. He thought it was
the siren, the All Clear. He was blind again, as he had been
ever since the bomb had fallen. He didn't know it was a lorry
until he stumbled into its path. In the moment before it struck
him he was wishing that just once, while his sight was
restored, he had seen Hester's face.

Everybody Needs a Little Love

Robert Bloch

It started out as a gag.

I'm sitting at the bar minding my own business, which was drinking up a storm, when this guy got to talking with me.

Curtis his name was, David Curtis. Big, husky-looking straight-arrow type; I figured him to be around thirty, same as me. He was belting it pretty good himself, so right off we had something in common. Curtis told me he was assistant manager of a department store, and since I'm running a video-game arcade in the same shopping mall we were practically neighbors. But talk about coincidence—turns out he'd just gotten a divorce three months ago, exactly like me.

Which is why we both ended up in the bar every night after work, at Happy Hour time. Two drinks for the price of one isn't a bad deal, not if you're trying to cut it with what's left after those monthly alimony payments.

"You think you got zapped?" Curtis said. "My ex-wife wiped me out. I'm not stuck for alimony, but I lost the house, the furniture and the car. Then she hits me for the legal fees and I wind up with zero."

"I read you," I told him. "Gets to the point where you want out so bad you figure it's worth anything. But like the old saying, sometimes the cure is worse than the disease."

"This is my cure," Curtis said, finishing his scotch and ordering another round. "Trouble is, it doesn't work."

49

"So why are you here?" I asked. "You ought to try that singles bar down the street. Plenty of action there."

"Not for me."Curtis shook his head. "That's where I met my ex. Last thing I need is a singles bar."

"Me neither," I said. "But sometimes it's pretty lonesome just sitting around the apartment watching the Late Show. And I'm not into cooking or housework."

"I can handle that." Curtis rattled his rocks and the bartender poured a refill. "What gets me is going out. Ever notice what happens when you go to a restaurant by yourself? Even if the joint is empty they'll always steer you to one of those crummy little deuce tables in back, next to the kitchen or the men's john. The waiter gives you a dirty look because a loner means a smaller tip. And when the crowd starts coming in you can kiss service good-bye. The waiter forgets about your order, and when it finally comes, everything's cold. Then, after you finish, you sit around 'til hell freezes, waiting for your check."

"Right on," I said. "So maybe you need a change of pace."

"Like what?"

"Like taking a run up to Vegas some weekend. There's always ads in the paper for bargain rates on airfare and rooms."

"And every damned one of them is for couples." Curtis thumped his glass down on the bar. "Two-for-one on the plane tickets. Double occupancy for the rooms."

"Try escort service," I told him. "Hire yourself a date, no strings—"

"Not on my income. And I don't want to spend an evening or a weekend with some yacky broad trying to make small talk. What I need is the silent type."

"Maybe you could run an ad for a deaf-mute?"

"Knock it off! This thing really bugs me. I'm tired of being treated like a cross between a leper and the Invisible Man."

"So what's the answer?" I said. "There's got to be a way—"

"Damn betcha!" Curtis stood up fast, which was a pretty good trick, considering the load he was carrying.

"Where you going?" I asked.

"Come along and see," he said.

Five minutes later I'm watching Curtis use his night-key to unlock the back door of the department store.

Ten minutes later he has me sneaking around outside a storeroom in the dark, keeping an eye out for the security guard.

Fifteen minutes later I'm helping Curtis load a window dummy into the back seat of his rental car.

Like I said, it started out as a gag.

At least that's what I thought it was when he stole Estelle.

"That's her name," he told me. "Estelle."

This was a week later, the night he invited me over to his place for dinner. I stopped by the bar for a few quickies beforehand and when I got to his apartment I was feeling no pain. Even so, I started to get uptight the minute I walked in.

Seeing the window dummy sitting at the dinette table gave me a jolt, but when he introduced her by name it really rattled my cage.

"Isn't she pretty?" Curtis said.

I couldn't fault him on that. The dummy was something special—blond wig, baby-blue eyes, long lashes, and a face with a kind of what-are-you-waiting-for smile. The arms and legs were what you call articulated, and her figure was the kind you see in centerfolds. On top of that, Curtis had dressed it up in an evening gown, with plenty of cleavage.

When he noticed me eyeballing the outfit he went over to a wall closet and slid the door open. Damned if he didn't have the rack full of women's clothes—suits, dresses, sports outfits, even a couple of nighties.

"From the store?" I asked.

Curtis nodded. "They'll never miss them until inventory, and I got tired of seeing her in the same old thing all the time. Besides, Estelle likes nice clothes."

I had to hand it to him, putting me on like this without cracking a smile.

"Sit down and keep her company," Curtis said. "I'll have dinner on the table in a minute."

I sat down. I mean, what the hell else was I going to do? But it gave me an antsy feeling to have a window dummy staring at me across the table in the candlelight. That's right, he'd put candles on the table, and in the shadows you had to look twice to make sure this was only a mannequin or whatever you call it.

Curtis served up a couple of really good steaks and a nice

tossed salad. He'd skipped the drinks-before-dinner routine; instead he poured a pretty fair Cabernet with the meal, raising his glass in a toast.

"To Estelle," he said.

I raised my glass too, feeling like a wimp, but trying to go along with the gag. "How come she's not drinking?" I asked.

"Estelle doesn't drink." He still didn't smile. "That's one of the things I like about her."

It was the way he said it that got to me. I had to break up that straight face of his, so I gave him a grin. "I notice she sin't eating very much either."

Curtis nodded. "Estelle doesn't believe in stuffing her face. She wants to keep her figure."

He was still deadpanning, so I said, "If she doesn't drink and she doesn't eat, what happens when you take her to a restaurant?"

"We only went out once," Curtis told me. "Tell the truth, it wasn't the way I expected. They gave us a good table all right, but the waiter kept staring at us and the other customers started making wise-ass remarks under their breath, so now we eat at home. Estelle doesn't need restaurants."

The straighter he played it the more it burned me, so I gave it another shot. "Then I guess you won't be taking her to Vegas after all?"

"We went there last weekend," Curtis said. "I was right about the plane-fare. Not only did I save a bundle, but we got the red-carpet treatment. When they saw me carrying Estelle they must have figured her for an invalid—we got to board first and had our choice of seats upfront. The stewardess even brought her a blanket."

Curtis was really on a roll now, and all I could do was go with it. "How'd you make out with the hotel?" I asked.

"No sweat. Double occupancy rate, just like the ads said, plus complimentary cocktails and twenty dollars in free chips for the casino."

I tried one more time. "Did Estelle win any money?"

"Oh no—she doesn't gamble." Curtis shook his head. "We ended up spending the whole weekend right there in our room, phoning room service for meals and watching closed-circuit TV. Most of the time we never even got out of bed."

That shook me. "You were in bed with her?"

"Don't worry, it was king-size, plenty of room. And I found out another nice thing about Estelle. She doesn't snore."

I squeezed off another grin. "Then just what does she do when you go to bed with her?"

"Sleep, of course." Curtis gave me a double take. "Don't go getting any ideas. If I wanted the other thing I could have picked up one of those inflatable rubber floozies from a sex-shop. But there's no hanky-panky with Estelle. She's a real lady."

"A real lady," I said. "Now I've heard everything."

"Not from her." Curtis nodded at the dummy. "Haven't you noticed? I've been doing all the talking and she hasn't said a word. You don't know how great it is to have someone around who believes in keeping her mouth shut. Sure, I do the cooking and the housework, but it's no more of a hassle than when I was living here alone."

"You don't feel alone anymore, is that it?"

"How could I? Now when I come home nights I've got somebody waiting for me. No nagging, no curlers in the hair— just the way she is now, neat and clean and well-dressed. She even uses that perfume I gave her. Can't you smell it?"

Damned if he wasn't right. I *could* smell perfume.

I sneaked another peek at Estelle. Sitting in the shadows with the candlelight soft on her hair and face, she almost had me fooled for a minute. Almost, but not quite.

"Just look at her," Curtis said. "Beautiful! Look at that smile!"

Now, for the first time, he smiled too. And it was his smile I looked at, not hers.

"Okay," I said. "You win. If you're trying to tell me Estelle is better company than most women, it's no contest."

"I figured you'd understand." Curtis hadn't changed his expression, but there was something wrong about that smile of his, something that got to me.

So I had to say it. "I don't want to be a party-pooper, but the way you come on, maybe there's such a thing as carrying a gag too far."

He wasn't smiling now. "Who said anything about a gag? Are you trying to insult Estelle?"

"I'm not trying to insult anybody," I told him. "Just remember, she's only a dummy."

"Dummy?" All of a sudden he was on his feet and coming

around the table, waving those big fists of his. "You're the one who's a dummy! Get the hell out of here before I—"

I got out, before.

Then I went over to the bar, had three fast doubles, and headed for home to hit the deck. I went out like a light but it didn't keep the dreams away, and all night long I kept staring at the smiles—the smile on his face and the smile on the dummy's—and I don't know which one spooked me the most.

Come to think of it, they both looked the same.

That night was the last night I went to the bar for a long time. I didn't want to run into Curtis there, but I was still seeing him in those dreams.

I did my drinking at home now, but the dreams kept coming, and it loused me up at work when I was hungover. Pretty soon I started pouring a shot at breakfast instead of orange juice.

So I went to see Dr. Mannerheim.

That shows how rough things were getting, because I don't like doctors and I've always had a thing about shrinks. This business of lying on a couch and spilling your guts to a stranger always bugged me. But it had got to where I started calling in sick and just sat home staring at the walls. Next thing you know, I'd start climbing them.

I told Mannerheim that when I saw him.

"Don't worry," he said. "I won't ask you to lie on a couch or take inkblot tests. The physical shows you're a little rundown, but this can be corrected by proper diet and a vitamin supplement. Chances are you may not even need therapy at all."

"Then what am I here for?" I said.

"Because you have a problem. Suppose we talk about it."

Dr. Mannerheim was just a little bald-headed guy with glasses; he looked a lot like an uncle of mine who used to take me to ballgames when I was a kid. So it wasn't as hard to talk as I'd expected.

I filled him in on my setup—the divorce and all—and he picked up on it right away. Said it was getting to be a common thing nowadays with so many couples splitting. There's always a hassle working out a new life-style afterwards and sometimes a kind of guilty feeling; you keep wondering if it was your fault and that maybe something's wrong with you.

We got into the sex bit and the drinking, and then he asked me about my dreams.

That's when I told him about Curtis.

Before I knew it I'd laid out the whole thing—getting smashed in the bar, stealing the dummy, going to Curtis's place for dinner, and what happened there.

"Just exactly what did happen?" Mannerheim said. "You say you had a few drinks before you went to his apartment—maybe three or four—and you drank wine with your dinner."

"I wasn't bombed, if that's what you mean."

"But your preceptions were dulled," he told me. "Perhaps he intended to put you on for a few laughs, but when he saw your condition he got carried away."

"If you'd seen the way he looked when he told me to get out you'd know it wasn't a gag," I said. "The guy is a nut-case."

Something else hit me all of a sudden, and I sat up straight in my chair. "I remember a movie I saw once. There's this ventriloquist who gets to thinking his dummy is alive. Pretty soon he starts talking to it, then he gets jealous of it, and next thing you know—"

Mannerheim held up his hands. "Spare me the details. There must be a dozen films like that. But in all my years of practice I've never read, let alone run across, a single case where such a situation actually existed. It all goes back to the old Greek legend about Pygmalion, the sculptor who made a statue of a beautiful woman that came to life.

"But you've got to face facts." He ticked them off on his fingers. "Your friend Curtis has a mannequin, not a ventriloquist's dummy. He doesn't try to create the illusion that it speaks, or use his hand to make it move. And he didn't create the figure, he's not a sculptor. So what does that leave us with?"

"Just one thing," I said. "He's treating this dummy like a real person."

Mannerheim shook his head. "A man who's capable of carrying a window dummy into a restaurant and a hotel—or who claims to have done so in order to impress you—may still just have taken advantage of your condition to play out an elaborate practical joke."

"Wrong." I stood up. "I tell you he believes the dummy is alive."

"Maybe and maybe not. It isn't important." Mannerheim

took off his glasses and stared at me. "What's important is that *you* believe the dummy is alive."

It hit me like a sock in the gut. I had to sit down again and catch my breath before I could answer him.

"You're right," I said. "That's why I really wanted out of there. That's why I keep having those damned dreams. That's why there's a drinking problem. Maybe I was juiced-up when I saw her, maybe Curtis hypnotized me, how the hell do I know? But whatever happens or didn't happen, it worked. And I've been running scared ever since."

"Then stop running." Dr. Mannerheim put his glasses on again. "The only way to fight fear is to face it."

"You mean go back there?"

He nodded at me. "If you want to get rid of the dreams, get rid of the dependency on alcohol, the first step is to separate fantasy from reality. Go to Curtis, and go sober. Examine the actual circumstances with a clear head. I'm satisfied that you'll see things differently. Then, if you still think you need further help, get in touch."

We both stood up, and Dr. Mannerheim walked me to the door. "Have a good day," he said.

I didn't.

It took all that weekend just to go over what he'd said, and another two days before I could buy his advice. But it made sense. Maybe Curtis had been setting me up like the shrink said; if not, then he was definitely a flake. But one way or another I had to find out.

So Wednesday night I went up to his apartment. I wasn't on the sauce, and I didn't call Curtis in advance. That way, if he didn't know I was coming, he wouldn't plan on pulling another rib—if it was a rib.

It must have been close to nine o'clock when I walked down the hall and knocked on his door. There was no answer; maybe he was gone for the evening. But I kept banging away, just in case, and finally the door opened.

"Come on in," Curtis said.

I stared at him. He was wearing a pair of dirty, wrinkled-up pajamas, but he looked like he hadn't slept for a week—his face was gray, big circles under his eyes, and he needed a shave. When we shook hands I felt like I was holding a sack of ice cubes.

"Good to see you," he told me, closing the door after I got inside. "I was hoping you'd come by so's I could apologize for the way I acted the other night."

"No hard feelings," I said.

"I knew you wouldn't hold it against me," he went on. "That's what I told Estelle."

Curtis turned and nodded across the living room, and in the dim light I saw the dummy sitting there on the sofa, facing the TV screen. The set was turned on to some old western movie, but the sound was way down and I could scarcely hear the dialogue.

It didn't matter, because I was looking at the dummy. She wore some kind of fancy cocktail dress, which figured, because I could see the bottle on the coffee table and smell the whiskey on Curtis's breath. What grabbed me was the stuff she was wearing—the earrings, and the bracelet with the big stones that sparkled and gleamed. They had to be costume jewelry, but they looked real in the light from the TV tube. And the way the dummy sat, sort of leaning forward, you'd swear it was watching the screen.

Only I knew better. Seeing the dummy cold sober this way, it was just a wooden figure, like the others I saw in the storeroom where Curtis stole it. Dr. Mannerheim was right; now that I got a good look the dummy didn't spook me anymore.

Curtis went over to the coffee table and picked up the bottle. "Care for a drink?" he asked.

I shook my head. "No, thanks, not now."

But he kept holding the bottle when he bent down and kissed the dummy on the side of its head. "How can you hear anything with the sound so low?" he said. "Let me turn up the volume for you."

And so help me, that's what he did. Then he smiled at the dummy. "I don't want to interrupt while you're watching, honey. So if it's okay with you, we'll go in the bedroom and talk there."

He moved back across the living room and started down the hall. I followed him into the bedroom at the far end and he closed the door. It shut off the sound from the TV set but now I heard another noise, a kind of chirping.

Looking over at the far corner I saw the birdcage on a stand, with a canary hopping around inside.

"Estelle likes canaries," Curtis said. "Same as my ex. She always had a thing for pets." He tilted the bottle.

I just stood there, staring at the room. It was a real disaster area—bed not made, heaped-up clothes lying on the floor, empty fifths and glasses everywhere. The place smelled like a zoo.

The bottle stopped gurgling and then I heard the whisper. "Thank God you came."

I glanced up at Curtis. He wasn't smiling now. "You've got to help me," he said.

"What's the problem?" I asked.

"Keep your voice down," he whispered. "I don't want her to hear us."

"Don't start that again," I told him. "I only stopped in because I figured you'd be straightened out by now."

"How can I? She doesn't let me out of her sight for a minute—the last time I got away from here was three days ago, when I turned in the rental car and bought her the Mercedes."

That threw me. "Mercedes? You're putting me on."

Curtis shook his head. "It's downstairs in the garage right now—brand new 280-SL, hasn't been driven since I brought it home. Estelle doesn't like me to go out alone and she doesn't want to go out either. I keep hoping she'll change her mind because I'm sick of being cooped up here, eating those frozen TV dinners. You'd think she'd at least go for a drive with me after getting her the car and all."

"I thought you told me you were broke," I said. "Where'd you get the money for a Mercedes?"

He wouldn't look at me. "Never mind. That's my business."

"What about your business?" I asked. "How come you haven't been showing up at work?"

"I quit my job," he whispered. "Estelle told me to."

"Told you? Make sense, man. Window dummies don't talk."

He gave me a glassy-eyed stare. "Who said anything about window dummies? Don't you remember how it was the night we got her—how she was standing there in the storage room waiting for me? The others were dummies all right, I know that. But Estelle knew I was coming, so she just stood there pretending to be like all the rest because she didn't want you to catch on.

"She fooled you, right? I'm the only one who knew Estelle was different. There were all kinds of dummies there, some real beauties, too. But the minute I laid eyes on her I knew she was the one.

"And it was great, those first few days with her. You saw for yourself how well we got along. It wasn't until afterwards that everything went wrong, when she started telling me about all the stuff she wanted, giving me orders, making me do crazy things."

"Look," I said. "If there's anything crazy going on around here, you're the one who's responsible. And you better get your act together and put a stop to it right now. Maybe you can't do it alone, the shape you're in, but I've got a friend, a doctor—"

"Doctor? You think I'm whacko, is that it?" He started shaking all over and there was a funny look in his eyes. "Here I thought you'd help me, you were my last hope!"

"I want to help," I told him. "That's why I came. First off, let's try to clean this place up. Then you're going to bed, get a good night's rest."

"What about Estelle?" he whispered.

"Leave that to me. When you wake up tomorrow I promise the dummy'll be gone."

That's when he threw the bottle at my head.

I was still shaking the next afternoon when I got to Dr. Mannerheim's office and told him what happened.

"Missed me by inches," I said. "But it sure gave me one hell of a scare. I ran down the hall to the living room. That damn dummy was still sitting in front of the TV like it was listening to the program and that scared me too, all over again. I kept right on running until I got home. That's when I called your answering service."

Mannerheim nodded at me. "Sorry it took so long to get back to you. I had some unexpected business."

"Look, Doc," I said. "I've been thinking. Curtis wasn't really trying to hurt me. The poor guy's so uptight he doesn't realize what he's doing anymore. Maybe I should have stuck around, tried to calm him down."

"You did the right thing," Mannerheim took off his glasses and polished them with his handkerchief. "Curtis is definitely psychotic, and very probably dangerous."

That shook me. "But when I came here last week you said he was harmless—"

Dr. Mannerheim put his glasses on. "I know. But since then I've found out a few things."

"Like what?"

"Your friend Curtis lied when he told you he quit his job. He didn't quit—he was fired."

"How do you know?"

"I heard about it the day after I saw you, when his boss called me in. I was asked to run a series of tests on key personnel as part of a security investigation. It seems that daily bank deposits for the store show a fifty-thousand dollar loss in the cash flow. Somebody juggled the books."

"The Mercedes!" I said. "So that's where he got the money!"

"We can't be sure just yet. But polygraph tests definitely rule out other employees who had access to the records. We do know where he bought the car. The dealer only got a down-payment so the rest of the cash, around forty thousand, is still unaccounted for."

"Then it's all a scam, right, Doc? What he really means to do is take the cash and split out. He was running a number on me about the dummy, trying to make me think he's bananas, so I wouldn't tumble to what he's up to."

"I'm afraid it isn't that simple." Mannerheim got up and started pacing the floor. "I've been doing some rethinking about Curtis and his hallucination that the dummy is alive. That canary you mentioned—a pity he didn't get it before he stole the mannequin."

"What are you driving at?"

"There are a lot of lonely people in this world, people who aren't necessarily lonely by choice. Some are elderly, some have lost all close relatives through death, some suffer an aftershock following divorce. But all of them have one thing in common—the need for love. No physical love, necessarily, but what goes with it. The companionship, attention, a feeling of mutual affection. That's why so many of them turn to keeping pets.

"I'm sure you've seen examples. The man who spends all his time taking care of his dog. The widow who babies her kitten. The old lady who talks to her canary, treating it like an equal."

I nodded. "The way Curtis treats the dummy?"

Mannerheim settled down in his chair again. "Usually they don't go that far. But in extreme cases the pretense gets out of hand. They not only talk to their pets, they interpret each growl or purr or chirp as a reply. It's called personification."

"But these pet-owners—they're harmless, aren't they? So why do you say Curtis might be dangerous?"

Dr. Mannerheim leaned forward in his chair. "After talking to the people at the store I did a little further investigation on my own. This morning I went down to the courthouse and checked the files. Curtis told you he got a divorce here in town three months ago, but there's no record of any proceedings. And I found out he was lying to you about other things. He was married, all right; he did own a house and furniture and a car. But there's nothing to show he ever turned anything over to his wife. Chances are he sold his belongings to pay off gambling debts. We know he did some heavy betting at the track."

"We?" I said. "You and who else?"

"Sheriff's department. They're the ones who told me about his wife's disappearance, three months ago."

"You mean she ran out on him?"

"That's what he said after neighbors noticed she was missing and they called him in this morning. He told them downtown that he'd come home from work one night and his wife was gone, bag and baggage—no explanation, no note, nothing. He denied they'd quarreled, said he'd been too ashamed to report her absence, and had kept hoping she'd come back or at least get in touch with him."

"Did they buy his story?"

Mannerheim shrugged. "Women do leave their husbands, for a variety of reasons, and there was nothing to show Curtis wasn't telling the truth. They put out an all-points on his wife and kept the file open, but so far no new information has turned up, not until this embezzlement matter and your testimony. I didn't mention that this morning, but I have another appointment this evening and I'll tell them then. I think they'll take action, once they hear your evidence."

"Wait a minute," I said. "I haven't given you any evidence."

"I think you have." Mannerheim stared at me. "According to the neighbors, Curtis was married to a tall blonde with blue eyes, just like the window dummy you saw. And his wife's name was Estelle.''

It was almost dark by the time I got to the bar. The Happy Hour had started, but I wasn't happy. All I wanted was a drink—a couple of drinks—enough to make me forget the whole thing.

Only it didn't work out that way. I kept thinking about what Mannerheim told me, about Curtis and the mess he was in.

The guy was definitely psyched-out, no doubt about that. He'd ripped off his boss, lost his job, screwed up his life.

But maybe it wasn't his fault. I knew what he'd gone through because I had been there myself. Getting hit with a divorce was bad enough to make me slip my gears, and for him it must have been ten times worse. Coming home and finding his wife gone, just like that, without a word. He never said so, but he must have loved her—loved her so much that when she left him he flipped out, stealing the dummy, calling it by her name. Even when he got to feeling trapped he couldn't give the dummy up because it reminded him of his wife. All this was pretty far-out, but I could understand. Like Mannerheim said, everybody needs a little love.

If anyone was to blame, it was that wife of his. Maybe she split because she was cheating on him, the way mine did. The only difference is that I could handle it and he cracked up. Now he'd either be tossed in the slammer or get put away in a puzzle-factory, and all because of love. His scuzzy wife got away free and he got dumped on. After Mannerheim talked to the law they'd probably come and pick him up tonight—poor guy, he didn't have a chance.

Unless I gave it to him.

I ordered up another drink and thought about that. Sure, if I tipped him off and told him to run it could get me into a bind. But who would know? The thing of it was, I could understand Curtis, even put myself in his place. Both of us had the same raw deal, but I'd lucked out and he couldn't take it. Maybe I owed him something—at least a lousy phone call.

So I went over to the pay phone at the end of the bar. This big fat broad was using the phone, probably somebody's cheating wife handing her husband a line about why she wasn't home. When I came up she gave me a dirty look and kept right on yapping.

It was getting towards eight o'clock now. I didn't know

when Dr. Mannerheim's appointment was set with the sheriff's department, but there wouldn't be much time left. And Curtis's apartment was only three blocks away.

I made it in five minutes, walking fast. So fast that I didn't even look around when I crossed in front of the entrance to the building's underground parking place.

If I hadn't heard the horn I'd have been a goner. As it was, there were just about two seconds for me to jump back when the big blue car came tearing up the ramp and wheeled into the street. Just two seconds to get out of the way, look up, and see the Mercedes take off.

Then I took off too, running into the building and down the hall.

The only break I got was finding Curtis's apartment door wide open. He was gone—I already knew that—but all I wanted now was to use the phone.

I called the sheriff's office and Dr. Mannerheim was there. I told him where I was and about seeing the car take off, and after that things happened fast.

In a couple of minutes a full squad of deputies wheeled in. They went through the place and came up with zilch. No Curtis, no Estelle—even the dummy's clothes were missing. And if he had forty grand or so stashed away, that was gone too; all they found was a rip in a sofa cushion where he could have hid the loot.

But another squad had better luck, if you can call it that. They located the blue Mercedes in an old gravel pit off the highway about five miles out of town.

Curtis was lying on the ground next to it, stone-cold dead, with a big butcher knife stuck between his shoulder blades. The dummy was there too, lying a few feet away. The missing money was in Curtis's wallet—all big bills—and the dummy's wardrobe was in the rear seat, along with Curtis's luggage, like he'd planned to get out of town for good.

Dr. Mannerheim was with the squad out there and he was the one who suggested digging into the pit. It sounded wild, but he kept after them until they moved a lot of gravel. His hunch paid off, because about six feet down they hit pay dirt.

It was a woman's body, or what was left of it after three months in the ground.

The coroner's office had a hell of a time making an ID. It turned out to be Curtis's wife, of course, and there were about twenty stab wounds in her, all made with a butcher knife like the one that killed Curtis.

Funny thing, they couldn't get any prints off the handle; but there were a lot of funny things about the whole business. Dr. Mannerheim figured Curtis killed his wife and buried her in the pit, and what sent him over the edge was guilt feelings. So he stole the dummy and tried to pretend it was his wife. Calling her Estelle, buying all those things for her—he was trying to make up for what he'd done, and finally he got to the point where he really thought she was alive.

Maybe that makes sense, but it still doesn't explain how Curtis was killed, or why.

I could ask some other questions too. If you really believe something with all your heart and soul, how long does it take before it comes true? And how long does a murder victim lie in her grave plotting to get even?

But I'm not going to say anything. If I told them my reasons they'd say I was crazy, too.

All I know is that when the Mercedes came roaring out of the underground garage I had only two seconds to get out of the way. But it was long enough for me to get a good look, long enough for me to swear I saw Curtis and the dummy together in the front seat.

And Estelle was the one behind the wheel.

The Yard

William F. Nolan

It was near the edge of town, just beyond the abandoned freight tracks. I used to pass it on the way to school in the mirror-bright Missouri mornings and again in the long-shadowed afternoons coming home with my books held tight against my chest, not wanting to look at it.

The Yard.

It was always spooky to us kids, even by daylight. It was old, had been in Riverton for as long as anyone could remember. Took up a full city block. A sagging wood fence (had it *ever* been painted?) circled all the way around it. The boards were rotting, with big cracks between many of them where you could see all the smashed cars and trucks piled obscenely inside, body to body, in rusted embrace. There were burst-open engines with ruptured water hoses like spilled guts, and splayed truck beds, split and swollen by sun and rain, and daggered windshields filmed with dark-brown scum. ("It's from people's brains, where their heads hit the glass," said Billy-Joe Gibson, and no one doubted him.)

The wide black-metal gate at the front was closed and padlocked most always, but there were times at night, *always* at night, when it would creak open like a big iron mouth and old Mr. Latting would drive his battered exhaust-smoky tow truck inside, with its missing front fenders and dented hood, dragging the corpse of a car behind like a crushed metal insect.

We kids never knew exactly where he got the cars—but there were plenty of bad accidents on the interstate, especially during the fall, when the fog would roll out from the Riverton woods and drape the highway in a breathing blanket of chalk white.

Out-of-towners who didn't know the area would come haul-assing along at eighty, then dive blind into that pocket of fog. You'd hear a squeal of brakes. Wheels locking. Then the explosion of rending metal and breaking glass as they hit the guardrail. Then a long silence. Later, sometimes a lot later, you'd hear the keening siren of Sheriff Joe Thompson's Chevy as he drove out to the accident. Anyway, we kids figured that some of those wrecked cars ended up in the Yard.

At night, when you passed the Yard, there was this sickly green glow shining over the piled up metal corpses inside. The glow came from the big arc lamp that Mr. Latting always kept lit. Come dusk, that big light would pop on and wouldn't go off till dawn.

When a new kid came to school in Riverton we knew he'd eventually get around to asking about the Yard. "You been inside?" he'd ask, and we'd say heck yes, plenty of times. But that was a lie. No kid I knew had ever been inside the Yard.

And we had a good reason. Mr. Latting kept a big gray dog in there. Don't know the breed. Some kind of mastiff. Ugly as sin on Sunday, that dog. Only had one good eye; the other was covered by a kind of veined membrane. Clawed in a fight maybe. The good eye was black as a chunk of polished coal. Under the dog's lumpy, short-haired skull its shoulders were thick with muscle, and its matted gray coat was oil-streaked and spotted with patches of mange. Tail was stubbed, bitten away.

That dog never barked at us, never made a sound; but if any of us got too near the Yard it would show its fanged yellow teeth, lips sucked back in silent fury. And if one of us dared to touch the fence circling the Yard that dog would slam its bulk against the wood, teeth snapping at us through the crack in the boards.

Sometimes, in the fall, in the season of fog, just at sunset, we'd see the gray dog drift like a ghost out the gate of the Yard to enter the woods behind Sutter's store and disappear.

Once, on a dare, I followed him and saw him leave the trees at the far edge of the woods and pad up the slope leading to the interstate. I saw him sitting there, by the side of the highway, watching the cars whiz by. He seemed to enjoy it.

When he swung his big head around to glare at me I cut out fast, melting back into the woods. I was shook. I didn't want that gray devil to start after me. I remember I ran all the way home.

I once asked my father what he knew about Mr. Latting. Said he didn't know anything about the man. Just that he'd always owned the Yard. And the dog. And the tow truck. And that he always wore a long black coat with the frayed collar turned up, even in summer. And always a big ragged hat on his head, with a rat-eaten brim that fell over his thin, pocked face and glittery eyes.

Mr. Latting never spoke. Nobody had ever heard him talk. And since he didn't shop in town we couldn't figure out where he got his food. He never seemed to sell anything, either. I mean, nobody ever went to the Yard to buy spare parts for their cars or trucks. So Mr. Latting qualified as our town eccentric. Every town has one. Harmless, I guess.

But scary just the same.

So that's how it was when I grew up in Riverton. (Always thought Riverton was a funny name for a place that didn't have a river within a hundred miles of it.) I was eighteen when I went away to college and started a new life. Majored in engineering. Just like my Dad, but he never did anything with it. I was thirty, with my own business, when I finally came back. To bury my father.

Mom had divorced him ten years earlier. She'd remarried and was living in Cleveland. Refused to come back for the funeral. My only sister was in California, with no money for the trip, and I had no brothers. So it was up to me.

The burial that fall, at Oakwood Cemetery, was bleak and depressing. Attendance was sparse—just a few of Pop's old cronies, near death themselves, and a scattering of my high school pals, as nervous and uncomfortable as I was. On hand just to pay their respects. Nothing in common between any of us, nothing left.

After it was over I determined to drive back to Chicago that same night. Riverton held no nostalgic attraction for me. Get Pop buried, then get the hell out. That was my plan from the start.

Then, coming from the cemetery, I passed the Yard.

I couldn't see anybody inside as I drove slowly past the padlocked gate. No sign of life or movement.

Of course, twelve long years had passed. Old Latting was surely dead by now, his dog with him. Who owned the place these days? Lousy piece of real estate if you'd asked me!

A host of dark memories rushed back, crowding my mind. There'd always been something foul about the Yard—something *wrong* about it. And that hadn't changed. I shuddered, struck by a sudden chill in the air. Turned the car heater up another notch.

And headed for the interstate.

Ten minutes later I saw the dog. Sitting at the wooded edge of the highway, on the gravel verge, at the same spot I'd followed it to so many years before. As my car approached it, the big gray animal raised its head and fixed its coal-chip eye on me as I passed.

The *same* dog. The same sightless, moon-fleshed eye on the right side of its lumped skull, the same mange-pocked matted fur, the same muscled shoulders and stubbed tail.

The same dog—or its ghost.

Suddenly I was into a swirl of opaque fog obscuring the highway. Moving much too fast. The apparition at the edge of the woods had shattered my concentration. My foot stabbed at the brake pedal. The wheels locked, lost their grip on the fog-damped road. The car began sliding toward the guardrail. A milk-white band of unyielding steel *loomed* at me. Into it. Head on.

A smashing explosion of metal to metal. The windshield splintering. The steering wheel hard into my chest. A snapping of bone. Sundered flesh. Blood. Pain. Darkness.

Silence.

Then—an awakening. Consciousness again. I blinked, focusing. My face was numb; I couldn't move my arms or legs. Pain lived like raw fire in my body. I then realized that the car was upside down, with the top folded around me like a metal shroud.

A wave of panic rippled over me. I was trapped, jackknifed inside the overturned wreck. I fought down the panic, telling myself that things could have been worse. Much worse. I could have gone through the windshield (which had splintered but was still intact); the car could have caught fire; I could have

broken my neck. At least I'd survived the accident. Someone
would find me. Someone.

Then I heard the sound of the tow truck. I saw it through the
windshield, through the spider-webbing of cracked glass,
coming toward me in the fog—the *same* tow truck I'd seen as a
boy, its front fenders missing, hood dented, its front bumper
wired together . . . The rumble of its ancient, laboring
engine was horribly familiar.

It stopped. A door creaked open and the driver climbed from
the cab. He walked over to my car, squatting down to peer in at
me.

Mr. Latting.

And he spoke. For the first time I heard his voice—like
rusted metal. Like something from a tomb. "Looks like you
went an' had yerself a smash." And he displayed a row of
rotting teeth as he smiled. His eyes glittered at me under the
wide brim of his ragged hat.

Words were not easy for me. "I . . . I'm . . . badly
hurt. Need to . . . get a doctor." I had blood in my mouth. I
groaned; pain was in me like sharp blades. All through my
body.

"No need to fret," he told me. "We'll take care'a you." A
dry chuckle. "Just you rest easy. Leave things to us."

I was very dizzy. It took effort just to breathe. My eyes lost
focus; I fought to remain conscious. Heard the sound of chains
being attached, felt the car lifted, felt a sense of movement, the
broken beat of an engine . . . Then a fresh wave of pain
rolled me into darkness.

I woke up in the Yard.

Couldn't be, I told myself. Not *here*. He wouldn't take me
here. I need medical care. A hospital. I could be dying.
Dying!

The word struck me with the force of a dropped hammer. I
was dying and he didn't care. He'd done nothing to help me; I
was still trapped in this twisted hulk of metal. Where were the
police? Mechanics with torches to cut me free? The ambulance?

I squinted my eyes. The pale green glow from the tall arc
lamp in the middle of the Yard threw twisting shadows across
the high-piled wreckage.

I heard the gate being slammed shut and padlocked. I heard

Latting's heavy boots, crunching gravel as he came toward me. The car was still upside down.

I attempted to angle my body around, to reach the handle of the driver's door. Maybe I could force it open. But a lightning streak of pain told me that body movement was impossible.

Then Latting's skeletal face was at the windshield, looking in at me through the splintered glass. A grin pulled at the skin of his mouth like a scar. "You all right in there?"

"God, no!" I gasped. "Need . . . a doctor. For Christ's sake . . . call . . . an ambulance."

He shook his head. "Got no phone to call one with here at the Yard," he said, in his rasping voice. "Besides that, you don't need no doctors, son. You got *us*."

"Us?"

"Sure. Me an' the dog." And the blunt, lumpy head of the foul gray animal appeared at the window next to Latting. His red tongue lolled wetly and his bright black unblinking eye was fixed on me.

"But . . . I'm bleeding!" I held up my right arm; it was pulsing with blood. "And I . . . I think I have . . . internal injuries."

"Oh, sure you got 'em," chuckled Latting. "You got *severe* internals." He leered at me. "Plus, your head's gashed. Looks like both yer legs is gone—an' your chest is all stove in. Lotta busted ribs in there." And he chuckled again.

"You crazy old fool!" I snapped. "I'll . . . I'll have the sheriff on you." I fought back the pain to rage at him. "You'll rot in jail for this!"

"Now don't go gettin' huffy," Latting said. "Sheriff ain't comin' in here. Nobody comes into the Yard. You oughta know that by now. Nobody, that is, but ones like you."

"What do you mean . . . like me?"

"Dyin' ones," the old man rasped. "Ones with mosta their bones broke and the heart's blood flowin' out of 'em. Ones from the interstate."

"You . . . you've done this before?"

"Sure. Lotsa times. How do you think we've kept goin' all these years, me an' the dog? It's what's up there on the interstate keeps us alive . . . what's inside all them mashed-up cars, all them rolled-over trucks. We *need* what's inside." He ruffled the mangy fur at the dog's neck. "Don't we, boy?"

In response, the big animal skinned back its slimed red lips and showed its teeth—keeping its obsidian eye fixed on me.

"This here dog is kinda unusual," said Latting. "I mean, he seems to just know *who* to pick out to cast the Evil Eye. Special ones. Ones like you that nobody's gonna miss or raise a fuss over. Can't have folks pokin' around the Yard, askin' questions. The ones he picks, they're just into the fog and gone. I tow 'em here an' that's that."

Numbly, through a red haze of pain, I remembered the fierce *intensity* of that single dark eye from the edge of the highway as I passed. Hypnotizing me, causing me to lose control and smash into the guardrail. The Evil Eye.

"Well, time to quit jawin' with ya and get this here job done," said Latting. He stood up. "C'mon, dog." And he led the animal away from the car.

I drew in a shuddering breath, desperately telling myself that some one must have heard the crash and reported it, that the sheriff would arrive any moment now, that I'd be cut free, eased onto cool crisp linen sheets, my skin gently swabbed of blood, my wounds treated . . .

Hurry, damn you! I'm dying. Dying!

A sudden, shocking, immediate smash of sound. Again and again and again. The cracked curve of safety glass in front of me was being battered inward by a series of stunning blows from Latting's sledge as he swung it repeatedly at the windshield.

"These things are gettin' tougher every year," he scowled, continuing his assault. "Ah, now . . . here she goes!"

And the whole windshield suddenly gave way, collapsing into fragments, with jagged pieces falling on my head and shoulders, cutting my flesh.

"There, that's better, ain't it?" asked the old man with his puckered-scar grin. "He can get at ya now with no bother."

Get at me?

The dog. Of course he meant the dog. That stinking horror of an animal. I blinked blood from my eyes, trying to push myself back, away from the raw opening. But it was useless. The pain was incredible. I slumped weakly against the twisted metal of the incaved roof, refusing to believe what was happening to me.

The gray creature was coming, thrusting his wide shoulders through the opening.

The fetid breath of the hellbeast was in my nostrils; his gaping mouth fastened to my flesh, teeth gouging; his bristled fur was rank against my skin.

A hideous snuffling, sucking sound . . . as I felt him draining me! I was being . . . *emptied* . . . into him . . . into *his foul body* . . . all of me . . . *all* . . .

I felt the need to move. To leave the Yard. The air was cold, edged with the promise of frost. The sky was steel gray above me.

It was good to move again. To run. To leave the town and the woods behind me.

It was very quiet. I gloried in the strong scent of earth and concrete and metal which surrounded me. I was *alive*. And strong again. It was fine to be alive.

I waited. Occasionally a shape passed in front of me, moving rapidly. I ignored it. Another. And another. And then, finally, the *one*. Happiness rushed through me. Here was one who would provide my life and strength and the life and strength of my master.

I raised my head. He saw me then, the one in the truck. My eye fixed on his as he swept past me with a metallic rush of sound. And vanished into the fog.

I sat quietly, waiting for the crash.

The Substitute

Gahan Wilson

None of the children was in a good mood even to begin with. It was a foul November morning and every boy and girl of them had been forced by their mothers to wear their hated galoshes, and of course the galoshes hadn't worked, the snow had been too high (it was a *particularly* foul November morning, even for the Midwest) and had poured in over the tops so that their feet had got wet and cold anyhow, in spite of their mothers.

They took off their galoshes, and their soggy coats and hats, and put them in their proper places by the hook with the right name on it, and then they marched into room 204 of Washington School, Lakeside, where the sixth grade was taught, and were, to the last one of them, fully prepared to be horrid.

And it was only then that they realized that their troubles had just begun, for when they looked up at the big desk by the windows, behind which their blond and pretty Miss Merridew, of whom they were all very, very fond, should by every right be sitting, there was, instead, a stranger, a person they had never seen in all their lives and wished they were not seeing now.

The stranger was a large, dark, balloonish woman. She seemed to be made up of roundness upon roundness; there was not a part of her that was not somehow connected with circularity from the coils of her thick, black hair, to the large, pearlish segments of her necklace and bracelets, to her round, wide, staring eyes with their dark irises set directly in the center of a roundness of white, which was a distinctly disconcerting effect since it made the eyes seem to stare at you so directly and penetratingly.

When the children were all settled at their desks and not one moment before, she stirred herself, making all those pearlish things rattle with a softly snakelike hiss, picked up the attendance sheet, consulted it very carefully with roundly pursed lips to indicate it was revealing many secrets to her, and when the class had become uncomfortable enough to make barely audible shifting noises, she looked up sharply and spoke.

"Good morning, students. I am Miss Or, that's O-R, and I will be your teacher for a time as poor Miss Merridew cannot be here due to an unfortunate, ah, accident. I am sure we will all get along just fine."

She paused to give a broad, rather fixed smile which the whole class disliked at once, and read off the attendance list, making little marks on the paper as she went along and studying the face of each student as they responded to their name. That done she stood, revealing that her roundness was not restricted to that part of her which showed over the desk, but continued through the length of her, down to a round, pearlish ball fixed to the toe of each of her black shoes, a decorative touch which none of the children ever remembered seeing on any Lakeside lady before, teacher or not. Her entire outfit, save for those pale, pearlish things, was black, unlike the colors of Miss Merridew's outfits which tended always to be cheerful and pleasantly sunny.

"Today we will have a very special lesson," she said, sweeping the children with another fixed smile and those strange, staring eyes. "We shall learn about a wonderful place which none of us have heard of before."

She moved over to the map holder fixed above the center of the blackboard, revealing a lightness of foot which was extraordinary in so large a person; she seemed to float from step to step. The map holder was an ingenious affair which contained an apparently inexhaustible supply of maps and charts of all descriptions which could be pulled down at choice like windowshades, and then caused to fly back up into hiding by a clever tug at their bottoms.

Miss Or selected a bright green tag which the sharper children did not remember seeing before, and unrolled a large, brightly-colored map new to them all.

"This is Aliahah," she said, "Ah-lee-ah-ah. Can you say that name, class?"

"Ah-lee-ah-ah," they said, more or less.

"That's fine. That's very good. Now, as you can see, Aliahah is extremely varied geographically, having mountain ranges, lush valleys, deserts, several large bodies of water, and an interesting coastline bordered by two different seas."

She paused and regarded the map with open affection while the children stared at it with varying degrees of disinterest.

"Mary Lou," said Miss Or, turning and fixing a thin, pale girl in the front row with her eyes which, now that the students had observed them in action, were seen to have the same near fixity in their sockets as those of sharks, "can you tell me how many major bodies of water there are in Aliahah?"

Mary Lou Gorman colored slightly, frowned, counted silently without moving her lips and answered, "Three."

"That is entirely correct," said Miss Or with a nod of her round head which made her thick hair float and weave in the air as if it weighed nothing at all, or was alive like so many snakes. "The most important one, Lake Gooki—"

There was the briefest of amused snortings from some members of the class at the sound of the name of Lake Gooki, but it was instantly silenced by an icy, vaguely dangerous glance from Miss Or's shark eyes.

"—is not only beautiful, but extremely useful, having no less than nine underwater mines, indicated by these pretty red triangles. The mines produce most of the radioactive ore needed for the war effort."

Leonard Bates rather tentatively raised a hand.

"Yes, Lennie?"

"Ah, Miss, ah . . ."

"Or, Lennie. My name is Miss Or."

"Miss, ah, Or," said Leonard, "I just wondered, was this going to be a test?"

"That's a good question, Lennie. No. There will be no test. However, it would be wise of you to remember as much as you can about Aliahah for the information will be most useful to you. Think of all this as a friendly attempt to familiarize you with a country which, I hope very much, you will come to love."

Leonard looked at Miss Or for a puzzled moment, then nodded and said, "Thank you, Miss, ah, Or."

Miss Or bestowed an odd, lingering glance on Leonard as she toyed absently with a pearlish thing or two on her necklace. Her nails were long and sharply pointed and painted a shiny black.

"Aliahah has only two cities of any size. Bunem, here in the north, and Kaldak in the midland plains."

She sent the map of Aliahah flying up into the holder with a smart pluck at its lower edge and pulled down a somewhat smaller map showing Kaldak, which she gestured at roundly with one round arm.

"Kaldak, being our main center of weapons manufacture, is levitational, if need be."

Harry Pierce and Earl Waters exchanged glances, and then Earl raised his hand.

"Yes, Earl?"

"Excuse me, Miss Or, but just what do you mean by 'levitational'?"

"Only that it can be floated to various locations in order to confuse enemy orientation."

Harry and Earl exchanged glances again, and this time made faces which Miss Or, turning back to the map with an alacrity which made her alarmingly weightless hair dance up from her skull in snakish hoops and coils, missed entirely.

"There are no less than two thousand seven hundred and ninety four factories working ceaselessly in Kaldak," said Miss Or, a new note of grimness creeping into her voice. "Ceaselessly."

She turned to the class, and there was no trace of her fixed smile now. She seemed, almost, to be anguished, and one or two of the children thought they caught a glimpse of a large, round tear falling from one of her staring, dark eyes, though it seemed incongruous.

"Do you realize," she said, "how many of us that keeps from the fighting? The glorious fighting?"

She turned with a sweep and a rattling hiss of her pearlish things, snapped the map of Kaldak back into the holder, and uncoiled an involved chart whose labyrinthine complexities seemed to mock any possibility of comprehension, certainly from that of the sixth grade of Washington School.

"It is very important," said Miss Or, looking over her black shoulder at them with her pale face, "that you understand everything of what I am going to tell you now!" And something about the roundness of her face and staring eyes, and something about how her round mouth worked in a circular, chewing fashion as she talked, put them all so much in mind of a shark staring at them, sizing them up—or was it a snake?—that they all drew back in their little seats behind their little desks, at the same time realizing it wasn't going to help at all.

And then she launched into a lecture of such intense and glorious inscrutability that it lost them all from its first sentence, from the first half of that sentence, from its first word, so that they could only boggle and cringe and realize that at last they had encountered what they had all dreaded encountering from their very first day at school: a teacher and a lesson which were, really and truly, completely and entirely, ununderstandable.

At the same moment Clarence Weed began, just began, to be able to see something peculiar about the long sides of the blackboard showing to the left and right of Miss Or's hanging graph. At first he assumed he was imagining it, but when it persisted and even clarified, he thought in more serious terms, thought about the light flashes he had seen just before coming down with influenza late last winter. But he'd only seen those lights out of the corners of his eyes, so to speak, as if they had been flicking far off to one side or even way around at his back, and the lights he was looking at now were directly in front of him, and besides, they didn't dim or blur if he squeezed his eyes shut for a second and then looked again; indeed, if anything, they seemed to get a little better defined.

"Of course," Miss Or was saying, following the spiraling curves of some symbol with the shiny, black, pointy fingernail of her left index finger, "density conforms with the number of seedlings loosened and the quantity surviving flotation to the breeding layer."

No, they did not blur or dim, nor, as he stared harder at them, did they continue to be nothing more than lights. Now he could make out edges, now forms, now there were the vague beginnings of three dimensionality.

"To be sure they will sometimes gomplex," Miss Or explained carefully. "There is always the possibility of a gomplex."

Clarence Weed looked across the aisle, trying to catch the eye of Ernie Price, then saw there was no need to give him any kind of signal as Ernie was leaning intently forward, studying the blackboard with all his might, so he went back to do some more of it himself.

And now he saw the shapes and spaces showing—what exactly was the process? Were these things showing through the blackboard? Or were they, somehow, starting to supplant it?—showing by their relationships a kind of scene. He was beginning to make out a sort of landscape.

"Any species so selected," Miss Or continued, "should count itself extravagantly fortunate."

There were things in a kind of formal grouping. He could not tell what the things were, nothing about them seemed familiar, but they were alive, or at least capable of motion. A kind of wind seemed to disturb them constantly, they were always fighting a tendency to drift to one side caused by some sort of endlessly pushing draft, and they reached out thin tendrils and clung to the objects about them so as not to be blown away. Clarence felt he could almost hear the wind, a sort of mournful, bitter sighing, but then he decided that *was* an illusion.

"The odds against such wonderful luck are easily several zahli sekutai. And yet you won!"

The beings, they were definitely beings and not things, were all staring straight out at him, at the class. He could see nothing which looked like eyes, could not even determine what part of the beings could be their equivalent of a head which would contain eyes, but he knew without question that they were looking, intently, at him and the other children.

He turned to see how Ernie was doing and in the process saw that all of them, every one of the children, were examining the blackboard with as much concentration as he had been, and then had what was perhaps the strangest experience of this entire adventure when he realized that even though he was looking at his classmates he was still seeing what they were seeing through the blackboard, exactly as if he were seeing it through all of their eyes, and he knew, at the same time, that they were seeing themselves through his eyes. They all seemed, somehow, to have joined.

"Though we have searched extensively," Miss Or was saying solemnly, "we have found no avenue of mental or psychic contact with the enemy. They are inscrutable to us, and we are inscrutable to them."

There had been all along something about the grouping of the beings which was teasingly near recognizable and at last Clarence realized what it was: their grouping was a mirror image of the class's grouping. They were assembled in four rows of five, just as the sixth grade was. And now he realized what else it was they reminded him of: balloons. They looked for all the world like a bunch of balloons of different shapes and colors such as you'd come across for sale in a circus or a fair.

Some were long and straight, some long and spiral; some, the majority, were almost perfectly round; some were a complex series of bulges of different sizes, and some were involved and elaborate combinations of some or all of these elements. In a weird sort of way this seemed to explain their lightness, their constant bobbing and sidewise slipping in the draft or wind which was so much a part of their world.

"Though there have been skeptics," Miss Or pronounced, "there is no doubt we shall eventually taste the fruits of victory, or at least of mutual annihilation."

But even now as Clarence watched them, the balloon beings were beginning some strange sort of group movement which, at first, he took to be an extreme change of posture on their parts; he even had a thought, though with no idea where it might have come from, that they were starting to engage in an elaborate magical dance ritual.

As the movements continued, though, he saw that they were much more extreme, much more basic than an ordinary shifting of parts, that these beings were involved in something a great deal more complicated than a changing of position. They were, he saw, actually engaged in a structural rearrangement of themselves.

At this point all the children of grade six gave a tiny, soft little sigh in unison, a sound so gentle that, perhaps very fortunately, Miss Or missed hearing it entirely, and Clarence Weed, along with Ernie Price, along with Harry Pierce and

Earl Waters and Mary Lou Gorman blurred and lost their edges and ceased to be any of those separate children.

The species, threatened severely and seeing that threat, went quickly and efficiently back to techniques long unused, abandoned since the tribal Cro-Magnon, tactics forsaken since the bold and generous experiment of giving the individual permission to separate from the herd in order to try for perilous, solitary excellence.

Now, faced with an alien danger serious enough to hint at actual extinction, the animal Man rejoined, temporarily abandoning the luxury of individuality and the tricky benefits of multiple consciousness in order to return to the one group mind, joining all strengths together for survival.

Meantime the beings on the other side of the blackboard had progressed significantly with their transformation. Gone now were the smooth, shiny surfaces and come instead were multiple depressions and extrusions, involved modelings and detailings. No longer were they reminiscent of balloons, now they looked like animated creatures in a crude cartoon with simple, splayed hands and blobby eyes, but they looked somewhat like humans, which was not so before.

"Not a retreat," intoned Miss Or, "but an expansion. Not a falling back, but a bold exploration!"

She looked skyward, smiling and starry-eyed, a figure in a patriotic mural. Around her the blackboard figures continued to take on something more like a structure based on bones and the fine points of the faces and fingers and even of costume trivia. Here was Helen Custer's belt with the doe's head buckle coming into focus, now, clearer and clearer, could you make out the round, black rubber patches pasted on the ankles of Dick Doub's gym shoes, and there was no mistaking the increasingly clear pattern of tiny hearts on Elsie Nonan's blouse.

But they were not Helen nor Dick nor Elsie forming there behind the blackboard. They were something quite else. Something entirely different.

"And if Aliahah, even sweet Aliahah, must perish in the flames and rays of war rather than fall into the power of vile invaders," Miss Or had now grown quite ecstatic in her posing before what she still took to be grade six of Washington School. One hand was clenched at her breast and the other raised to take hold of yet another tab from the map holder's inventory, her shark eyes glistening freely with sentimental tears, "its noble race shall survive, at whatever cost!"

The beings, now completely convincing simulations of grade six, began to form a column, two abreast, leading to the graph chart and, on perfect cue, Miss Or smartly sent the chart up into hiding in the map holder and pulling down a long, wide sheet, far bigger than even the map of Aliahah, a design altogether different from anything that had come before, a clearly potent cabalistic symbol which, from its linear suggestions of perspective and its general shape, could represent nothing other than some sort of hermetic door, a pathway for Miss Or's race—her identity with the ominous creatures on the other side of the blackboard was certainly now established beyond any shade of doubt—an entry for the invasion of our own dear planet, Earth.

"Let me show the way!" cried Miss Or joyfully, and all the round, pearlish baubles on her suddenly lit up brightly in orange and magenta, doubtless the colors of Aliahah, as she stepped forward, and with a broad and highly theatrical gesture of invitation to the beings which were even now advancing in step toward the sinister opening she had provided for them, shouted, *"Let me be th—"*

But, unfortunately for Miss Or, unfortunately for her approaching countrybeings, what had been the sixth grade of Washington School rose as one creature, strode forward, lifted her—she was, as her floating hair and prancing steps had suggested, extremely light—and flung her through the door where she impacted on her fellow Aliahahians much as a bowling ball strikes a line of ninepins, and the whole group of them no sooner gave a great wail of despair, when the sheet bearing the drawing of the door flew up into the map holder with a huge puff of smoke and a fine shower of sparks.

It was less than a quarter hour later that Michael O'Donoghue, the school's hard working janitor, experienced the greatest shock and surprise of his life since birth when he opened a storage closet of the main assembly hall with its biographical murals showing pivotal scenes from George Washington's life, and, sprawling with all the abandon of a Raggedy Ann, out tumbled the comely body of Miss Merridew, the regular and rightful teacher of the sixth grade.

Under the concerned ministrations of Mr. O'Donoghue together with the hastily-summoned school nurse, Leska

Haldeen, and under the steady but alarmed gaze of Lester Baxter, the school principal, Miss Merridew was soon restored to consciousness and near to her regular state of health.

Her first thought, of course, was for the children, and so nothing would do but that she must hurry off with O'Donoghue, Haldeen, Baxter and a growing number of curious and worried others in tow, to see if her charges were safe.

They seemed to be, but a careful looking over of all of them showed that, without exception, they were in a peculiar, groggy state, blinking and gaping vaguely at nothing and looking for all the world, as Mr. O'Donoghue observed, "as if they'd been freshly born."

Of course they were asked many questions, not just that day, off and on for some weeks after, but none of the children ever seemed to remember anything at all about what had happened, or, if they did, none of them ever chose to tell.

It was noticed, however, that they all seemed to be very pleased with themselves, even if for no particular reason, and Lucy Barton did mention something vague to her parents just before drifting off to sleep that night, something about a nasty creature that somehow got into the classroom, but they couldn't find out from her whether it was a bug or a rat or what.

The next day Miss Merridew found she was unable to operate the map holder so Mr. O'Donoghue took it to the basement to have a look at it and found that someone must have been tampering with it maliciously for it was indeed jammed and when he took it apart in order to repair it, he saw that some sort of odd conflagration had taken part in its interior. Apparently a flammable substance had been packed into it, set afire, and not only warped its works severely enough to put them beyond Mr. O'Donoghue's abilities to set it right again, but burnt all the maps so badly that there was nothing legible left of any one of them except for a small part of Iowa, and one other fragment which had peculiar, glowing colors in some strange, exotic design.

That was far from the oddest aspect of the little scrap, for Mr. O'Donoghue found that if he held it close to his ear with the designed part uppermost, he could hear a continual, complicated squeaking noise which sounded exactly as if a mutltitude of tiny beings were trapped in a confined space and endlessly crying in horror and panic as they unsuccessfully tried to escape.

Now from that description it might seem that the sound would be extremely disturbing and depressing to hear, but Mr. O'Donoghue found, quite to the contrary, that it gave him great satisfaction to hold the little fragment to his ear for minutes on end, and that the tiny screaming and turmoil, far from being in any way unpleasant, always gave him great satisfaction, and that the screams actually made him chuckle and never failed to cheer him up if he happened to be feeling gloomy.

After dinner that Thanksgiving he showed the fragment to his grandchildren and showed them how to listen to it, and when they heard it they begged him to let them keep it and he didn't, of course, have the heart to refuse.

They took it with them and, while they cherished it dearly and delighted in showing it off to all their friends, it was lost track of through the years and never seen or heard by any human being ever again.

Maurice and Mog

James Herbert

They had laughed at him, but who had the last laugh now? Who had survived, who had lived in comfort, confining though it might be, while others had died in agony? Who had foreseen the holocaust years before the Middle East situation finally bubbled over to world conflict? Maurice Joseph Kelp, *that's* who.

Maurice J. Kelp, the insurance agent (who knew better about future-risk?)

Maurice Kelp, the divorcee (no one else to worry about).

Maurice, the loner (no company was more enjoyable than his own).

He had dug the hole in his back garden in Peckham five years ago, much to the derision of his neighbors (who was laughing now, eh? Eh?), big enough to accommodate a large-sized shelter (room enough for four actually, but who wanted other bodies fouling his air, thank you very much). Refinements had been saved for and fitted during those five years, the shelter itself, in kit form, costing nearly £3,000. Accessories such as the hand-and-battery-operated filtration unit (£350 secondhand) and the personal radiation measuring meter (£145 plus £21.75 VAT) had swollen the costs, and fitting extras like the foldaway wash basin and the own-flush toilet had not been cheap. Worth it, though, worth every penny.

The prefabricated steel sections had been easy to assemble

and the concrete filling-in had been simple enough, once he had read the instruction book carefully. Even fitting the filter and exhaust units had not proved too difficult, when he had fully comprehended what he was supposed to be doing, and the shelter duct connections had proved to be no problem at all. He had also purchased a cheap bilge pump, but mercifully had had no reason to use it. Inside he had installed a bunk bed with foam mattress, a table (the bed was his chair) a heater and Grillogaz cooker, butane gas and battery operated lamps, storage racks filled with tinned and jarred food, dried food, powdered milk, sugar, salt—in all, enough to last him two months. He had a radio with spare batteries (although once below he'd only received crackling noises from it), a medical kit, cleaning utensils, an ample supply of books and magazines (no girlie stuff—he didn't approve of that sort of thing), pencils and paper (including a good stock of toilet paper), strong disinfectants, cutlery, crockery, tin opener, bottle opener, saucepans, candles, clothing, bedding, two clocks (the ticking had nearly driven him crackers for the first few days—he didn't even notice it now), a calendar, and a twelve-gallon drum of water (the water never used for washing dishes, cutlery, or drinking, without his Milton and Maw's Simpla sterilizing tablets).

And oh yes, one more recent acquisition: a dead cat.

Just how the wretched animal had got into his tightly-sealed shelter he had no way of knowing (the cat wasn't talking) but he guessed it must have crept in there a few days before the bombs had dropped. Rising tension in world affairs had been enough to spur Maurice into FINAL PREPARATIONS stage (as four or five similar crises had since he'd owned the shelter) and the nosy creature must have sniffed its way in as he, Maurice, had scurried back and forth from house to shelter, leaving open the conning tower hatch (the structure was shaped like a submarine with the conning tower entrance at one end rather than in the middle). He hadn't discovered the cat until the morning after the holocaust.

Maurice remembered the doomsday vividly, the nightmare impressed onto the back of his brain like a finely detailed mural. God, how frightened he'd been! But then, how smug afterwards.

The months of digging, assembling, equipping—enduring the taunts of neighbors!—had paid off. "Maurice's Ark," they had laughingly called it, and now he realized how apt that description was. Except, of course, it hadn't been built for bloody animals.

He sat bolt upright on the bunk bed, nauseated by the foul smell, but desperate to draw in the thinning air. His face was pale in the glare of the gas lamp.

How many would be alive out there? How many neighbors had died not laughing? Always a loner, would he now be truly alone? Surprisingly, he hoped not.

Maurice could have let some of them in to share his refuge, perhaps just one or two, but the pleasure of closing the hatch in their panic-stricken faces was too good to resist. With the clunking of the rotary locking mechanism and the hatch airtight-sealed against the ring on the outside flange of the conning tower, the rising and falling sirens had become a barely heard wailing, the sound of his neighbors banging on the entrance lid just the muffled tapping of insects. The booming, shaking of the earth had soon put a stop to that.

Maurice had fallen to the floor clutching the blankets he had brought in with him, sure that the thunderous pressure would split the metal shell wide open. He lost count of how many times the earth had rumbled and, though he could not quite remember, he felt perhaps he had fainted. Hours seemed to have been lost somewhere, for the next thing he remembered was awaking on the bunk bed, terrified by the heavy weight on his chest and the warm, fetid breath on his face.

He had screamed and the weight was suddenly gone, leaving only a sharp pain across one shoulder. It took long, disoriented minutes to scrabble around for a torch, the absolute darkness pressing against him like heavy drapes, only his imagination illuminating the interior and filling it with sharp-taloned demons. The searching torch beam discovered nothing, but the saturating lamp light moments later revealed the sole demon. The ginger cat had peered out at him from beneath the bed with suspicious yellow eyes.

Maurice had never liked felines at the best of times, and they, in truth, had never cared much for him. Perhaps now, at the worst of times (for those up there, anyway) he should learn to get along with them.

"Here, moggy," he had half-heartedly coaxed. "Nothing to be afraid of, old son or old girl, whatever you are." It was a few days before he discovered it was "old girl."

The cat refused to budge. It hadn't liked the thundering and trembling of this room and it didn't like the odor of this man. It hissed a warning and the man's sideways head disappeared from view. Only the smell of food a few hours later drew the animal from cover.

"Oh, yes, typical that is," Maurice told it in chastising tones. "Cats and dogs are always around when they can sniff grub."

The cat, who had been trapped in the underground chamber for three days without food or water or even a mouse to nibble at, felt obliged to agree. Nevertheless, she kept at a safe distance from the man.

Maurice, absorbed more by this situation than the one above, tossed a chunk of tinned stewed meat towards the cat, who started back, momentarily alarmed, before pouncing and gobbling.

"Yes, your belly's overcome your fright, hasn't it?" Maurice shook his head, his smile sneering. "Phyllis used to be the same, but with her it was readies," he told the wolfing, disinterested cat, referring to his ex-wife who had left him fifteen years before after only eighteen months of marriage. "Soon as the pound notes were breathing fresh air she was buzzing round like a fly over a turd. Never stayed long once the coffers were empty, I can tell you. Screwed every last penny out of me, the bloody bitch. Got her deserts now, just like the rest of them!" His laugh was forced, for he still did not know how secure he was himself.

Maurice poured half the meat into a saucepan on the gas burner. "Have the rest later tonight," he said, not sure if he was talking to the cat or himself. Next he opened a small can of beans and mixed the contents in with the cooking meat. "Funny how hungry a holocaust can make you." His laughter was still nervous and the cat looked at him quizzically. "All right, I suppose you'll have to be fed. I can't put you out, that's for sure."

Maurice smiled at his own continued humor. So far he was handling the annihilation of the human race pretty well.

"Let's see, we'll have to find you your own dinner bowl. And something for you to do your business in, of course. I can dispose of it easily enough, as long as you keep it in the same place. Haven't I seen you before somewhere? I think you belonged to the colored lady two doors along. Well, she won't be looking for you anymore. It's quite cozy down here, don't you think? I may as well just call you Mog, eh? Looks like we're going to have to put up with each other for a while . . ."

And so, Maurice J. Kelp and Mog had teamed up to wait out the holocaust.

By the end of the first week, the animal had ceased her restless prowling.

By the end of the second week, Maurice had grown quite fond of her.

By the end of the third week, though, the strain had begun to tell. Mog, like Phyllis, found Maurice a little tough to live with. Maybe it was his weak but sick jokes. Maybe it was his constant nagging. It could have been his bad breath. Whatever, the cat spent a lot of time just staring at Maurice and a considerable amount of time avoiding his stifling embrace.

Maurice soon began to resent the avoidance, unable to understand why the cat was so ungrateful. He had fed her, given her a home! Saved her life! Yet she prowled the refuge like some captive creature, shrinking beneath the bunk bed, staring out at him with baleful, distrusting eyes as if . . . as if . . . yes, as if he were going mad. The look was somehow familiar, in some way reminding him of how . . . of how Phyllis used to stare at him. And not only that, the cat was getting sneaky. Maurice had been awakened in the dead of night more than once by the sound of the cat mooching among the food supplies, biting its way into the dried food packets, clawing through the cling-film capped half-full tins of food.

The last time Maurice had really flipped, really lost control. He had kicked the cat and received a four-lane scratch along his shin in return. If his mood had been different, Maurice might have admired the nimble way Mog had dodged the missiles directed at her (a saucepan, canned fruit—the portable own-flush loo).

The cat had never been the same after that. It had crouched in corners, snarling and hissing at him, slinking around the scant furniture, skulking beneath the bunk bed, never using the plastic litter tray that Maurice had so thoughtfully provided, as though it might be trapped in that particular corner and bludgeoned to death. Or worse.

Soon after, while Maurice was sleeping, Mog had gone on to the offensive.

Unlike the first time when he had woken to find the cat squatting on his chest, Maurice awoke to find fierce claws sinking into his face and Mog spitting saliva at him, hissing in a most terrifying manner. With a screech, Maurice had tossed the manic animal away from him, but Mog had immediately returned to the attack, body arched and puffed up by stiffened fur.

They had faced each other from separate ends of the bed, Maurice cringing on the floor, fingers pressed against his deeply gashed forehead and cheek (he hadn't yet realized part of his ear was missing), the cat perched on the bedclothes, hunchbacked and snarling, eyes gleaming a nasty yellow.

She came for Maurice again, a streaking ginger blur, a fury of fur, all fangs and sharp-pointed nails. He raised the blankets just in time to catch the cat and screeched as the material tore. Maurice ran when he should have used the restraining bedcovers to his advantage; unfortunately, the area for escape was limited. He climbed the small ladder to the conning tower and crouched at the top (the height was not more than eight feet from hatch to floor), legs drawn up and head ducked against the metal lid itself.

Mog followed and claws dug into Maurice's exposed buttocks. He howled.

Maurice fell, not because of the pain, but because something crashed to the ground above them, causing a vibration of seismic proportions to stagger the steel panels of the bunker. He fell and the cat, still clutching his rear end, fell with him. It squealed briefly as its back was broken.

Maurice, still thinking that the wriggling animal was on the attack, quickly picked himself up and staggered toward the other end of the bunker, wheezing air as he went. He scooped up the saucepan from the Grillogaz to defend himself with and looked in open-mouthed surprise at the writhing cat. With a whoop of glee, Maurice snatched up the bedcovers and raced back to the helpless creature. He smothered Mog and thrashed her body with the saucepan until the animal no longer moved and tiny squeals no longer came from beneath the blankets. Then he picked up a flat-bottomed cylinder of butane gas, using both hands to lift it, and dropped it on a bump where he imagined Mog's head to be.

Finally he sat on the bed, chest heaving, blood running from his wounds, and giggled at his triumph.

Then he had to live with the decomposing body for another week.

Not even a triple layer of tightly-sealed polythene bags, the insides liberally dosed with disinfectant, could contain the smell, and not even the chemicals inside the Porta Potti toilet could eat away the carcass. In three days the stench was unbearable; Mog had found her own revenge.

And something else was happening to the air inside the shelter. It was definitely becoming harder to breathe and it wasn't only due to the heavy cat odor. The air was definitely becoming thinner by the day, and lately, by the hour.

Maurice had intended to stay inside for at least six weeks, perhaps eight if he could bear it, all-clear sirens or not; now, with no more than four weeks gone, he knew he would have to risk the outside world. Something had clogged the ventilation system. No matter how long he turned the handle of the Microflow Survivaire equipment for, or kept the motor running from the twelve-volt car battery, the air was not replenished. His throat made a thin wheezing noise as he sucked in, and the stink cloyed at his nostrils as if he were immersed in the deepest, foulest sewer. He had to have good, clean air, radiation packed or not; otherwise he would die a different sort of slow death. Asphyxiation accompanied by the mocking smell of the dead cat was no way to go. Besides, some pamphlets said fourteen days was enough for fallout to have dispersed.

Maurice rose from the bed and clutched at the small table, immediately dizzy. The harsh white glare from the butane gas lamp stung his red-rimmed eyes. Afraid to breathe and more afraid not to, he staggered toward the conning tower. It took all his strength to climb the few rungs of the ladder and he rested just beneath the hatch, head swimming, barely inflated lungs protesting. Several moments passed before he was able to raise an arm and jerk open the locking mechanism.

Thank God, he thought. Thank God I'm getting out, away from the evil sodding ginger cat. No matter what it's like out there, no matter who or what else has survived, it would be a blessed relief from this bloody stinking shithouse.

He allowed the hatch to swing down on its hinge. Powdered dust covered his head and shoulders, and when he had blinked away the tiny grains from his eyes, he uttered a weak cry of dismay. He now understood the cause of the crash just a week before: the remains of a nearby building, undoubtedly his own house, had finally collapsed. And the rubble had covered the ground above him, blocking his air supply, obstructing his escape exit.

His fingers tried to dig into the concrete slab, but hardly marked the surface. He pushed, he heaved, but nothing shifted. Maurice almost collapsed down the ladder, barely able to keep his feet at the bottom. He wailed as he stumbled around the bunker looking for implements to cut through the solid wall above, the sound rasping and faint. He used knives, forks, anything with a sharp point to hammer at the concrete, all to no avail, for the concrete was too strong and his efforts too weak.

He finally banged dazedly at the blockage with a bloodied fist.

Maurice fell back into what was now a pit and howled his frustration. Only the howl was more like a wheeze, the kind a cat might make when choking.

The plastic-covered bundle at the far end of the shelter did not move but Maurice, tears forcing rivulets through the dust on his face, was sure he heard a faint, derisory *meow*.

"Never liked cats," he panted. "Never."

Maurice sucked his knuckles, tasting his own blood, and waited in his private, self-built tomb. It was only a short time to wait before shadows crept in on his vision and his lungs became flat and still, but it seemed an eternity to Maurice. A lonely eternity, even though Mog was there to keep him company.

Angel's Exchange

Jessica Amanda Salmonson

"Ah, my brother angel Sleep, I beg a boon of thee," said grimacing Death.

"It cannot be," answered Sleep, "that I grant a gift of slumber to you, for Death must be forever vigilant in his cause."

"That is just it," said Death. "I grow melancholy with my lot. Everywhere I go, I am cursed by those I strive most to serve. The forgetfulness of your gift brings momentary respite and would help a wearied spirit heal."

"I can scarce believe you are greeted with less enthusiasm than I!" exclaimed the angel Sleep, appalled and incredulous. "Despite the transience of the gift I bring to mortals, they seem ever happy to have had it for a time. Your own gift is an everlasting treasure, and should be sought more quickly than mine."

"Aye, some seek me out, but never in joyous mind," said Death, his voice low and self-pitying. "You are praised at morning's light, when people have had done with you. Perhaps it is the very impermanence of your offering which fills them with admiration; the gift itself means little."

"I cannot see that that is so," said Sleep, though not affronted by the extrapolation. "What I would give for your gift held to my breast! Do you think there is anything so weary as Sleep itself? Yet I am denied your boon, as you are denied mine; I, without a moment's rest, deliver it to others, like a starving grocery boy on rounds. It is my ceaseless task to give humanity a taste of You, so they might be prepared. Yet you say they meet you with hatred and trepidation. Have I, then, failed my task?"

"I detect an unhappiness as great as mine," said Death, a rueful light shining in the depths of his hollow eyes.

"Brothers as we are," said Sleep, "it is sad to realize we know so little of the other's sentiment. Each of us is unhappy with our lot. This being so, why not trade professions? You take my bag of slumber, and I your bag of souls; but if we find ourselves dissatisfied even then, we must continue without complaint."

"I would not mind giving you my burden and taking up yours," said Death. "Even if I remain sad, I cannot believe I would be sadder; and there is the chance things would improve for me."

So Death and Sleep exchanged identities. Thereafter, Sleep came nightly to the people of the world, a dark presence, sinister, with the face of a skull; and thereafter, Death came, as bright and beautiful as Gabriel, with as sweet a sound. In time, great cathedrals were raised, gothic and somber, and Sleep was worshipped by head-shaven, emaciated monks. Thereafter, beauty was considered frightening. The prettiest children were sacrificed in vain hope of Death's sweet face not noticing the old.

Thus stands the tale of how Death became Sleep and Sleep became Death. If the world was fearful before, it is more so now.

Hidey Hole

Steve Rasnic Tem

Every house Jennifer had ever lived in had a hidey hole. A secret place at the back of a closet, or behind a door, or under a porch. A place where thoughts were private and where you could be anything you wanted to be. She thought that maybe each house came that way. Or better still, maybe you dreamed the hidey holes up in your head because you just had to have them, and that made them appear. Like magic.

Jennifer had never gone inside any of her hidey holes, not at any of the many houses she'd lived in. She'd always been too afraid.

Instead she went inside herself and dreamed about what it would be like to be inside those hidey holes. The dreams weren't always nice.

Here the hidey hole was under the brick porch, on the cold north side beside a bush where nobody went, not even her parents. Her mom said the dirt was too poor to plant a flower bed there. Six or seven bricks were missing to make the hole. It was the only opening under the porch—everything else was all brick. Jennifer could see black dirt there, and if she stood several feet away—which was the closest she would ever get to the hidey hole—she saw an old moldy shoe and a brown bottle a couple of feet inside.

This was her twelfth house, hers and her mom's—that was more houses than she was years old. She had a dad this time,

not just Mom's boyfriend, and Mom promised her he was
going to last. He wasn't too bad, kind of grumpy sometimes
but then he read stories to her sometimes and took her places
and told her, really told her, that he loved her. None of them
had ever done that before.

But she was big for her age. Maybe a little fat, "baby fat"
her new dad called it and laughed a little. And taller than
anyone else in her class. "Big-boned," her new grandmother
called it, and gave her a brownie and some milk. Her new dad
didn't like her grandmother doing that. He said it just
encouraged her to eat too much.

He said it was okay to be bigger than the other kids, but he
made her run all the time just the same. And made her take
classes. And made her wear clothes that made her look not so
big.

He said he cared, and that was pretty okay. But he didn't like
her being fat. She could tell. Her mom was always saying she
was fat because she was lazy and because she didn't care about
herself. Her new dad didn't like her mom saying those things to
her, but she'd always been saying those things, so Jennifer
didn't think she'd stop it now.

Besides, Jennifer didn't think it bothered her so much
anymore. Not so much. She'd just lie on her bed and pretend
she was in the hidey hole. She'd make a picture about what it
was like inside the hidey hole. She'd make a picture of a little
dog in the hidey hole she could pet. She'd make a picture of a
bunch of comic books and sodas all covered with ice like on
the TV. She'd make a picture of a bag of cookies, and flowers
growing there even though it was so dark, and the ground was
so poor.

But most of the pictures she made were mean ones. Snakes
and lizards with long tongues, black beetles and white wigglers
eating rotting dead things and old underwear, horrible things
she couldn't name that squirmed and dug and scraped the
ground at the bottom of the hidey hole.

She thought it was probably pretty bad to be thinking those
things, but she couldn't help it. They just came that way. And it
made things feel a little better that they came—she thought that
was pretty weird, and a pretty bad thing, too. Maybe she was
just bad all the way through.

But she would never go *inside* a hidey hole. Not one single
one of them. She was much too afraid. Something might

happen to her for making all those mean things. Maybe—and this was hard to think about—maybe she'd just turn into a mean thing *herself*. So she'd never go inside one. She'd just make pictures inside her head instead.

There was just one more problem she had, besides being big for her age. That was Robert. Robert was five years old. Robert was her new little brother.

A long time ago Jennifer's new dad had had another wife, and Robert was their baby. Then she did something real bad and so she didn't live there anymore. Robert wasn't a baby anymore. Jennifer liked babies; babies were cute. Robert was her new dad's little son, and her little brother.

Jennifer's new dad loved little Robert a whole lot.

But that was okay. He was supposed to. Because he was a good daddy.

The problem was that Robert was just too little to be much fun. And every time her new dad wanted to take her some place, little Robert wanted to go, too. And her new dad usually let him.

And her new dad was all the time stopping her from yelling at Robert, or from shoving him away when he got into her business. Her new dad kept saying she didn't always know how big she was, and she could hurt him. He called that "bullying." Jennifer didn't understand. Robert just kept making her mad at him, and she didn't want him making her mad. It scared her to be mad.

Her mom always said she had a mean temper.

Now today Robert was wanting to play with her some more. He wanted her to take him outside.

"Let's play soldier!" he kept saying, real loud.

Jennifer just looked at him. He *was* kind of cute when he was all excited like that about something. And sometimes she actually *liked* playing with him. Her new dad said Robert "looked up to her." That was kind of nice.

But he was too little for her. And she didn't feel like playing outside.

"Let's play soldier!" he screamed.

"Hush! You'll get us both in trouble!"

"I'll tell Dad you . . . hit me!" Robert looked happy that he said that.

"I don't think he'd believe you."

"Mom would."

Jennifer figured he was right. And just then her mom did come in.

"What's going on here?" Her mom looked like she just got out of bed. Her hair looked dirty. Jennifer thought that her mom wasn't very pretty anymore. It made her wonder why she was always telling Jennifer, that *she* didn't look good.

Robert looked real sad. He was pretty good at looking sad. "Jennifer won't play wif me."

"Go out and play with him, Jennifer."

"But, Mom . . ."

"Just do what I said. It's better than having you two yelling at each other down here, waking me up."

So Robert ran outside, Jennifer walking right behind him, trying not to say anything. But then Robert ran toward the north side of the house.

Jennifer felt a hurt in her chest. "Don't!" She'd yelled it so loud Robert stopped and turned around. He looked surprised, and a little scared. "Let's play someplace else," she said.

He looked at her a little while and then said, "Don't want to!" He turned and kept running toward that side of the house.

"Robert!" Suddenly Jennifer was running toward that side of the house, too.

When she rounded the corner Robert was crouched down in front of the hole.

"*No*, Robert!"

He turned and stared at her. "It ain't your hole," he said, "Dad and me had this house before you ever came."

Jennifer's chest hurt again. For a little bit it was hard to breathe. She was watching wide-eyed as he started to crawl through the hole. "Don't go in there!"

He stopped and turned his head. "It ain't your hole!"

Jennifer wanted to tell him it was her place, her secret special place that she'd made herself because she pictured it and thought about it and knew the kind of things that might be there. But she wouldn't crawl into the hidey hole herself; she was much too afraid. So how could it be hers?

"It's not safe." It was all she could think of to say.

Robert looked a little worried. "Why not?"

"There's things in it, crawly things. And . . . things with long thin legs to wrap around you." She shivered just saying it. Pictures were coming into her head she tried to keep out.

Robert looked at her with his little lip sticking out. She

might have thought he was cute then if she wasn't so mad at him. "I don't believe you," he said. "You're lying."

"No, I'm not."

"Yes you are and God hates liars. He burns 'em up!"

There were more pictures fighting to get inside Jennifer's had. She kept looking at Robert real hard, thinking about him being her little brother, trying to think about the times she liked him. It got harder and harder. "Go on in, then! I don't *care!*"

She screamed it out so quick, she didn't even know she was going to say it. Robert was already halfway into the hole before she thought to take it back. "No! Robert, come back!"

And in her panic, she let the pictures come into her head.

A thin line dropped onto Robert's back, followed by another, then another. She could see his little yellow T-shirt bulge in the places where the lines, the legs, pressed in.

He had just begun screaming when the last long leg wrapped around his backside and pulled him in. Then he stopped screaming.

Jennifer turned and ran.

They never found Robert. Finally the police decided her new dad's old wife had come and got him, and so they had to find *her*. But nobody knew where she was. Jennifer told them all she was in the backyard when Robert ran around to the front. That was the last she ever saw him.

Her new dad was very sad. Sometimes he just held Jennifer in his lap for a long time, real tight, and didn't say a word.

Her mom just looked at her. But at least she didn't say bad things about her anymore. Just once she said, real quiet, "You're going to drive this one away, too, aren't you?" Jennifer wasn't sure what she meant.

Jennifer knew she was bad inside. She saw the pictures of her badness in her head. They were real mean and real ugly.

That's why she never went inside any of the hidey holes. Because that's where she'd always kept her badness so no one could see it.

But she missed Robert. She'd liked her little brother a lot, more than she ever knew. After all, he was the only one she'd ever had. Maybe she'd even loved Robert, but she decided she really didn't know what that meant.

She was going to have to go visit the hidey hole real soon now. Just like Robert. Just like Robert, she was going to have to go inside.

Long After Ecclesiastes

Ray Bradbury

Long after Ecclesiastes:
The First Book of Dichotomy,
The Second Book of Symbiosis,
What do they say?
Work away.
Make do.
Believe.
Conceive
That by the bowels of Christ
It may be true—
There's more to Matter
Than me and you.
There's Universe
Terse
In the microscope.
With hope find Elephant
    beyond—
God's fond of vastness there.
And everywhere? spare parts!
This large, that small!
His All spreads forth in seas
Of multiplicities
While staying mere.
Things do adhere, then fly apart;

The heart pumps one small tide
While brides of Time train by in
    Comets' tails.
Flesh jails our senses;
All commences or stops short
To start again.
The stars are rain that falls on
    twilight field.
All's yield, all's foundering to
    death.
Yet in an instant
God's sweet breath sighs Life
    again.
All's twain yet all is twin
While, micro-midge within,
Dire hairy mammoth hides in
    flea.
I hop with him!
And trumpet to the skies!
All dies?
No, all's reborn.
The world runs to its End?
No: Christmas Morn
Where my small candle flickers
    in the dark.
My spark then fuses Catherine
    Wheel
Which ricochets wild flesh in
    all directions;
Resurrections of hope and will
    I feel.
Antheaps of elephants do mole
    in me.
In good Christ's crib by shore of
    Galilee
We all step forth to feast
On star in East which rises in
    pure shouts.
We hug our doubts, but love,
For we're above as well as low;
Our bodies stay, our senses go
And pull old blood along;

We move to grave ourselves on
    Moon and Mars
And then, why not, the stars?
But always mindful on the way
    to sense
Where flesh and Nothing
    stop/commence;
Where shuttling God in swift
    osmosis
Binds abyss sea
In space born flea
And give us war-mad men some
    hope
To fire-escape psychosis,
Moves tongues to say
What's day is night, night-day,
What's lost to sight is found
The Cosmic Ground which
    shrinks us small
But dreams us tall again.
Our next desire? Space!
We race to leap into that fire,
To Phoenix-forth our lives.
God thrives in flame,
Do we game and play,
God and Man one name?
Under pseudonym,
Does God scribble us,
We Him?
Give up being perplexed,
Here's a text that's final,
God, the spinal cord,
We, the flesh of Lord.
In the Pleiades,
Read both, if you please.
Immortality's prognosis
Scriptured, shaped, designed,
Palmer penned and signed:
The First Book of Dichotomy!
The Second Book of
Symbiosis!

The Night Is Freezing Fast

Thomas F. Monteleone

It started with a curse—albeit a mild one.

"Oh *damn!*" cried Grandma from the kitchen. When ten-year-old Alan heard her cursing, he knew she was serious.

Grandpa eased the Dubuque newspaper down from his face, and spoke to her. "What's the matter?"

"I ran out of shortnin' for this cake . . . and if you want a nice dessert for Christmas dinner, you'll get yourself into town and get me some more."

"But it's a *blizzard* goin' on out there!" said Grandpa.

Grandma said nothing. Grandpa just sighed as he dropped his paper, shuffled across the room to the foyer closet.

Alan watched him open the door and pull out snow boots, a beat-up corduroy hat, and a mackinaw jacket of red and black plaid. He turned and looked wistfully at Alan, who was sitting in on the floor half-watching a football game.

"Want to take a ride, Alan?"

"Into town?"

"Yep. 'Fraid so."

"In the blizzard?"

Grandpa sighed, stole a look toward the kitchen. "Yep."

"Yeah! That'll be *great* fun," he said.

Alan ran to the closet and pulled on the heavy, rubber-coated boots, a knit watch cap, and scarf. Then he shook into the goose down parka his mom had ordered from the L. L. Bean mail-order place. It was so *different* out here in Iowa.

"Forty-two years with that woman and I don't know how she figures she can . . ."

Grandpa had just closed the door to the mud porch behind them. He was muttering as he faced into the stinging slap of the December wind, the bite of the ice-hard snowflakes attacking his cheeks. Alan heard on the radio that there would be roof-high drifts by morning if it kept up like this.

Grandpa stepped down to the path shoveled toward the garage. It was already starting to fill in and would need some new digging out pretty soon.

The hypnotic effect of the snow fascinated Alan. "Do you get storms like this all the time, Grandpa?"

" 'Bout once a month this bad." Grandpa reached the garage door, threw it up along its spring-loaded tracks. He shook his head and shivered from the wind chill. "I don't know about you, but *I'd* rather be with your mom and dad, takin' that cruise right about now."

"No way! This is going to be the first *real* Christmas I ever had!"

"Why? Because it's a *white* one?" Grandpa chuckled as he opened the door of the four-wheel-drive Scout, climbed in.

"Sure," said Alan "Haven't you ever heard that song?"

Grandpa smiled. "Oh, I think I've heard it a time or two . . ."

"Well, that's what I mean. It *never* seems like Christmas in L.A.—even when it *is* Christmas!" Alan jumped into the Scout and slammed the door. The blizzard awaited them.

Grandpa eased the Scout from the driveway to Route 14A. Alan looked out across the flat landscape of the other farms in the distance, and felt disoriented. He could not tell where the snowy land stopped and the white of the sky began. When the Scout lurched forward out onto the main road it looked like they were constantly driving smack into a white sheet of paper, a white nothingness.

It was scary, thought Alan. Just as scary as driving into a pitch-black night.

"Oh, she picked a fine time to run out of something for that danged cake! Look at it, Alan. It's goin' to be a regular *white-out*, is what it is."

Alan nodded. "How do you know where you're going, Grandpa?"

Grandpa harrumphed. "Been on this road a million times, boy. Lived here all my life! I'm not about to get lost. But my god, it's *cold* out there! Hope this heater gets going pretty soon . . ."

They drove on in silence except for the skrunch of the tires on the packed snow and *thunk-thunk* of the wiper blades trying to move off the hard new flakes that pelted the glass. The heater still pumped chilly air into the cab and Alan's breath was almost freezing as it came out of his mouth.

He imagined that they were explorers on a faraway planet—an alien world of ice and eternally freezing winds. It was an instantaneous, catapulting adventure of the type only possible in the minds of imaginative ten-year-olds. There were creatures out in the blizzard—great white hulking things. Pale, reptilian, evil-eyed things. Alan squinted through the windshield, ready in his gun turret if one turned on them. He would blast it with his laser cannons . . .

"What in *heck?*" muttered Grandpa.

Abruptly, Alan was out of his fantasy world as he stared past the flicking windshield wipers. There was a dark shape standing in the center of the white nothingness. As the Scout advanced along the invisible road, drawing closer to the contrasted object, it became clearer, more distinct.

It was a man. He was standing by what must be the roadside, waving a gloved hand at Grandpa.

Braking easily, Grandpa stopped the Scout and reached across to unlock the door. The blizzard rushed in ahead of the stranger, slicing through Alan's clothes like a cold knife. "Where you headed?" cried Grandpa over the wind. "I'm going as far as town . . ."

"That'll do," said the stranger.

Alan caught a quick glimpse of him as he pushed into the back seat. He was wearing a thin coat that seemed to hang on him like a scarecrow's rags. He had a black scarf wrapped tight around his neck and a dark blue ski mask that covered his face under a floppy-brimmed old hat. Alan didn't like that—not being able to see the stranger's face.

"Cold as hell out there!" said the man as he smacked his gloved hands together. He laughed to himself, then: "Now there's a funny expression for you, ain't it? 'Cold as hell.'

Don't make much sense, does it? But people still say it, don't they?''

"I guess they do," said Grandpa as he slipped the Scout into gear and started off again. Alan looked at the old man, who looked like an older version of his father, and thought he saw an expression of concern, if not apprehension, forming on the lined face.

"It's not so funny, though . . ." said the stranger, his voice lowering a bit. "Everybody figures hell to be this *hot* place, but it don't *have* to be, you know?"

"Never really thought about it much," said Grandpa, jiggling with the heater controls. It was so cold, thought Alan. It just didn't seem to want to work.

Alan shivered, uncertain whether or not it was from the lack of heat, or the words, the voice of the stranger.

"Matter of fact, it makes more sense to think of hell as full of all kinds of *different* pain. I mean, fire is so unimaginative, don't you think? Now, *cold* . . . something as cold as that wind out there could be just as bad, right?" The man in the back seat chuckled softly beneath the cover of the ski mask. Alan didn't like that sound.

Grandpa cleared his throat and faked a cough. "I don't think I've really thought much about that either," he said as he appeared to be concentrating on the snow-covered road ahead. Alan looked at his grandfather's face and could see the unsteadiness in the old man's eyes. It was the look of fear, slowly building.

"Maybe you should . . ." said the stranger.

"Why?" said Alan. "What do you mean?"

"It stands to reason that a demon would be comfortable in any kind of element—as long as it's harsh, as long as it's cruel."

Alan tried to clear his throat and failed. Something was stuck down there, even when he swallowed.

The stranger chuckled again. "Course, I'm getting off the track . . . we were talking about figures of speech, weren't we?"

"You're the one doing all the talking, mister," said Grandpa.

The stranger nodded. "Actually, a more appropriate expression would be 'cold as the *grave*' . . ."

"It's not *this* cold under the ground," said Alan defensively.

"Now, how would *you* know?" asked the stranger slowly. "You've never been in the grave . . . not *yet*, anyway."

"That's enough of that silly talk, mister!" said Grandpa. His voice was hard-sounding, but Alan detected fear beneath the thin layer of his words.

Alan looked from his grandfather to the stranger. As his eyes locked in with those behind the ski mask, Alan felt an ice pick touch the tip of his spine. There was something about the stranger's eyes, something dark which seemed to lurch and caper violently behind them.

A dark chuckle came from the back seat.

"Silly talk? *Silly?*" asked the stranger. "Now what's silly and what's serious in the world today? Who can *tell* anymore?! Missiles and summit conferences! Vampires and garlic! Famine and epidemics! Full moons and maniacs!"

The words rattled out of the dark man and chilled Alan more deeply than the cold blast of the heater fan. He looked away and tried to stop the shiver which raced up and down his backbone.

"Where'd you say you was goin', Mister?" asked Grandpa as he slowly eased off the gas pedal.

"I didn't say."

"Well, how about sayin'—right now."

"Do I detect hostility in your voice, sir? Or is it something else?" Again came the deep-throated, whispery chuckle.

Alan kept his gaze upon the white on-white panorama ahead. But he was listening to every word being exchanged between the dark stranger and his grandfather, who was suddenly assuming the proportions of a champion. He listened but he could not turn around, he could not look back. There was a fear gripping him now. It was a gnarled spindly claw reaching up for him, out of the darkness of his mind, closing in on him with a terrible certainty.

Grandpa hit the brakes a little too hard, and even the four-wheel-drive of the Scout couldn't keep it from sliding off to the right to gently slap a bank of plowed snow. Alan watched his grandfather as he turned and stared at the stranger.

"Listen, Mister, I don't know what your game is, but I don't find it very amusin' like you seem to . . . And I don't appreciate the way you've dealt with our hospitality."

Grandpa glared at the man in the back seat, and Alan could

feel the courage burning behind the old man's eyes. Just the sight of it gave Alan the strength to turn and face the stranger.

"Just trying to make conversation," said the man in a velvety-soft voice. It seemed to Alan that the stranger's voice could change any time he wanted it to, could sound any way at all. The man in the mask was like a ventriloquist or a magician, maybe . . .

"Well, to be truthful with you, Mister," Grandpa was saying. "I'm kinda tired of your 'conversation,' so why don't you climb out right here?"

The eyes behind the mask flitted between Grandpa and Alan once, twice. "I see . . ." said the voice. "No more silly stuff, eh?"

The stranger leaned forward, putting a gloved hand on the back of Alan's seat. The hand almost touched Alan's parka and he pulled away. He knew he didn't want the stranger touching him. Acid churned in his stomach.

"Very well," said the dark man. "I'll be leaving you now . . . but one last thought, all right?"

"I'd rather not," said Grandpa, as the man squeezed out the open passenger's door.

"But you will . . ." Another soft laugh as the stranger stood in the drifted snow alongside the road. The eyes behind the mask darted from Grandpa to Alan and back again. "You see, it's just a short ride we're all taking . . . and the night is freezing fast."

Grandpa's eyes widened a bit as the words drifted slowly into the cab, cutting through the swirling, whipping-cold wind. Then he gunned the gas pedal. "Good-bye, Mister . . ."

The Scout suddenly leaped forward in the snow with such force that Alan didn't have to pull the door closed—it slammed shut from the force of the acceleration.

Looking back, Alan could see the stranger quickly dwindle to nothing more than a black speck on the white wall behind them.

"Of all the people to be helpful to, and I have to pick a danged nut!" Grandpa forced a smile to his face. He looked at Alan and tapped his arm playfully. "Nothin' to worry about now, boy. He's behind us and gone."

"Who you figure he was?"

"Oh, just a nut, son. A kook. When you get older you'll realize that there's lots of 'funny' people in the world."

"You think he'll still be out on the road when we go back?"

Grandpa looked at Alan and tried to smile. It was an effort and it didn't look anything at all like a real smile.

"You were afraid of him, weren't you, boy?"

Alan nodded. "Weren't *you?*"

Grandpa didn't answer for an instant. He certainly *looked* scared. Then: "Well, kinda, I guess. But I've known about his type. Everybody runs into 'im . . . sooner or later, I guess."

"Really?" Alan didn't understand what the old man meant. Grandpa looked ahead. "Well, here's the store . . ."

After parking, Grandpa ran into the Food-A-Rama for a pound of butter while Alan remained in the cab with the engine running, the heater fan wailing, and the doors locked. Looking out into the swirling snow, Alan could barely pick out single flakes anymore. Everything was blending into a furiously thick, white mist. The windows of the Scout were blank sheets of paper, he could see *nothing* beyond the glass.

Suddenly there was a dark shape at the driver's side, and the latch rattled on the door handle. The lock flipped up and Grandpa appeared with a small brown paper bag in his hand. "Boy, it's blowin' up terrible out here! What a time that woman has to send us out!"

"It looks worse," said Alan.

"Well, maybe not," said Grandpa, slipping the vehicle into gear. "Night's coming on. When it gets darker, the white-out won't be as bad."

They drove home along Route 28, which would eventually curve down and cross 14A. Alan fidgeted with heater fan and the cab was finally starting to warm up a little bit. He felt better, but he couldn't get the stranger's voice out of his mind.

"Grandpa, what did that man mean about 'a short ride' we're all taking? And about the night freezing fast?"

"I don't rightly know what he meant, Alan. He was a kook, remember? He probably don't know himself what he meant by it . . ."

"Well, he sure did make it sound creepy, didn't he?"

"Yes, I guess he did," said Grandpa as he turned the wheel onto a crossing road. "Here we go, here's 14A. Almost home, boy! I hope your grandmother's got that fireplace hot!"

The Scout trundled along the snowed-up road until they reached a bright orange mailbox that marked the entrance to Grandpa's farm. Alan exhaled slowly, and felt the relief spreading into his bones. He hadn't wanted to say anything, but the white-white of the storm and the seeping cold had been bothering him, making him get a terrible headache, probably from squinting so much.

"*What* in—?" Grandpa eased off the accelerator as he saw the tall, thin figure standing in the snow-filled rut of the driveway.

"It's *him,* Grandpa . . ." said Alan in a whisper.

The dark man stepped aside as the Scout eased up to him. Angrily, Grandpa wound down the window, and let the storm rush into the cab. He shouted past the wind at the stranger. "You've got a lot of nerve comin' up to my house!"

The eyes behind the ski mask seemed to grow darker, unblinking. "Didn't have much choice," said the chameleon-voice.

Grandpa unlocked the door, and stepped out to face the man. "What do you mean by that?"

Soft laughter cut through the howl of the wind. "Come now! You *know* who I am . . . and *why* I'm here."

The words seemed to stop Grandpa in his tracks. Alan watched the old man's face flash suddenly pale. Grandpa nodded. "Maybe," he said, "but I never knew it to be like this . . ."

"There are countless ways," said the stranger "Now excuse me, and step aside . . ."

"What?" Grandpa sounded shocked.

Alan had climbed down from the Scout, standing behind the two men. He could hear naked terror couched in the back of his grandfather's throat, the trembling fear in his voice. Without realizing it, Alan was backing away from the Scout. His head was pounding like a jackhammer.

"Is it the *woman?!*" Grandpa was asking in a whisper.

The dark man shook his head.

Grandpa moaned loudly, letting it turn into words. "No! Not *him!* No, you can't mean it!"

"Aneurysm . . ." said the terribly soft voice behind the mask.

Suddenly Grandpa grabbed the stranger by the shoulder, and spun him around, facing him squarely. "No!" he shouted, his face twisted and ugly. "Me! Take me!"

"Can't do it," said the man.

"Grandpa, what's the matter?!" Alan started to feel dizzy.

The pounding in his head had become a raging fire. It hurt so bad he wanted to scream.

"Yes you can!" yelled Grandpa. "I *know* you can!"

Alan watched as Grandpa reached out and grabbed at the tall thin man's ski mask. It seemed to come apart as he touched it, and fell away from beneath the droopy brimmed hat. For an instant, Alan could see—or at least he *thought* he saw—*nothing* beneath the mask. It was like staring into a night sky and suddenly realizing the *endlessness*, the eternity of it all. To Alan, it was just an eye-blink of time, and then he saw, for another instant, white, angular lines, dark hollows of empty sockets.

But the snow was swirling and whipping, and Grandpa was suddenly wrestling with the man, and the ache in his head was almost blinding him now. Alan screamed as the man wrapped his long thin arms around his grandfather and they seemed to dance briefly around in the snow.

"Run, boy!" screamed Grandpa.

Alan turned toward the house, then looked back and he saw Grandpa collapsing in the snow. The tall, dark man was gone.

"Grandpa!" Alan ran to the old man's side as he lay face up, his glazed eyes staring into the storm.

"Get your grandmother . . . quick," said the old man. "It's my heart."

"Don't die, Grandpa . . . not now!" Alan was frantic and didn't know what to do. He wanted to get help, but he didn't want to leave his grandfather in the storm like this.

"No choice in it," he said. "A deal's a deal."

Alan looked at his grandfather, suddenly puzzled. "What?"

Grandpa winced as new pain lanced his chest. "Don't matter now . . ." The old man closed his eyes and wheezed out a final breath.

Snowflakes danced across his face, and Alan noticed that his headache, like the dark man, had vanished.

The Old Men Know

Charles L. Grant

There was an odd light in the yard in the middle of November.
A curious light. And puzzling.

The weather was right for the time of the year: clouds so
close they might have been called overcast were it not for the
stark gradations of dark and light gray, for the bulges that
threatened violence, for the thin spots that promised blue; a
wind steady but not strong, damp and cold but only hinting at
the snow that would fall not this time but too soon for comfort;
the look of things in general, with the grass still struggling to
hang onto its green, the shrubs tented in burlap, the trees
undecided—some newly bare, others with leaves intact and
tinted, colors that didn't belong to the rest of the land.

Those colors were precious now. They were the only break
in desolation until spring, not even the snow promising much
more than slush or the mark of passing dogs or the dark tracks
of creatures, mechanical and living. Those colors were loved,
and cherished, and unlike the same ones that filled most of
October, these were mourned because they marked the end of
the end of change. To see them now meant the air no longer
smelled like smoke, that the sunsets would be bleak, that the
brown they'd become would fill gutters and driveways with
work, not with pleasure.

But the light was curious, and so then were the colors.

From my second-story study window I could see a maple

111

tree in the middle of the backyard. It wasn't tall, but its crown was thick enough to provide ample summer shade, and a pile of leaves big enough for the neighborhood children to leap into after I'd spent an hour raking them up. Its color this year was a yellow laced with red, made all the more brilliant because the tall shrubs and trees behind it had lost their leaves early and provided the maple with a background glum enough to make it stand out.

Now it was almost glowing.

I looked up from my accounts and stared at it, leaned away and rubbed my eyes lightly, leaned forward again and squinted.

"Hey," I said, "come here and look at this."

A whispering of skirts, and Belle came to the desk, stood behind me and put her hands on my shoulders. She peered through the window, craned and looked down into the yard as close to the house as she could.

"What?"

"Don't you see it?" I pointed to the tree.

"Yeah. Okay."

"Doesn't it look sort of odd to you?"

"Looks like a tree to me."

If she had said yes, I would have agreed, watched it a few moments more and returned to paying the bills; if she had said no, I would have pressed her a little just to be sure she wasn't kidding; but she had been, as she was increasingly lately, flippant without the grace of humor. So I rose, walked around the desk and stood at the window. The sill was low, the panes high, and I was able to check the sky for the break in the clouds that had let in the sun just enough to spotlight the maple. There was none, however, and I checked the room's other three windows.

"Caz, I think you have a blur on your brain."

"Don't be silly."

She followed me around the room, checked as I did, muttering incomprehensibly, and just low enough to bother me. And when I returned to the desk she sat on it, crossed her legs and hiked up the plaid skirt to the middle of her thighs.

"Sailor," she said, "you've been at sea too long. Wanna have a good time?" Her slippered foot nudged my knee. She winked and turned slightly to bring my gaze to her chest. "What do you say, fella? I'm better than I look."

I almost laughed, and didn't because that's what she wanted

me to do. When we'd met at a party five years ago, I had kept to myself in a corner chair, nursing a weak drink I didn't want, eavesdropping on conversations I didn't want to join. I was having fun. I preferred being alone, and I entertained the fantasy of my being invisible, a harmless voyeur of the contemporary scene, unwilling, and perhaps unable, to make any commitments. Then Belle had come over in dark blue satin, pulled up an ottoman and given me the same lines she'd just spoken in the study. I'd laughed then, and surprised myself by talking to her. All night, in fact, without thinking we might end up in bed. We exchanged phone numbers and addresses, and I didn't see or think of her again for another six months. Until the next party I couldn't get out of. This time we stayed together from the moment I walked in the door, and six months after that she moved in with me.

She didn't want to get married because she said it would spoil all her best lines; I didn't want to get married because then I wouldn't be able to be alone again.

"Caz," she said then, dropping the pose and readjusting her skirt, "are you okay?"

I shrugged without moving. "I guess so. I don't know. It's the weather, I imagine. It's depressing. And this," I said with a sweep of my hand to cover the bills, "doesn't help very much."

"That is an understatement." She stood and kissed my forehead, said something about getting dinner ready, come down in ten or fifteen minutes, and left without closing the door. I did it for her. Softly, so she wouldn't think I was annoyed. Then I went back to the window and watched the maple glow until the glow faded, twilight took over, and the dead of November was buried in black.

The next day, Belle dropped me at the park on her way to work. When I kissed her good-bye, I think she was surprised at the ardor I showed; I certainly was. Generally, I couldn't wait to be rid of her. Not that I didn't like her, and not that I didn't love her, but I still blessed those hours when we were apart. It not only made our time together more imporant, but it also allowed me time to myself.

To sit on the benches, to walk the paths, to leave the park and head into town. Listening to people. Watching them. Every so often, when I was feeling particularly down, hoping that one of them would come up to me and say, hey, aren't you

Caz Rich, the children's book guy? They never did, but I sometimes spent hours in bookstores, waiting for someone to buy one of my books.

Well, not really *my* books.

I don't write them, I illustrate them. Mostly books about what I call critters, as opposed to creatures—silly monsters, silly villains, silly any bad thing to take the sting out of evil for the little kids who read them.

Some of the shopkeepers, once they'd gotten used to seeing me around, asked what it was like to be a house-husband while the wife was out doing whatever she was doing. In this case, it was managing a string of five shops catering to those who bought labels instead of clothes. I used to correct them, tell them I was a commercial artist who worked at home, but when they smiled knowingly and kept it up each time they asked, I gave up and said that I liked it just fine, and as soon as I figured out what I was going to be when I grew up, my wife could stay home like a good wife should.

They didn't care much for that and didn't talk much to me again, but as I often said to Foxy, life in the fast lane has its price, too.

I grinned at myself then, and looked around to see if Foxy was out.

He was, with his cronies.

They were sitting on the high step of the fountain in the middle of the park. The water had been turned off a month ago, and the marble bowl was filling with debris from the trees and passersby. Foxy and his men kept unofficial guard on it, to keep the brats from tossing their candy wrappers in it, and to keep the teens from pissing there whenever they had too much beer.

Only one person I know of complained to the police about the harassment, and the police suggested slyly to Belle that unless she had mischief of her own up her sleeve there was no discernible harm done so please, miss, no offense but get lost.

Foxy grinned when he saw me, stood up and held out his hand. He was at that age when age didn't matter, and when a look couldn't tell you what it was anyway. His skin was loose here and tight there, his clothes the same, and his hair was always combed, and always blown by the wind. Unlike the others, he never wore a hat because, he'd once confided, he'd read in a magazine that using one of those things was a guarantee of baldness.

"Caz!" he said cheerily. His grip was firm, his blue eyes bright, his mouth opened in a grin that exposed his upper gums. "Caz, the boys and me were just talking about you."

The boys numbered five, all of an age, all of a color, and all of them smelling like attics in spring. They grunted their greetings as I walked around the fountain, shaking hands, noting the weather and generally not saying much at all. Chad was busy knitting himself a winter sweater with nimble fat fingers that poked out of fingerless gloves; Streetcar was reading; so were Dick O'Meara and his brother, Denny; and Rene didn't like me so he hardly acknowledged my presence beyond an ill-concealed sideways sneer. Once done with the formalities, Foxy and I headed off toward the far end of the park, where a hot dog vendor waited patiently under his striped umbrella for the offices to let out so he could feed them all lunch.

"So how's Miss Lanner?"

"Same. Fine."

Foxy nodded.

"You?"

Foxy shrugged. He wore a worn Harris tweed jacket buttoned to the chest, a soft maroon scarf that served as a dashing tie, his pants didn't match and sometimes neither did his shoes. "Could be better, but it's the weather, you know? Thinking about going to Florida before I get the chilblains."

"A trip would do you good."

He laughed. "Sure, when I win the lottery."

Foxy used to be an attorney, spent it all as he made it, and now lived on his Social Security and what other folks in their charity deemed fit to give him. He didn't mind charity; he figured he'd earned it. Age, to him, was a privilege, not a curse.

We passed a few others as we made our way west. It was raw, and what pedestrians there were rushed along their shortcuts instead of admiring the views. And by the time we reached the stand, made our choices and turned around, the park was deserted except for the boys at the fountain.

"Any inspiration lately?" he asked around a bite of his lunch.

"Only that when I see you I want to open a savings account."

He laughed and poked me hard on the arm, shook his head

and sighed. "Misspent youth, Caz, m'boy. You'd be wise to take a lesson from your elders."

Dick and Denny had finished their books by the time we'd returned and were attempting to find ways to keep the cold off their bald pates. Rene was pitching pebbles at the pigeons. Streetcar was dozing. Chad, however, looked up at Foxy, looked at me, and smiled sadly.

"Saw it again, Fox," he said. His face was more beard than flesh, his coat the newest of the lot. He should have been warm, but his teeth were chattering.

"You're kidding."

"While you were gone," and he pointed over my shoulder.

I looked automatically, and saw nothing but the grass, the trees, and a wire litter basket half-filled with trash.

Foxy didn't move.

"Saw what?" I asked.

"Gonna call?" Foxy said.

"Nope," Chad told him. "What's the use?"

"I guess."

"Saw what?"

Foxy patted his friend's shoulder and walked me up the path to the corner, stopped and looked back. "It's sad, Caz, real sad. Chad sees things. More and more of them every day. This week it's bank robbers."

"But you can't see the bank from—" I stopped, ashamed I hadn't picked it up right away. "Oh."

He nodded, tapped a temple. "At least he doesn't bother the police. If he did, I don't think we'd see him here much longer."

I was sympathetic, but I was also getting cold, so we spoke only a few minutes more before I headed home, taking the shortest route instead of picking streets at random; and once inside, I turned up the furnace to get warm in a hurry. Then I went upstairs and stood at my desk. I knew I should work; there were two contracts at hand, both of them fairly good, and the possibility I might get a chance to do a critter calendar for kids.

There was little enough wealth involved in what I did for a living, but there had been sufficient in the past five years so that Belle wouldn't have to worry if she ever decided to pack it in and stay home. I didn't know how I'd handle that, but since there didn't seem much chance of it, I seldom thought about it—only when I was feeling old-fashioned enough to want her home, with me, the way it had been for my father, and his father before him.

Being a liberated male when you're ten is easy; when you're over thirty, however, it's like mixing drugs—today it's cool and I don't mind because it doesn't limit my freedom or alter my perspectives; tomorrow it's a pain in the ass and whatever happened to aprons and babies.

And when I got in moods like that, I did what I always do—I worked.

So hard that I didn't hear Belle come home, didn't hear though I sensed her standing in the doorway watching for a moment before she went away, leaving me to my critters, and my make-believe children.

An hour later, I went downstairs, walked into the kitchen and saw that it was deserted. Nothing on the stove. Nothing on the table. I went into the living room, and it was empty, and so was the dining room. Frowning, and seeing her purse still on the hall table, I peered through a front window and saw her on the porch. A sweater was cloaked around her shoulders, and she was watching the empty street.

When I joined her she didn't turn.

"Chilly," I said.

It was dark, the streetlamps on, the leaves on the lawn stirring for their nightmoves.

"What are we going to do, Caz?"

"Do? About what?"

I couldn't see her face, and she wouldn't let me put an arm around her shoulders.

"I had lunch with Roman today."

Hell and damnation, the writing on the wall. Lunch with Roman today, several times over the past few months, a day-trip into New York to do some buying during the summer. Roman Carrell was the manager of one of her bigger shops, younger than both of us, and hungrier than I. If the husband is always the last to know, I wondered where I fit in. On the other hand, maybe he was only a good friend, and a shoulder to cry on whenever I got into one of my moods.

She pulled the sweater more snugly across her chest. "He says he wants to marry me, Caz."

"Lots of people do. You're beautiful."

Her head ducked away. "I am not."

"Well, I think you are, and since I'm an artist experienced in these things, you'll have to believe me."

Another one of our lines. Dialogue from a bad show that also happened to be my life.

Jesus.

I leaned back against the railing, looking at her sideways. "Do you want to marry him?"

Suddenly, there was gunfire, so much of it I knew it wasn't a backfiring car or truck. We both straightened and stared toward downtown, then I ran inside and grabbed my Windbreaker from the closet.

"What the hell are you doing?" she demanded, grabbing my arm as I ran out again.

The gunshots were replaced by what sounded like a hundred sirens.

"Nosy," I said, grinning. "Want to come along?"

"You'll get hurt, stupid."

I probably was, but in a town this size the only shots ever heard came from the occasional hunter who thought a Chevy was a deer. This was something else, some excitement, and as I ran down the walk I hoped to hear Belle trying to catch up. She didn't. I wasn't surprised.

I reached the park about the same time a hundred others did, and we saw patrol cars slanted all over the street, their hoods aimed at a jewelry store a few doors in from the intersection. An ambulance was there, and spotlights poked at the brick walls while a dozen cops strode back and forth in flak jackets, carrying shotguns and rifles and pushing the crowd back.

I made my way to the front in about ten minutes, just in time to see two attendants loading a stretcher into the van. There was blood on the sidewalk, and the shop's glass doors were blown inward. No one had seen anything, but from those I talked to it must have been a hell of a battle.

Belle didn't say anything when I finally got home; she was already in bed, the alarm clock set, and my pajamas laid out on my side of the mattress.

She left before I woke up.

"Well," I said to Foxy two afternoons later, "Chad's crystal ball needs a little polishing, huh?"

He grinned, turned to Dick and Denny who were feeding a lone squirrel from a popcorn bag, and asked if they'd mind holding the fort while he and I took a short walk. They said no,

Streetcar was busy plucking leaves from the fountain, and Rene didn't bother to turn around.

Once we reached the far end of the path, Foxy stopped and faced me. "Chad's dead," he said.

"Oh hell, no."

"Yeah. Bad heart. Last night. His daughter called me. He went in his sleep."

I didn't say anything except to ask which funeral parlor he was in, then walked to the florist and sent the old guy some flowers. I didn't work at all that afternoon, and Belle didn't come home for dinner.

While I waited for her in the living room—TV on and unwatched, newspaper in my lap unfolded and unread—I listened to the leaves racing across the lawn ahead of the wind, and couldn't help hearing the sound of Chad dying. I paced until the wind died, then drank a couple of tasteless beers, waited until midnight, and went to bed.

Belle didn't return the next day either, which was too bad because that maple glowed again and I wanted her to see it before the clouds closed off the sun.

I called the shop, finally, all the shops, and kept just missing her according to the clerks. Roman was out as well, and I didn't need a plank across the back of my head to know I'd been deserted. Instead of bemoaning and ranting, however, I worked, which in itself is a sort of reaction—the yelling went into the drawings, the tears into the ink. It worked until I couldn't hold a pen any longer, until I was back downstairs and there was no one to talk to.

Alone was one thing; lonely was something else.

Still, I didn't lose my temper.

I decided instead to be noble about it all. After all, we weren't married, weren't even contemplating it, and if that's what Belle wanted then that's what she would have. Maybe she'd grow tired of the little prick; maybe she'd come back and maybe she wouldn't. So I didn't call again, and I worked as hard as I ever had over the next several days, only once going down to the park where I noticed Streetcar was gone, taken away, Foxy said, by the men in pretty white because he was talking about an atom bomb dropping into the middle of town.

"A crock," said Rene, and said nothing more.

Dick and Denny were nervous but they kept on reading, the same book, and I didn't ask why.

And a week to the day after she'd left, Belle came back.

I was in the kitchen fixing lunch when she walked in, sat at the table and smiled.

"Have a nice trip?" I said.

"So-so."

I couldn't help it—I yelled. "Goddamnit, Lanner, where the hell have you been?"

There was no contrition; she bridled. "Thinking, driving, screwing around," she said coldly. "You're not my husband, you know."

"No, but Christ, it seems to me I have a few rights around here. A little common courtesy wouldn't have killed you."

She shrugged and picked at something invisible on her lip.

"Are you back?" I said, sounding less than enthusiastic.

"No."

"A little more thinking, driving, screwing around?"

"I need it," she told me.

"Then get it." I turned my back to her, kept it there while I fussed with the skillet where my eggs were scrambling, kept it there until she got up and left. Then I tossed the skillet into the sink, threw the plate against the wall, picked up the drain where the clean dishes were stacked and threw it on the floor. I knocked over her chair. I punched the refrigerator and screamed when I heard at least one of my knuckles cracking.

Then I left without cleaning up, marched to the park and dropped onto a bench. Sat there. Blindly. Until Dick and Denny came up to me, twins in rags with paperback books in their hands.

"We saw it, you know," Dick said with a glance to Denny, who nodded. "We saw it yesterday."

"Saw what," I grumbled.

They hesitated.

"Gentlemen," I said, "I'm really very tired. It's been a bad day and it's not even two." I managed a smile. "Would you mind?"

"But we saw it!" Dick insisted as Denny tugged at his sleeve. "We really did see it."

"Yeah, okay," I said.

"So here." And before I could move they had shoved both their books into my hands. "They're really good," said Dick. "I won't tell you the end, though, it would spoil it, and I hate when somebody does it to me."

Denny nodded solemnly.

Foxy came up then, put his arms around the two men's shoulders and looked an apology at me. "Let's go, boys," he said, steering them away. Another look, and I shook my head in sympathy. The sanity, not to mention the mortality, rate among the guys at the fountain was getting pretty serious. But they were all in the same decade, with the weather as raw as it was, and their health not the best, so it wasn't all that surprising.

It was, on the other hand, depressing, and I left before Foxy could return and tell me the latest from the geriatric book of fairy tales.

The newspaper I picked up on my way home didn't help my mood any. The Middle East was blowing up, Washington was squabbling, the state senate was deadlocked on a bill to improve education, there were a handful of murders, a kidnapping, and two bus crashes on the outskirts of town. Great. Just what I needed to read when I had twenty-one more critters to draw that needed a light touch, not a scalpel.

I tossed the paper onto the kitchen table and cleaned up the broken crockery; then I poured myself a glass of soda and sat down, hands on my cheeks, hair in my eyes, until suddenly I frowned. I picked up the paper, snapped over a couple of pages and read the story about the first bus crash. At first I didn't recognize the name; then I realized that among the eight dead had been poor old Streetcar Mullens.

"Well, shit," I said to the empty room. "Shit."

Two days later, Dick and Denny were dead as well, their boarding house burned down; they had been sleeping at the time.

I was on my way out the door when Belle drove up in front of the house. She didn't get out of the car, but rolled down the passenger side window. I leaned over and waited.

"Aren't you glad to see me?"

"I might be," I said flatly, "but a couple of friends of mine died last night. In a fire."

"Oh, I'm sorry." She polished the steering wheel with her gloved hands, then straightened the silk scarf tossed around her neck. "Anyone I know?"

"No," I said, realizing how much of my life she never knew at all. "A couple of guys from the park."

"Oh, them," she said. "For God's sake, Caz, when are you

going to get friends your own age? Christ, you'll be old before your time if you're not careful." She looked at me then. "I take it back. You *are* old, only you don't know it."

"And what does that make you?" I laughed. "The world's oldest teenaged swinger?" I leaned closer, hearing the sound of dishes smashing on the floor. "He's too young for you, Belle. The first wrinkle you sprout will send him packing."

She glared, and her hands fisted. "You bastard," she said softly. "At least I'm getting the most out of . . . oh, what's the use."

She would have cheerfully cut my throat then, and I astonished myself in the realization that I wouldn't have let her. "You're leaving then?"

She hesitated before nodding.

"And you want to be sure I'm not around when you and young Roman come for your things because you want to spare my old man's feelings."

"You don't have to talk that way."

"No, but I am."

She swallowed. "If you had needed me, if only you had needed me."

"I did, don't be silly."

She shook her head. "No, Caz, you didn't. Not in the way it counted."

There were tears in her eyes. I don't know how long they'd been there, but they began to make me feel like a real bastard. She had a point, I suppose, but it had taken her a hell of a long time to find the courage to make her move. And to be truthful, I was relieved. When she drove away, I was almost light-headed because someone had finally done something, taken a step, and now things would change. A selfish, perhaps even cowardly way to look at it, but as I made my way to the park I couldn't yet feel much guilt. Maybe later. Maybe later, in the dark, with no one beside me.

Foxy was sitting glumly in his usual place, and Rene was beside him.

"God, I'm sorry," I said as I approached them.

"Thank you, Caz," Foxy said without moving. His face was pale, his eyes dark and refusing to meet my gaze. In his lap his hands trembled.

Rene looked up. "Go away," he said sourly. "You ain't got no right here."

My exchange with Belle had drained my patience, and I grinned mirthlessly at him. "Shut up, Rene. I'm sick of your grousing."

"Oh, are you?" he said. "And how about if I'm sick and tired of you coming around here all the time, prying into what's none of your business? Huh? Suppose I'm tired of that?"

"Rene, hold it down," Foxy said wearily.

I was puzzled, because I hadn't the faintest idea what he was talking about, or why Foxy had suddenly lost his verve. Even after Streetcar's death the old man had managed to keep his good humor; now, his head seemed too heavy for his neck, and his hands still danced over the broadcloth of his lap.

"I'm not going to argue," I said, turning away. "I just wanted to give you my sympathy, that's all. I'm not being nosy."

But Rene wouldn't let it go.

"No? Then why are you all the time talking about what we see, huh? Why are you all the time asking about that?"

"He's a writer," Foxy snapped at him. "He's naturally curious."

"He ain't a writer, he draws pictures."

It was dumb, but I didn't leave. I had nowhere I wanted to go, and this for the time being was better than nothing.

"I illustrate," I corrected, almost primly, looking hard at Rene with a dare for contradiction. "I draw things for kids in books—which you're right, I don't write—and sometimes I do it for myself, all right? I draw houses and people and animals and critters and . . . and . . ." I looked around, feeling a surge of heat expand in my chest, and burn my eyes. "And trees, okay? The way they grow, the way they look in different seasons, the way they glow when there's no sun, the way they look when they've been hit by lightning. Christ!"

I stalked away and had almost reached the street when I heard Foxy calling. I looked back and saw him beckoning, while Rene yanked so hard on his arm that he toppled from the step to the concrete. I ran back, ready to exchange Belle for Rene and beat the hell out of both of them. But when I got there, Foxy was sitting up and Rene was sitting above him.

"What did you mean, about the trees?" Foxy said as soon as I was close enough to hear.

"Just what I said."

"Damn."

"Damn what?" I frowned. Rene wasn't talking, so I knelt and smiled. "Hey, is that what you guys have been seeing here in the park? A tree glowing sort of?" I poked Foxy's arm. "Hey, there's nothing wrong with that. It's the light. A break in the clouds, that's all. Hollywood does it all the time. Jeez, you didn't have to lie to me, the burglars and stuff. Good God, Foxy, I told you I saw it, too."

He took my hand and held it; his fingers were ice, his grip was iron, and his eyes seemed farther back, black in his skull. "You see it for the dying," he said. "You see it for the dying."

He wouldn't talk to me after that, and Rene only scowled, and I finally went home after eating out. I felt, oddly, a hundred times better than when I'd left, and I even started to do a little work. Two hours later I was still at it, when I looked up and saw the tree.

It was dark outside; night had crept up on me while my pens were flying.

It was dark outside, and the maple tree was glowing.

The stars were out, but there was no moon.

And the maple tree was glowing.

I switched off the lights, and nothing changed; I hurried downstairs and stood at the back door, and nothing changed; I ran outside, and the tree was glowing. Gold, soft, and casting no shadows.

I was afraid to walk up and touch it. Instead, I went back in and sat at the kitchen table, watching for nearly an hour until the tree faded. Then I grabbed up a newspaper and began scribbling dates and names in the largest margins I could find. When I was done, I shook my head and did it again. After the second time, I had convinced myself that the old men in the park, if they had seen what I had, had been given glimpses of the future. Deaths. Accidents. And they were afraid of what they saw, so they made up stories to go with their age, with the failing of their minds. And they were afraid of what they saw, afraid of what it meant, and they died. A heart attack, a probable stroke, two men probably drunk in their rooms and not hearing the alarm.

"Jesus," I whispered.

And the telephone rang.

I thought it might be Belle, ready to tell me she'd be over to clear out her things.

But it was Foxy, and before he had a chance to say anything

more than his name, I told him what I'd discovered and, if it were true, what it might mean.

"My God, Foxy," I said, fairly jumping with excitement, "think of what you guys can do, think of the people you can save."

"Caz, wait a minute."

"I know, I know—you don't want to be thought of as freaks, and I don't blame you. But God, Foxy, it's incredible!" I wound the cord around my wrist and stared grinning at the ceiling. "You know that, you know it's incredible, right? But look, you've got to tell me how you know where it's going to be and things like that. I mean, all I can see is the tree and nothing else. How do you know where the accident is going to be?"

"I don't."

"Impossible. Chad didn't just guess, you know. Do you *know* the odds on something like that?"

I wasn't making sense; I didn't care. Belle was leaving me, and I didn't care; the books weren't going right, and I didn't care. Something else was fine, and I was feeling all right.

"It was Chad in the store that night, Caz."

"So look, are you going to tell—" I stopped, straightened, blinked once very slowly. "Chad?"

"He needed the money. He knew he was going to die, so he decided to give it a try, to see if he could change it." There was a pause. A long pause to be sure I was listening and not just hearing. "It was Chad shot down that night, Caz. He was carrying a toy gun."

"Wait!" I said loudly, sensing he was about to hang up. "Foxy, wait. He *knew* he was going to die?"

Another pause, and I could hear him breathing as if he were drowning.

"*I* saw it today, Caz. I saw the tree. I know."

And he hung up.

I didn't want to go to the park the next day, but I did. Rene was sitting at the fountain, and he was alone.

"Where's Foxy?" I asked angrily.

"Where do you think?" he said, and pointed at the ground.

"He . . . he said he saw the tree yesterday."

Rene shrugged. And looked suddenly up at me and grinned. "So did you. A couple of times."

"But . . ." I looked around wildly, looked back and spread my hands. "But my God, aren't you afraid?"

"When you know it's done, it's done, right, old man?" And he grinned even wider.

There were a number of people walking through the park that day, but it didn't bother me—I hit him. I leaned back and threw a punch right at the side of his head, and felt immense satisfaction at the astonishment on his face as he spilled backward and struck his skull against the fountain's lip. He was dead. I knew it. And I knew then he had seen the tree and hadn't told me. So I ran, straight for home, and fell into the kitchen.

No prophecy except knowing when you'll die.

No change except for the method of the dying.

I had seen the tree glow, and I was going to die, and the only thing he didn't tell me was how long it was before it all happened.

There was fear, and there was terror, and finally in the dark there was nothing at all. Rene was right; when you had no choice, there was nothing but deciding you might as well get on with your work. At least that much would be done; at least there'd be no loose ends.

I started for the staircase, and the front door opened, and Belle came in.

I almost wept when I saw her, knowing instantly she'd been right—I'd not really needed her before, not the way it should have been. But I needed her now, and I wanted her to know it.

"Oh, Belle," I said, and opened my arms to gather in her comfort.

And gave her the perfect target for the gun in her hand.

Splatter
A Cautionary Tale

Douglas E. Winter

Apocalypse Domani. In the hour before dawn, as night retreated into shadow, the dream chased Rehnquist awake. The gates of hell had opened, the cannibals had taken to the streets, and Rehnquist waited alone, betrayed by the light of the coming day. Soon, he knew, the zombies would find him, the windows would shatter, the doors burst inward, and the hands, stained with their endless feast, would beckon to him. They would eat of his flesh and drink of his blood, but spare his immortal soul; and at dawn, he would rise again, possessed of their hunger, their quenchless thirst, to view a grave new world through the vacant eyes of the dead next door.

The Beyond. "And you will face the sea of darkness, and all therein that may be explored." Tallis tipped his wineglass in empty salute. "So much for the poet." He glanced back along the east wing of the Corcoran Gallery, its chronology of Swiss impressionists dominated by Zweig's "L'Aldila," an ocean-scape of burned sand littered with mummified remains. His attorney, Gavin Widmark, steered him from the bar and forced a smile: "Perhaps a bit more restraint." Tallis slipped a fresh glass of Chardonnay from the tray of a passing waiter. "Art," he said, his voice slurred and overloud, "is nothing but the absence of restraint." Across the room, a blond woman faced them with a frown. "Ah, Thom," Widmark said, gesturing toward her. "Have you met Cameron Blake?"

Cannibal Ferox. Memory: the angry rain washing over Times Square, scattering the Women's March Against Pornography into the ironic embrace of ill-lit theater entrances. She stood beneath a lurid film poster: "Make Them Die Slowly!" it screamed, adding, as if an afterthought, "The Most Violent Film Ever!" And as she waited in the sudden shadows, clutching a placard whose red ink had smeared into a wound, she surveyed the faces emerging from the grindhouse lobby: the wisecracking black youths, shouting and shoving their way back onto the streets; the middle-aged couple, moving warily through the unexpected phalanx of stern-faced women; and finally, the young man, alone, a hardcover novel by Thomas Tallis gripped to his chest. His fugitive eyes, trapped behind thick wire-rimmed glasses, seemed to caution Cameron Blake as she stood with her sisters, hoping to take back the night.

Dawn of the Dead. At the shopping mall, the film posters taunted Rehnquist with the California dream of casual, sunbaked sex: for yet another summer, teen tedium reigned at the fourplex. He visited instead the video library, prowling the ever-thinning shelves of horror films—each battered box a brick in the wall of his defense—and wondering what he would do when they were gone. At the cashier's desk, he had seen the mimeographed petition: PROTECT YOUR RIGHTS—WHAT YOU NEED TO KNOW ABOUT H.R. 1762. But he didn't need to know what he could see even now, watching the shoppers outside, locked in the time-step of the suburban sleepwalk. "This was an important place in their lives," he said, although he knew that no one was listening.

Eaten Alive. "After all," said Cameron Blake as another slide jerked onto the screen, a pale captive writhing in bondage on a dusty motel room bed, "what is important about a woman in these films is not how she feels, not what she does for a living, not what she thinks about the world around her . . . but simply how she bleeds." The slide projector clicked, and the audience fell silent. The next victim arched above a makeshift worktable, suspended by a meat hook that had been thrust into her vagina. Moist entrails spilled, coiling, onto the gore-stained floor below. From the back of the lecture hall, as the shocked whispers rose in protest, came the unmistakable sound of someone laughing.

Friday the 13th. He had decided to rent an eternal holiday favorite, and now, on his television screen, the bottle-blond game-show maven staggered across the moonlit beach, her painted lips puckered in a knowing smile. "Kill her, Mommy, kill her," she mouthed, a singsong soliloquy that he soon joined. The obligatory virgin fell before her, legs sprawled in an inviting wedge, and the axe poised, its shiny tip moistened expectantly with a shimmer of blood. Rehnquist closed his eyes; all too soon, he knew, we would visit the hospital room where the virgin lay safe abed, wondering what might still lurk at Camp Crystal Lake. But he imagined instead a different ending, one without sequel, one without blood, and he knew that he could not let it be.

The Gates of Hell. On the first morning of the hearings on H.R. 1762, Tallis mounted the steps to the Rayburn Building to observe the passionate parade: the war-film actor, pointing the finger of self-righteous accusation; the bearded psychiatrists, soft-spoken oracles of aggression models and impact studies; the schoolteachers and ministers, each with a story of shattered morality; and then the mothers, the fathers, the battered women, the rape victims, the abused children, lost in their tears and in search of a cause, pleading to the politicians who sat in solemn judgment above them. He saw, without surprise, that Cameron Blake stood with them in the hearing room, spokesman for the silent, the forgotten, the bruised, the violated, the sudden dead.

Halloween. That night, alone in his apartment, Rehnquist huddled with his videotapes, considering the minutes that would be lost to the censor's blade. Sometimes, when he closed his eyes, he envisioned stories and films that never were, and that now, perhaps, never would be. As his television flickered with the ultimate holiday of horror, he watched the starlet's daughter, pressed against the wall, another virgin prey to an unwelcome visitor; but as her mouth opened in a sound-less scream, his eyes closed, and he saw her in her mother's place, heiress to that fateful room in the Bates Motel, a full-color nude trapped behind the shower curtain as the arm, wielding the long-handled knife, stiffened and thrust, stiffened and thrust again. And as her perfect body, spent, slipped to the blood-sprinkled tile, he opened his eyes and grinned: "It *was* the Boogeyman, wasn't it?"

Inferno. "No, my friends," pronounced the Reverend Wilson Macomber, scowling for the news cameras as he descended the steps of the Liberty Gospel Church in Clinton, Maryland. "I am speaking for our children. It is *their* future that is at stake. I hold in my hand a list . . ." The flashguns popped, and the minicams swept across the anxious gathering, then focused upon the waiting jumble of wooden blocks, doused with kerosene. Macomber suddenly smiled, and his flock, their arms laden with books and magazines, videotapes and record albums, smiled with him. He thrust a paperback into the eye of the nearest camera. "This one," he laughed, "shall truly be a firestarter." He tossed the book onto the waiting pyre, and proclaimed, with the clarity of unbending conviction, "Let there be light." And the flames burned long into the night.

Just Before Dawn. As she rubbed at her eyes, the headache seemed to flare, then pass; she motioned to the graduate student waiting at the door. Cameron Blake saw herself fifteen years before, comfortable in t-shirt and jeans, hair tossed wildly, full of herself and the knowledge that change lay just around the corner. She saw herself, and knew why she had left both a husband and a Wall Street law firm for the chance to teach the lessons of those fifteen years. Change did not lie in wait. Change was wrought, often painfully, and never without a fight. In the student's hands were the crumpled sheets of an awkward polemic: "Only Women Bleed: DePalma and the Politics of Voyeurism." In her eyes were the wet traces of self-doubt, but not tears; no, never tears. Cameron Blake smoothed the pages and unsheathed her red pen. "Why don't we start with *Body Double*?"

The Keep. Tallis silenced the stereo and stared into the blank screen of his computer. He had tried to write for hours, but his typing produced only indecipherable codes: words, sentences, paragraphs without life or logic. Inside, he could feel only a mounting silence. He looked again to the newspaper clippings stacked neatly on his desk, a bloody testament to the power of words and images: Charles Manson's answer to the call of the Beatles' "Helter Skelter"; the obsession with *Taxi Driver* that had almost killed a president; the parents who had murdered countless infants in bedroom exorcisms. He drew his last novel, *Jeremiad*, from the bookshelf, and wondered what deaths had been rehearsed in its pages.

The Last House on the Left. Congressman James Stodder overturned the cardboard box, scattering its contents before the young attorney from the American Civil Liberties Union. He carefully cataloged each item for the subcommittee: black market photographs of the nude corpse of television actress Lauren Hayes, taken by her abductors moments after they had disemboweled her with a garden trowel; a videotape of Lucio Fulci's twice-banned *Apoteosi del Mistero;* an eight-millimeter film loop entitled *Little Boy Snuffed*, confiscated by the FBI in the back room of an adult bookstore in Pensacola, Florida; and a copy of the Clive Barker novel *Requiem*, its pages clipped at its most infamous scenes. "Now tell me," Stodder said, his voice shaking and rising to a shout, "which is fact and which is fiction?"

Maniac. Rehnquist keyed the volume control, drawn to the montage of violent film clips that preceded the C-SPAN highlights of the Stodder subcommittee. A film critic waved a tattered poster, savoring his moment before the cameras: "This is," he exclaimed, "the single most reprehensible film ever made. The question that should be asked is: are people so upset because the murderer is so heinous or because the murderer is being portrayed in such a positive and supportive light?" Rehnquist twisted the television dial, first to the top-rated police show, where fashionable vice cops pumped endless shotgun rounds into a drug dealer; then to the news reports of bodies stacked like cords of wood at a railhead in El Salvador; and finally to the solace of M-TV, where Mick Jagger cavorted in the streets of a ruined city, singing of too much blood.

Night of the Living Dead. In the beginning, he remembered, there were no videotapes. There were no X ratings, no labels warning of sex or violence, no seizures of books on library shelves, no committees or investigations. In the beginning, there were dreams without color. There was peace, it was said,

and prosperity; and he slept in that innocent belief until the
night he had awakened in the back seat of his car, transfixed by
the black-and-white nightmare, the apocalypse alive on the
drive-in movie screen: "They're coming to get you, Barbara,"
the actor had warned. But Rehnquist knew that the zombies
were coming for him, the windows shattering, the doors
bursting inward. The dead, he had learned, were alive and
hungry—hungry for him—and the dreams, ever after, were
always the color red.

Orgy of the Blood Parasites. The gavel thundered again, and
as the shouts subsided, Tallis returned to his prepared state-
ment. "Under the proposed legislation," he read, without
waiting for silence, "whether or not the depiction of violence
constitutes pornography depends upon the perspective that the
writer or the film director adopts. A story that is violent and
that simply depicts women"—he winced at the renewed chorus
of indignation—"that simply depicts women in positions of
submission, or even display, is forbidden, regardless of the
literary or political value of the work taken as a whole. On the
other hand, a story that depicts women in positions of equality
is lawful, no matter how graphic its violence. This . . ." He
paused, looking first at James Stodder, then at each other
member of the subcommittee. "This is thought control."

Profondo Rosso. Widmark led him through the gauntlet of
reporters outside the Rayburn Building. Tallis looked to the
west, but saw only row after row of white marble façades.
"This is suicide," Widmark said. "You realize that, don't you?
Take a look at this." He flourished an envelope stuffed with
photocopies of news clippings and book reviews, then handed
Tallis a letter detailing the lengthy cuts that Berkley had
requested for the new novel. Tallis tore the letter in half,
unread. "I need a drink," he said, and waved to the blond
woman who waited for him on the steps below. No one noticed
the young man in wire-rimmed glasses who stood across the
street, washed in the deep red of the setting sun.

Quella Villa Accanto il Cimitero. Rehnquist had found the
answer on the front page of the *Washington Post,* while
reading its reports of the latest testimony before Stodder's
raging subcommittee. There, between boldfaced quotations

from a midwestern police chief and a psychoanalyst with the unlikely name of Freudstein, was a clouded news photograph labeled GEORGETOWN PROFESSOR CAMERON BLAKE; its caption read, "Violence in fiction, film, may as well be real." His fingers had traced the outline of her face with nervous familiarity—the blond hair, the thin lips parted in anxious warning, the wide dark eyes of Barbara Steele. When he raised his hand, he saw only the dark blur of newsprint along his fingertips. He knew then what he had to do.

Reanimator. They shared a booth at the Capitol Hilton coffee shop, trading Bloody Marys while searching for a common ground. The conversation veered from Lovecraft to the latest seafood restaurant in Old Town Alexandria; then Tallis, working his third cocktail, told of his year in Italy with Dario Argento, drawing honest laughter with an anecdote about the mistranslated script for *Lachrymae*. She countered with the story of the graduate student who had called him the most dangerous writer since Norman Mailer. "That's quite a compliment," he said. "But what do you think?" Cameron Blake shook her head; "I told her to try reading you first." As they left the hotel, he paused at the newsstand to buy a paperback copy of *Jeremiad*. "A gift for your student," he said, but when he reached to take her hand, she hesitated. In a moment, he was alone.

Suspiria. "Hello." It was his voice, hardly more than a sigh, that surprised Cameron Blake. The door slammed shut behind her, and he passed from the shadows into light, barring her way. She stepped back, taking the measure of the drab young man who had invaded her home; she thought, for a moment, that they had once met, strangers in a sudden rain. "I want to show you something," Rehnquist said; but as she pushed past him, intent on reaching the telephone, the videocassette that he had offered to her slipped away, shattering on the hardwood floor. In that moment, as the tape spooled lifelessly onto the floor, their destiny was sealed.

The Texas Chainsaw Massacre. Tallis hooked the telephone on the first ring. He had been waiting for her to call, but the voice at the other end, echoing in the hiss of long distance, was that of Gavin Widmark; it was his business voice, friendly but measured, and could herald only bad news. Berkley, despite three million copies of *Jeremiad* in print, had declined to publish the new novel. If only he would consider the proposed cuts . . . If only he would mediate the level of violence . . . If only . . . Without a word, Tallis placed the receiver gently back onto its cradle. He tipped another finger of gin into his glass and stared into the widening depths of the empty computer screen.

The Undertaker and His Pals. She knew, as Rehnquist unfolded the straight razor, that there would be no escape. A dark certainty inhabited his eyes as he advanced, the light shimmering on the blade, and she pressed against the wall, watching, waiting. "For you, Cameron," he said. The razor flashed, kissing his left wrist before licking evenly along the vein. She squeezed her eyes closed, but he called to her—"For you, Cameron"—and she looked again as the fingers of his left hand toppled to the carpet in a rain of blood. "For you, Cameron." The razor poised at his throat, slashing a sudden grin that vomited crimson across his chest, and as he staggered out into the street, blood trailing in his wake, she found that she could not stop watching.

Videodrome. Every picture tells a story, thought Detective Sergeant Richard Howe, stepping aside to clear the police photographer's field of vision. He knew that the prints on his desk tomorrow would seem to depict reality, their flattened images belying what he had sensed from the moment he arrived: the bloodstains splattering the floor of the Capitol Hill townhouse had been deeper and darker than any he had ever seen. He would not easily forget the woman's expression when he told her that the shorn fingertips were slabs of latex, the blood merely a concoction of corn syrup and food coloring. He looked again to the shattered videocassette, sealed in the plastic evidence bag: DIRECTED BY DAVID CRONENBERG read the label. He couldn't wait for the search warrant to issue; turning over this guy's apartment was going to be a scream.

The Wizard of Gore. When the first knock sounded at the door, Rehnquist set aside his worn copy of *Jeremiad*, marked at its most frightening passage: "and at dawn, he would rise again, possessed of their hunger, their quenchless thirst, to view a grave new world through the vacant eyes of the dead next door." At his feet curled the thin plastic tubing, stripped from his armpit and drained of stage blood. "It's not real," he said, and the knocking stopped. "It's *never* been real." The window to his left shattered, glass spraying in all directions; then the door burst inward, yawning on a single hinge, and the hands, the beckoning hands, thrust toward him. The long night had ended. The zombies had come for him at last.

Xtro. The Reverend Wilson Macomber rose to face the Stodder subcommittee, his deep voice echoing unamplified across the hearing room. "I don't know if anybody else has done this for you all, but I want to pray for you right now, and I want to ask everyone in this room who fears God to bow their head." He pressed a tiny New Testament to his heart. "Dear Father . . . I pray that you will destroy wickedness in this city and in every wicked city. I pray that you draw the line, as it is written here, and those that are righteous, let them be righteous still, and they that are filthy, let them be filthy still . . ." At the back of the hearing room, his face etched in the shadows, Tallis shifted uneasily. In Macomber's insectile stare, mirrored by the stony smile of James Stodder, the haunted eyes of Cameron Blake, he knew that it was over. As the vote began on H.R. 1762, he turned and walked away, into the sudden light of a silent day.

Les Yeux Sans Visage. Months later, in another kind of theater, green-shirted medical students witnessed the drama of stereotactic procedures, justice meted out in the final reel. "The target," announced the white-masked lecturer, gesturing with his scalpel, "is the cingulate gyrus." Here he paused for effect, glancing overhead to the video enlargement of the patient's exposed cerebral cortex. "Although some prefer to make lesions interrupting the fibers radiating to the frontal lobe." The blade moved with deceptive swiftness, neither in extreme close-up nor in slow motion; but the blood, which jetted for an instant across the neurosurgeon's steady right hand, was assuredly real.

Zombie. In an hour like many other hours, Rehnquist smiled as the warder rolled his wheelchair along the endless white corridors of St. Elizabeth's Hospital. He smiled at his new-found friends, with their funny number-names; he smiled at the darkened windows, crisscrossed with wire mesh to keep him safe; he smiled at the warmth of the urine puddling slowly beneath him. And as the wheelchair reached the end of another hallway, he smiled again and touched the angry scar along his forehead. He asked the warder—whose name, he thought, was Romero—if it was time to sleep again. He liked to sleep. In fact, he couldn't think of anything he would rather do than sleep. But sometimes, when he woke, smiling into the morning sun, he wondered why it was that he no longer dreamed.

Czadek

Ray Russell

"The gods are cruel" is the way Dr. North put it, and I could not disagree. The justice of the gods or God or Fates or Furies or cosmic forces that determine our lives can indeed be terrible, sometimes far too terrible for the offense; a kind of unjust justice, a punishment that outweighs the crime, not an eye for an eye but a hundred eyes for an eye. As long as I live, I'll never be able to explain or forget what I saw this morning in that laboratory.

I had gone there to do some research for a magazine article on life before birth. Our local university's biology lab has a good reputation, and so has its charming director, Dr. Emily North. The lab's collection of embryos and fetuses is justly famous. I saw it this morning, accompanied by the obliging and attractive doctor. Rows of gleaming jars, each containing a human creature who was once alive, suspended forever, eerily serene, in chemical preservative.

All the stages of pre-birth were represented. In the first jar, I saw an embryo captured at the age of five weeks, with dark circles of eyes clearly visible even that early. In the next jar, I saw an example of the eight-week stage, caught in the act of graduating from embryo to fetus, with fingers, toes, and male organs sprouting. On we walked, past the jars, as veins and arteries became prominent: eleven weeks . . . eighteen weeks (sucking its thumb) . . . twenty-eight weeks, ten inches long, with fully distinguishable facial features.

It was a remarkable display, and I was about to say so when I saw a jar set apart from the others that made me suddenly stop. "My God," I said, "what's that?"

Dr. North shook her head. Her voice was shadowed by sadness as she replied, "I wish I knew. I call it Czadek."

There used to be (and perhaps still are?) certain dry, flavorless wafers, enemies of emptiness, which, when eaten with copious draughts of water, coffee, or other beverage, expanded in the body, swelling up, ballooning, becoming bloated, inflated, reaching out, ranging forth, stretching from stomach wall to stomach wall, touching and filling every corner, conquering and occupying the most remote outposts of vacuous void; in that way creating an illusion of having dined sumptuously, even hoggishly, scotching hunger, holding at bay the hounds of appetite, and yet providing no nourishment.

Estes Hargreave always reminded me of those wafers, and they of him. Other things have brought him to mind, over the years. When, for example, I encountered the publicity for a Hollywood film (ten years in the making, a budget of sixty million dollars, etc.) and was able to check the truth of those figures with the producer, who is a friend of mind, the thought of Estes promptly presented itself. What my friend told me was that the movie actually had been made in a little over *one* year and had cost about *six* million dollars. As he revealed this, in the living room of my apartment, over the first of the two vodka gimlets that are his limit, the image of Estes absolutely took over my mind, expanding in all directions like one of those wafers. I saw him as he had been, a very tall but small-time actor, indignantly resigning from Equity, a move he'd hoped would be shocking, sending ripples of pleasant notoriety throughout Thespia. But it had gone unnoticed. The only reason I remembered it was because I'd been a small-time actor myself in those days, and I'd been present at the resignation. Where was Estes now? Was he alive? I hadn't heard of him in years.

"That stuff you see in the papers," said my guest, the producer, "that's the work of my P. R. guy, a very good man with the press. I asked him to pick me up here in about half an hour, by the way, hope you don't mind. He's set up an interview with one of the columnists for this afternoon, to plug the product. I wouldn't do an interview without him. He's great, this fellow."

Intuition flared like brushfire through my brain. "Did he used to be an actor?"

"As a matter of fact, I think he did, a long time ago."

(I knew it!)

"Is his name Estes Hargreave?"

"No. Wayne McCord."

"Oh."

Talk about anticlimax. My intuition, it seemed, was not so much brushfire as backfire. The reason I had homed in on poor old Hargreave was because he had always employed a Rule of Ten when reporting the statistics of his life. He just added a zero to everything. If he received a fee of, say, $200 for an acting engagement, he airily let it drop that "they paid me two grand," or, if a bit more discretion was advisable, he would resort to ambiguity—"they laid two big ones on me"—knowing that, if challenged, he could always claim that by "big ones" he had meant "C-notes." His annual income—which, according to him, averaged "a hundred G's, after taxes"—was, by this same rule, closer to $10,000 in the real world. *Before* taxes.

He applied the Rule of Ten to his very ancestry. His branch of the Hargreaves had been in the United States for a hundred and fifty years prior to his birth, he would proudly claim; but he and I had grown up in the same neighborhood, and I knew that his parents had arrived in this country just fifteen years before he had come squalling into the world, bearing their spiky Central European surname, which he changed after graduating high school and before being drafted into the Army (World War II). "First Lieutenant Hargreave" was another figment of his fecund mind: he never rose above the rank of buck private, and, in fact, took a lot of kidding with the phrase, "See here, Private Hargreave," a paraphrase of the title of Marion Hargrove's bestseller. I used to wonder why he didn't say he'd been a captain or a major, as long as he was making things up, but that was before I tumbled to his Rule. In the Army rankings of those days, First Lieutenant was exactly ten rungs from the bottom: (1) Private, (2) PFC, (3) Corporal, (4) Sergeant, (5) Staff Sergeant, (6) Tech Sergeant, (7) Master Sergeant, (8) Warrant Officer, (9) Second Lieutenant, (10) First Lieutenant.

The Rule of Ten was applied to his losses and expenditures too. "I dropped a hundred bucks last night in a poker game" could safely be translated as $10. A new wardrobe had set him back "three and a half thou," he once announced; but his tailor also happened to be mine, and I quickly learned that Hargreave had spent $350 on two suits at $150 each plus a parcel of shirts and ties totaling $50.

There were, of course, areas that needed no amplification: his height, for instance, which was impressively towering without embellishment. It was to Hargreave's credit that he never felt compelled to *diminish* any numbers even when it might have seemed advantageous to do so: He never peeled any years off his age, and, to the best of my knowledge, was meticulously honest in his relations with the IRS.

Hargreave was clever. If Truth-times-Ten resulted in an absurd, unbelievable figure, he still produced that figure, but as a deliberate hyperbole. There was the time he was involved in a vulgar brawl with a person of slight frame who weighed not much more than a hundred pounds, and yet had flattened him. This was particularly humiliating to Hargreave because his opponent in that brawl was a woman. In recounting the incident, Hargreave first made use of another favorite device, simple reversal, and said that he, Hargreave, had flattened "the other guy." He did not, of course, claim that his opponent weighed a thousand pounds. Not exactly. But he did say, with a chuckle and a smile, "This bruiser tipped the scales at about half a ton." The Rule of Ten was thus preserved by lifting it out of the literal, into the jocular figurative.

When it came to matters of the heart, Hargreave applied a Rule of Ten to the Rule of Ten itself. For example, the oft-repeated boast that he bedded "two new chicks every week" (or 104 per year) was his hundredfold inflation of the actual annual figure, 1.4—the fraction representing misfires: couplings left unconsummated due to this or that dysfunction. Of course, I'm guessing about these intimate matters, but it's an educated guess, supported by the testimony of talkative ladies.

There were some Hargreavean inflations, however, that did not conveniently fit into the Rule of Ten or the Rule of Ten times Ten. The infamous *Macbeth* affair was one of these. That time, he utilized an asymmetrical variant somewhere between those two Rules—sort of a Rule of Thirty-Seven and a Half. A summer theater group had made the understandable mistake of

booking him to play leads in a season of open air repertory—
I say understandable because his brochure (a handsomely
printed work of fabulistic fiction) would have fooled anybody. "Mr. Hargreave has appeared in over fifty Broadway
plays" was one of its claims. He'd appeared in five, as walk-
ons, or over five, if you count the one that folded in New
Haven and never got to Broadway. " 'OF OVERPOWERING
STATURE . . . PRODIGY!'—*Brooks Atkinson.*" Atkinson
had indeed written those words about Hargreave, though
without mentioning his name: ". . . But focus was diverted
from Mr. Olivier's great scene by the unfortunate casting of a
background spear-carrier of overpowering stature, who seemed
to be nearly seven feet tall. It was impossible to look at anyone
else while this prodigy was on stage." Hargreave was actually
only six eight, but he may have been wearing lifts. (I've often
wondered if he realized that Atkinson had used "prodigy" not
in the sense of "genius" but in its older meaning of *lusus
naturae* or gazingstock . . .)

Anyway, the brochure was an impressive document, and
considering the fact that the prodigy it described was available
for a reasonable $150 per week (or, as he later put it, "a thou
and a half"), it was not surprising that the outdoor theater
snapped him up. There were half a dozen stunning photos in
the brochure, as well, showing Hargreave in makeup for
everything from *Oedipus Rex* to *Charley's Aunt*, as well as in
the clear: he was a good-looking chap.

The first production of the summer had lofty aspirations:
Macbeth, uncut, with faddish borrowings from other productions: a thick Scots burr (in homage to the Orson Welles film)
and contemporary military uniform (shades of several Shakespearean shows, including the "G. I." *Hamlet* of Maurice
Evans, but dictated by economy rather than experimentalism).
To this outlandish medley was superimposed incidental music
filched from both operatic versions of the tragedy, those of
Verdi and Bloch (oil and water, stylistically), rescored for
backstage bagpipes.

Hargreave wasn't to blame for any of this, of course, even
though he went on record as praising the "bold iconoclastic
flair" of the production—which may have been no more than
diplomacy rather than his own vivid absence of taste. No,
Hargreave's transgression was the interminable interpolation
he wrote into the classic script and performed on opening

night, after first taking great care *not* to seek the approval of the director. What he did, exactly, was to apply the aforementioned Rule of Thirty-Seven and a Half to the familiar couplet—

> I will not be afraid of death and bane
> Till Birnam Forest come to Dunsinane

—bloating it up to a rant of seventy-five lines. If that doesn't seem particularly long as Shakespearean speeches go, be reminded that, of Macbeth's other major speeches, "Is this a dagger" is only thirty-two lines in length, "If it were done" but twenty-eight, and "Tomorrow and tomorrow and tomorrow" a scant ten.

The production, as I've said, was uncut, retaining even those silly witch-dance scenes considered by some scholars to be non-Shakespearean in origin. Hargreave's seventy-five leaden lines—delivered in no great hurry—made an already long evening in the theater seem endless to the mosquito-punctured audience. I wasn't there, thanks for large mercies, but plenty of people were, and their reports all coincide to form one of the minor legends of contemporary theatrical lore.

The worst part of this depressing farrago was what happened after the seventy-fifth and final line had been bellowed. The spectators, mesmerized into mindless automata, to their everlasting shame gave Hargreave a standing ovation lasting a clamorous sixty seconds (ten minutes, according to him). Maybe they just wanted to stretch their legs.

The drama critic of the local paper did not join in the ovation. Although not enough of a scholar to spot the interpolation as such, he knew what he didn't like. Hence, he allotted only one sentence to the male lead: "In the title role, Estes Hargreave provided what is certainly the dullest performance I have ever seen in twenty-two years of theater-going." There's a divinity that protects ham actors: the linotypist drunkenly substituted an "f" for the "d" in "dullest," resulting in a rave review that Hargreave carried in his wallet until it disintegrated into lacework.

Surprisingly, the unscheduled interpolation did not in itself cause Hargreave to be fired—or not so surprisingly, perhaps, considering the standing ovation and the lucky typo. What cooked his goose was his demand that, for the remaining *Macbeth* performances that season, the programs be overprinted with the line, "ADDITIONAL VERSES BY ESTES

HARGREAVE." That broke the camel's back. He was handed his walking papers, and his understudy took over for the rest of the season. Hargreave, naturally, gave it out that he had quit. "I ankled that scene, turned my back on a grand and a half a week rather than prostitute my art."

But the director had his revenge. He reported Hargreave's behavior to Actors Equity (enclosing a copy of the seventy-five-liner that I've treasured to this day), and his complaint, added to others that had been lodged from time to time, not to mention the persistent rumors that Hargreave often worked for much less than Equity scale, caused him to be casually called on the carpet before an informal panel of his peers that included me.

"Sit down, Estes," I said chummily, "and let's hear your side of all this." He sat. With a grin, I added, "Preferably in twenty-five words or less. Nobody wants to make a Federal case out of it."

Hargreave did not return my grin. He looked me straight in the eye. Then he looked the other members straight in the eye, one by one. He cleared his throat.

"I stand before you," he said, hastily rising from his chair, "a man thoroughly disgusted with the so-called 'legitimate' stage and with this 'august' body. I am sickened by the East Coast snobbery that persists in promulgating the myth that the almighty stage is superior to the art of film. I have given my life, my dedication, *my blood* to the stage—and how have I been rewarded? Oh, I'm not saying I haven't made a good living. I'm not saying I haven't received glowing reviews from the most respected critics of our time. I'm not saying I haven't been mobbed by hordes of idolatrous fans. But all of this is Dead Sea fruit when I find myself here before a group of greasepaint junkies, none of whom are better actors than I, all of whom have the infernal gall to set themselves up as holier-than-thou *judges* of my behavior. Well, I am not going to give you the satisfaction. I hear they're preparing to do a remake of that classic film, *Stagecoach*, out there in the 'despised' West. Yes, I hear that clarion call, and I am going to answer it. I have been asked to test for the role John Wayne created in the original version. An artist of my experience and caliber does not usually deign to audition or do screen tests, of course, but I have no false pride. I will test for that role. And I will get it.

You clowns will have my formal resignation in tomorrow's mail."

I never knew how he did it. Was it a kind of genius? Did he have a built-in computer in his head? I only know that later, when we played back the tape that one of our cagier members had secretly made of the proceedings, and had a stenographer transcribe it for us, I discovered to my wonder that Hargreave's resignation speech totaled exactly ten times the length I had waggishly requested of him: two hundred and fifty words on the button, if you think of "so-called" as two words. I had to admire the man. He was a phony, he had no talent, he was as corny as a bumper sticker, but he was so consistently and flagrantly appalling in everything he did that he was like a living, breathing, walking, talking piece of junk art. Whether or not he actually tested for the John Wayne role, I don't know. Maybe he did. I tend to doubt it. At any rate, the job went to Alex Cord.

The doorbell rang.

"That must be my man now," said my guest, draining his second and last drink. I got to my feet, opened the door, and looked up into a smiling, sun-browned, middle-aged but very familiar face, on top of a tall—prodigiously tall—frame.

"Estes!" I cried.

"Long time no see," he said, jovially, in the pidgin of our youth.

My intuition began brushfiring again, quickly making the John Wayne/Alex Cord/Wayne McCord connection, and I realized that Hargreave, after his *Stagecoach* disappointment, had taken on the names of both actors, probably in the hope that their good fortune would be mystically transferred to him. In a way, it had. He looked happy. He radiated success. He had found his true vocation.

"Come on in!" I boomed, genuinely glad to see him. "Have a drink!"

He shook his head. "No time. Can I have a rain check?" Addressing his employer, he said, "We'd better shake a leg or we'll be late. It's close to rush hour and we have to fight about ten miles of crosstown traffic."

"No, Wayne," the producer said with an indulgent sigh, "it's just eight short blocks up the street. An easy stroll. We could both use the exercise."

That was two or three summers ago. I ran into my producer friend again earlier this year, and asked about Wayne. He shrugged. "Had to let him go. He suffered a . . . credibility gap, I guess you could call it. People just stopped believing him. I suppose it was bound to happen. I mean, how long can you tamper with the truth the way he did, and hope to get away with it? There's always a price tag, my friend, a day of reckoning, know what I mean? Anyway, I gave him the sack. No, I don't know where he is now, but I'll bet a nickel he's still in show business."

"The gods are cruel," Dr. Emily North said this morning as she told me about the creature in the jar:

"Some friends of mine had mentioned it, how they'd seen it in a little traveling carnival. But I had to see for myself, so I drove to the outskirts of town and managed to get there just as they were packing up to move on. It was a real relic of a show, the kind of thing I'd thought had gone out of style. Shabby, sleazy, tasteless, probably illegal. But I did see what I went to see. Czadek was all they called him. Like the name of one of those outer-space villains on a TV show. But he wasn't rigged out in outer-space gear. He was dressed like a cowboy—Stetson hat, chaps, lariat. He twirled the lariat, and did a not-very-good tap dance. And he smiled   a desperate, frightened smile, full of anguish. I tried to talk to him but he didn't answer. He couldn't speak—or wouldn't, I never knew which. A few months later, when he died, the owner of the carnie phoned me long distance and asked me if I wanted to buy the cadaver for scientific purposes. So there he is. In a jar. Without his cowboy costume. Naked as a fetus, but not a fetus. An adult human male of middle age, well nourished and perfectly proportioned, quite handsome, in fact. But only eight inches tall . . ."

No, I can't explain it. I won't even try. But I think about those words "A day of reckoning" and "The gods are cruel" and "How long can you tamper with the truth the way he did, and hope to get away with it?" I recall some lines from Estes' awful amplification of *Macbeth*—

For by this fatal fault I was cast down,
Ay, to damnation, by mine own fell hand!
None but myself to censure or to blame . . .

—and I think of Estes, who stood six feet, eight inches tall without his shoes. Eighty inches. Exactly ten times taller than the creature in the jar. The tiny dead man with the hauntingly familiar face. And I remember the original surname by which Estes was known before he changed it. A spiky Central European name . . .

Wordsong

J. N. Williamson

When true magic came in the mail, the probability was that this literary legerdemain was conceived by one of the Rays, Richards or Roberts. Occasionally, a Dennis, Jim or David showed up in the by-line and, more rarely, a Steve. For whatever occult reason, none of the fiction I preferred for the anthologies I edited seemed ever to be written by a man with a less popular given name: Donald or George, say, Randolph or Oscar. Unfailingly, Johns, Alans, Bills, and Toms.

The anomaly puzzled me as much as did the given names of the women whose yarns I selected; because in the case of the ostensible gentle sex, the obverse was true. Ladies dipping in my pool of fictive possibilities always seemed to be named Ardath, Mona, Bari or Lisa, Jeannette or Annette or Jessica, Tabbie or Tanith. Not a Mary, Helen, Linda or Jane in sight! Indeed, the only woman writer I read with frequency—outside the genre—was named Eudora.

Yet the greatest stories ever submitted for my collections were written by someone with a name that presented no clue to the writer's gender. And while I eagerly accepted each magical tale from that mysterious pen, I was never allowed to publish even *one* of them.

Before explaining this strange sequence of events, please permit me to express the mystical hope that the presence, or essence, of that extraordinary artist is somehow conveyed to the present, excellent fictional works I was allowed—through the kind offices of the publisher—to offer you. If anything of Wordsong's storytelling sorcery becomes a part of you as it has become a bewitching part of me, you may count yourself blessed.

It was when I was assembling material for the first anthology bearing my name as editor that I initially read those enchanting, pseudonymous writings. And I was sent another Wordsong story each time I began another anthology. Each was created on the foundation of a new or basically fresh idea, and each plot sprung from characterizations which were incredibly lifelike, mesmeric in their psychological insight. When I declare that each idea appeared new, I mean what I say. Those of you who have ever seen an old book entitled *Plotto*, which boasted that every idea a writer might need was contained in it, may imagine how surprised and delighted I was. Almost any other wordworker I knew would have been tempted to develop the ideas alone, confident that their thrilling originality would lead to the invention of a memorable yarn. But the mystery author who sent the four tales to me had found the self-control and possessed the forethought to turn each story into something fully fleshed—without a vestige of the vignette—with the result that all four were so perfectly completed that to apply a blue pen's mark anywhere on their pages might have been a sin in the face of God.

Anybody who has submitted their work to me knows now, I believe, how exceptional and extraordinary were the writings of Wordsong.

My appreciation seemed almost unprofessional to me; my near-worship appalled me. But I perceived that Wordsong's emergence gave me the opportunity of a Mencken or a Max Perkins to recognize and advance genius. When I'd finished reading that first story, I was so overcome by how fulfilled it was that I felt . . . *redeemed*.

Then I learned that I was only to be permitted to *read*. Not present.

For the first time during my life in the second half of the century, I'd come upon a fiction writer who very literally wrote simply for the love of writing. At first, it appeared blasphemous. In time, it came to seem almost divine. But whether I was trapped editorially between heaven and hell or not, I was suffused with the heady and not-uncharitable sense of dis-

covery; moments after I'd devoured that first story, I was eager
to accept and buy it. Who "Wordsong" might be, I had no
idea; it was all but impossible to believe a newcomer had
created it. I thought of the giants of the genre who'd resorted to
pseudonyms in the past, but I could not recognize the ineffable
style. And at that moment, I did not know I would never even
have the chance to see the author's signature on a canceled
check.

It was the telephone call—with the writer's instructions—
which, coming moments after my first reading, provided much
of the information I've given to you. I told the frustrating
genius on the other end that I insisted upon paying for the tale,
since that would tie it up, prevent other editors from obtaining
it; he or she might experience a change of heart. "If you truly
appreciate it that much," the voice murmured in my ear, "you
may—but you must do so in cash."

That, of course, was an outrage. I said I would do the best I
could. "That is all anyone should seek from you," came the
reply. When I strove to learn *why* cash, and no publication, the
connection was broken instantly.

Still, I did what I'd said I would; the publisher was a
gentleman and, while he wasn't sanguine about the transaction,
he allowed it. Quite riskily, I sent Wordsong's payment to the
address with which I'd been provided—a rural route box
located in one of those states no one ever recalls when trying to
name all the fifty variegated slices of America; a wilder, freer,
less-populated state—and a town even expert gazetteers forget
to list.

Permission was never granted me to include that marvelous
yarn. The identical, bewildering conditions were repeated
when I was gathering new tales for further anthologies. Every
time, my exquisite pride, my editorial zeal, was dashed by a
phone call in which I was asked if I "appreciated" the new
work, told that I would never be allowed to publish it, and left
with the self-bestowed obligation of purchasing the story. Deep
inside, I think, I hoped one day to have enough of these fictive
gems to assemble a veritable king's ransom of a story
collection—the sort that would add my name as editor to those
of Campbell, Boucher, Grant, Schiff, Derleth and the rest. To
be truthful, there were times when I was annoyed, almost
angered by the way Wordsong "let" me provide payment for
material no one else would read except the publisher (eventual-

ly, quite reasonably, he demanded to read what he had paid for).

As well, I became . . . well . . . haunted by the writer's unusual voice as it reached me during our phone conversations. Consistently, ours was a dreadful connection and the author's voice, each time, was marked by shadowed vocal pauses so lacking in inflection that it would have sounded remote even with a good connection. And each call, that voice was masculine and feminine at once, though not in the androgynous sense. There was power to it; its integrity was implicit and the peculiar melding of strength and gentleness always rendered Wordsong's sex unimportant until after we had hung up and I was left to shake my head in despair and wonderment.

When the fourth story arrived, the situation began to change: it got worse. *Not* the tale; oh, no. If anything, it was the best. I have never read a work of fiction—that's the plain truth—that so aroused my every emotion, made me laugh and cry, filled me with horror, wonder, and suspense, and finally thrilled me with its unique, amazingly apt ending. The fault was in the inevitable, damned phone call—and Wordsong's ultimate declaration that this fourth story would be the *final* one.

I was informed why, at last. But I'm unable to tell anybody else, except to the degree that readers of this bizarre history are able to perceive the reason. The complete truth. It's here, and all about you.

My decision seconds after our last phone discussion—which was more a one-sided tirade, since I begged at first and I was shouting by the end of it—was to try, in person, to wrest Wordsong's permission to publish from him, or her. Failing that, maybe I might have learned more from meeting the genius, gained some inkling into the author's reasons.

I found I could fly most of the way to the hamlet in the forgettable state but not without being obliged to make a series of connecting flights throughout the journey. No one cared to go there, save I. The trip was at my expense; I hadn't dared try the patience of the publisher again. It had also occurred to me that he might wish to fly there with me and, I admit it, I had such a feeling of personal mission that I was unwilling to share my meeting with the enigmatic author. After finally arriving in the town of my destination, I learned to my dismay that I'd need to rent an eight-year-old jalopy from the one auto rental service in a forty-mile radius and drive myself.

Soon, I was on dirt roads no one but the rural mail carrier had maneuvered, surely, since the Korean conflict. There was a look to the dust in the road of sullen permanence, of a settling, even a reclaiming, that was virtually hostile. It curled up from beneath the tires of my aged auto like fringes of white hair round the neck of a retired businessman who had retained certain powerful and unpleasant influences. I wasn't aided by the ‑drastic change of weather. I'd left wintry, mopey Indianapolis behind and it was hot here, stifling because of the heat given off by the straining engine. The farther I went down the dirt road, never catching sight of another person or vehicle, the more my imagination strove to get the better of me. What, I wondered, if Wordsong was . . . literally . . . a *ghost writer?* One who, unsuccessful in life, so yearned to make a mark on this earth that he had clung to partial existence by pale hands locked to his desk, to try once more—with some special insights muttered in his ear at the instant of juxtaposition with eternity.

I roused myself to think about books, the creative production of other authors, and recalled what Eudora Welty wrote: "It had been startling and disappointing . . . to find out that story books had been written by *people,* that books were not natural wonders . . ." The entire process of "thinking up" fiction, when one reflected upon it, was more extraordinary than anyone had quite admitted, even *other-natural,* for want of a better word. It consisted in part of dissociative ideas which the author imagined would link together intriguingly, viably, toward some point, yet the source of the ideas themselves was often impossible to trace. It was also—

A short series of mailboxes rose on posts at the edge of the dirt road, like high, plump grave markers. After I'd followed the road for miles, they became the first evidence that Wordsong, that anyone at all, endured in that loneliness. Of course, with my window rolled down, I checked each one out; but I discovered only that I had chosen the correct rural route. No "Wordsong" was revealed to me and most of the other names were partly or wholly eradicated by time and erosion.

With no other choice, I proceeded on the road and, for another few moments, the roiling clouds of utterly quiet, clearly protesting dust enveloped the old car. Dust and the further stillness of land untenanted and deserted by man, devoid of human improvement, bewitched me; and I smiled, starting to understand the source of my writer's inspiration. By now it was dusk and the road had come to seem unending, ceaseless; a person living here, for any length of time, might sooner or later conclude that the road did *not* end but went on, and on, winding through wild worlds beyond the imagination even of a writer who called himself—or herself—Wordsong.

And of course, eventually, such a creative soul would nonetheless attempt to capture it all on paper.

Then I saw the next mailbox, over the berm to my right, and quickly realized that I saw no other in the distance. Braking sharply with a creature's squeal that was jarring, shocking, I parked just behind the rusted mail container and stared for the first time toward the place where a house should stand.

I saw it, though the wind continued to swirl the dust, its noise as strident as a dying old woman's; or rather, saw the foundation and two adamant walls of a house that might have been built at Nathaniel Hawthorne's time—or used as the model for something Hawthorne wrote. Scarcely, I saw, too— or believed that I saw—a similarly insubstantial or incomplete figure beside one standing wall. Alighting from the car with alacrity, I started to call out but the amorphous form was gone—if it had been there. It seemed I had moved in surprised recognition and, in doing so, stepped beyond the limits of an unperceivable dimensional allowance.

There was nothing in the ruins and they'd been abandoned. There was no sign of life as I tended to identify it; yet there were . . . sensations, I suppose. Distant, discernible reflections of lives once lived there and others that continued to do so, submerged in the depths of the untrod, weed-strewn lot like underwater entities.

In a mailbox with the correct number, I found no mail; none. It appeared not to have been used for decades, but the curt vertical lid had been left open. Trembling because I fancied that something I'd be unable to see might sweep down that road and drown me in that crawly, fertile, deserted lot, I started to close the box. Give up; drive off.

But at the rear of the container I found a healthy, vivaciously alarmed mother bird of a kind I couldn't identify and, around her, several scrawny infants. I must have made a sound because the mother flew at me then, screaming as she relinquished her young and escaped, voiceless again, on the rising surfer sky. I watched that flight, feeling regretful kinship, hoping she'd return; then I peered in once more at the baby birds.

They were squirming in a nest made of the cash—the generous dollar bills—I had paid Wordsong for those perfect and magical stories.

I sat behind the wheel of the rented car for more than an hour, but the mother bird didn't return. I attempted to figure it out, the best I was able, and remembered something else Eudora Welty had written in her valuable little Harvard book of memories, *One Writer's Beginnings:* "It isn't my mother's voice, or the voice of any person I can identify, certainly not my own." She spoke of the voice she always heard whenever she read, or wrote. "It is to me," she wrote, "the voice of the story . . . itself."

The Wordsong work was that. The stories had risen from this ruin of a house, the neglect of a land man no longer required, of a dirt road going from somewhere to elsewhere; they had no birth, could have no death. They existed. They were. They wished to be read; once. And the other Wordsong stories were everywhere and all around me, further than the eye perceived, down a road that stretched from one appreciative reader's belief into fantasy, and infinity.

Down by the Sea
Near the Great Big Rock

Joe R. Lansdale

Down by the sea near the great big rock, they made their camp and toasted marshmallows over a small, fine fire. The night was pleasantly chill and the sea spray cold. Laughing, talking, eating the gooey marshmallows, they had one swell time; just them, the sand, the sea and the sky, and the great big rock.

The night before they had driven down to the beach, to the camping area; and on their way, perhaps a mile from their destination, they had seen a meteor shower, or something of that nature. Bright lights in the heavens, glowing momentarily, seeming to burn red blisters across the ebony sky.

Then it was dark again, no meteoric light, just the natural glow of the heavens—the stars, the dime-size moon.

They drove on and found an area of beach on which to camp, a stretch dominated by pale sands and big waves, and the great big rock.

Toni and Murray watched the children eat their marshmallows and play their games, jumping and falling over the great big rock, rolling in the cool sand. About midnight, when the kids were crashed out, they walked along the beach like fresh-found lovers, arm in arm, shoulder to shoulder, listening to the sea, watching the sky, speaking words of tenderness.

"I love you so much," Murray told Toni, and she repeated the words and added, "and our family, too."

154

They walked in silence now, the feelings between them words enough. Sometimes Murray worried that they did not talk as all the marriage manuals suggested, that so much of what he had to say on the world and his work fell on the ears of others, and that she had so little to truly say to him. Then he would think: What the hell? I know how I feel. Different messages, unseen, unheard, pass between us all the time, and they communicate in a fashion words cannot.

He said some catch phrase, some pet thing between them, and Toni laughed and pulled him down on the sand. Out there beneath that shiny-dime moon, they stripped and loved on the beach like young sweethearts, experiencing their first night together after long expectation.

It was nearly two A.M. when they returned to the camper, checked the children and found them sleeping comfortably as kittens full of milk.

They went back outside for awhile, sat on the rock, and smoked and said hardly a word. Perhaps a coo or a purr passed between them, but little more.

Finally they climbed inside the camper, zipped themselves into their sleeping bag and nuzzled together on the camper floor.

Outside the wind picked up, the sea waved in and out, and a slight rain began to fall.

Not long after Murray awoke and looked at his wife in the crook of his arm. She lay there with her face a grimace, her mouth opening and closing like a guppie, making an "uhhh, uhh," sound.

A nightmare perhaps. He stroked the hair from her face, ran his fingers lightly down her cheek and touched the hollow of her throat and thought: What a nice place to carve out some fine, white meat . . .

What in hell is wrong with me? Murray snapped inwardly, and he rolled away from her, out of the bag. He dressed, went outside and sat on the rock. With shaking hands on his knees, buttocks resting on the warmth of the stone, he brooded. Finally he dismissed the possibility that such a thought had actually crossed his mind, smoked a cigarette and went back to bed.

He did not know that an hour later Toni awoke and bent over

him and looked at his face as if it were something to squash. But finally she shook it off and slept.

The children tossed and turned. Little Roy squeezed his hands open, closed, open, closed. His eyelids fluttered rapidly.

Robyn dreamed of striking matches.

Morning came and Murray found that all he could say was, "I had the oddest dream."

Toni looked at him, said, "Me, too," and that was all.

Placing lawn chairs on the beach, they put their feet on the rock and watched the kids splash and play in the waves; watching as Roy mocked the sound of the *Jaws* music and made fins with his hands and chased Robyn through the water as she scuttled backwards and screamed with false fear.

Finally they called the children from the water, ate a light lunch, and, leaving the kids to their own devices, went in for a swim.

The ocean stroked them like a mink-gloved hand. Tossed them, caught them, massaged them gently. They washed together, laughing, kissing—

Then tore their lips from one another as up on the beach they heard a scream.

Roy had his fingers gripped about Robyn's throat, had her bent back over the rock and was putting a knee in her chest. There seemed no play about it. Robyn was turning blue.

Toni and Murray waded toward the shore, and the ocean no longer felt kind. It grappled with them, held them, tripped them with wet, foamy fingers. It seemed an eternity before they reached shore, yelling at Roy.

Roy didn't stop. Robyn flopped like a dying fish.

Murray grabbed the boy by the hair and pulled him back, and for a moment, as the child turned, he looked at his father with odd eyes that did not seem his, but looked instead as cold and firm as the great big rock.

Murray slapped him, slapped him so hard Roy spun and went down, stayed there on hands and knees, panting.

Murray went to Robyn, who was already in Toni's arms, and on the child's throat were blue-black bands like thin, ugly snakes.

"Baby, baby, are you okay?" Toni said over and over. Murray wheeled, strode back to the boy, and Toni was now yelling at him, crying, "Murray, Murray, easy now. They were just playing and it got out of hand."

Roy was on his feet, and Murray, gritting his teeth, so angry he could not believe it, slapped the child down.

"Murray," Toni yelled, and she let go of the sobbing Robyn and went to stay his arm, for he was already raising it for another strike. "That's no way to teach him not to hit, not to fight."

Murray turned to her, almost snarling, but then his face relaxed and he lowered his hand. Turning to the boy, feeling very criminal, Murray reached down to lift Roy by the shoulder. But Roy pulled away, darted for the camper.

"Roy," he yelled, and started after him. Toni grabbed his arm.

"Let him be," she said. "He got carried away and he knows it. Let him mope it over. He'll be all right." Then softly: "I've never known you to get that mad."

"I've never been so mad before," he said honestly.

They walked back to Robyn, who was smiling now. They all sat on the rock, and about fifteen minutes later Robyn got up to see about Roy. "I'm going to tell him it's okay," she said. "He didn't mean it." She went inside the camper.

"She's sweet," Toni said.

"Yeah," Murray said, looking at the back of Toni's neck as she watched Robyn move away. He was thinking that he was supposed to cook lunch today, make hamburgers, slice onions; big onions cut thin with a freshly sharpened knife. He decided to go get it.

"I'll start lunch," he said flatly, and stalked away.

As he went, Toni noticed how soft the back of his skull looked, so much like an over-ripe melon.

She followed him inside the camper.

Next morning, after the authorities had carried off the bodies, taken the four of them out of the bloodstained, fire-gutted camper, one detective said to another:

"Why does it happen? Why would someone kill a nice family like this? And in such horrible ways . . . set fire to it afterwards?

The other detective sat on the huge rock and looked at his partner, said tonelessly, "Kicks maybe."

• • •

That night, when the moon was high and bright, gleaming down like a big spotlight, the big rock, satiated, slowly spread its flippers out, scuttled across the sand into the waves, and began to swim toward the open sea. The fish that swam near it began to fight.

Outsteppin' Fetchit

Charles R. Saunders

Motion Picture and Television Home and Hospital—1988

The old man's body was so small and frail it barely made a dent in the hospital bed. But the orderly was still hard-pressed to hold him down.

"Naw!" the old man shouted as he bucked and heaved against the arms that pinned his shoulders to the mattress. *"Naw!"*

"God-*damn*, why can't you hold your old ass still?" the orderly grunted. He pushed harder, feeling the indentation of sharp-edged collarbones on his palms. He kept his gaze averted from the wrinkle-embedded eyes of the patient. Those eyes were looking at him as though he were the Klan incarnate—and the only white thing about him was his uniform.

Suddenly a large hand attached to a heavyweight arm shoved the orderly aside so hard he had to shoot both hands in front of him to cushion a collision with the wall. He looked back to the bed and saw Nurse Henrietta cradling the old man in her arms.

"What the *hell* did you do that for, woman?" the orderly shouted.

"Go to the nurses' station," Henrietta said without looking at him. "Wait for me there."

The orderly walked out of the room. He'd only been working at MPTHH a week, but he already knew better than to mess with Henrietta, who was big enough to play linebacker

159

for the L.A. Rams. As he shut the door behind him, he heard Henrietta crooning to the old man: "It's all right, Peanut. Nobody gon' hurt you. You be okay . . ."

The orderly sat quietly at the scarred table. A Styrofoam cup of machine coffee steamed in front of him. He paid no attention to it. He was waiting for Henrietta, and wondering if he was about to be fired. The job had been so damned *hard* to come by—

Henrietta came in like a queen. She eased herself into the chair opposite the orderly's. Despite her bulk, the chair accepted her without protest.

Probably give up a long time ago, the orderly thought sourly. Aloud, he commenced to cop a rote version of his "save my gig" plea.

"I wasn't tryin' to hurt him, ma'am. I just come in to check on him, like I'm suppose to. That old man take one look at me and try to crawl off his bed. I was tryin' to keep him from fallin' off and hurtin' hisself."

Henrietta looked at him.

"Save your bull-tickey," she said. "You don't know what the problem is. I *do*. Now I'ma tell you."

The orderly didn't say anything.

"You ever see any of Peanut's movies?" she asked.

"Naw. Peanut Posey was before my time."

"Wasn't before mine," she said. "He was just about the funniest thing on the screen back them. He even outdid ol' Stepin Fetchit. Made a movie with Step and stole the show. Peanut so little and so *cute*, he could get away with near everything. They used to say he 'outstepped Fetchit.' Made him a lot of money, bein' his cute little self."

"You mean, bein' a cute little Tom."

Henrietta fixed him with a gaze flat as a tabletop. "Who you think cleared the road for all you young bloods today?" she asked.

"You the one changin' the subject."

Henrietta gave him the short "humph" that signified how ignorant she thought he was. But she went on with her story.

"Peanut was *real* popular with the ladies. I remember seein' a picture of him settin' on Lena Horne's lap. He went through women faster'n he went through his money. Naturally, some of them women had babies. There was this one son . . ."

• • •

New Jersey Turnpike—1969

Flame stepped on the accelerator of his T-Bird. He zoomed past the slower cars on the pike and shot the finger at one driver with an AMERICA—LOVE IT OR LEAVE IT bumper sticker. A landscape of oil refineries, fast-food restaurants, gas stations, and liquor supermarkets blurred by, as though he were driving underwater. Flame wiped his eyes.

He was making his routine New York-to-Philly run, as he'd done for the past three years. His destination: Douglass University, just outside Philadelphia; close to the Maryland border. Ordinarily, he'd be on his way to make another of the militant speeches that had earned him his fiery nickname. Now—

It had happened after a meeting of Righteous Liberation at the Harlem YMCA. The revolution was getting its ass kicked and something had to be done. At this meeting, the rhetoric was hot as ever. But concrete courses of action remained elusive.

After the meeting broke up in a flurry of "Right on's" and soul handshakes, Flame heard a familiar voice behind him.

"Hold up, Bro."

Flame stopped reluctantly. He didn't like the voice or its owner: Brother Do-Nasty.

When Flame turned, his eyes locked with Do-Nasty's. Do-Nasty motioned Flame beneath the stairwell for a private conversation.

"What you want, man?" Flame asked. "I got to get back to Douglass."

"I know who your daddy is—Bro."

Flame closed his eyes. His stomach heaved as though he were suffering from a Ripple hangover.

"What you talkin' about, fool?" he said. "I told you *I* don't even know who my father is."

"You know, you always sayin' if you lyin' you flyin'. Keep talkin' *that* shit and you be one air-*borne* motherfucker!"

Flame shook his head. The words wouldn't go away. Do-Nasty never had liked him. Flame was too tight with the sisters, and Do-Nasty just couldn't get over no matter what he did. Now, Do-Nasty had dug up the dirt again. Flame's hands wanted to reach out and close around Do-Nasty's neck. But he knew Do-Nasty wouldn't be talking if he hadn't already told somebody else.

"What you want, man?" he asked wearily.

"You a okay cat, Flame. But it won't do the Revolution no good at all if word get out that you *Peanut Posey's* son. Now there *ways* to keep *this* shit quiet. But you still got to go, man. Get *out* of the Revolution. Why don't you take up actin' lessons?"

He laughed. Nastily. Flame wanted to hurt him. But there was nothing he could do.

He'd walked out of the YMCA, got into his T-Bird, driven through the tunnels and tollgates, and hit the pike. The car was loaded with revolutionary literature—much of it written by him. And there was also a semiautomatic rifle hidden under the front seat.

Now, something was wrong with Flame's windshield. The Jersey landscape was flickering in and out of view like a badly-spliced piece of film. New images overlaid the unsteady outlines of Gino's Hamburgers and the A&P—images he had never fully succeeded in blocking from his memory . . .

His mother used to show him old Peanut Posey movies on a secondhand Bell & Howell projector. When he was a child, Flame looked at the grainy, jumpy rendition of the comedian's antics and fell off his chair laughing.

"That your Daddy," his mother would say. "He send us money every month so we can live decent."

"Why he don't live with us?" Flame would ask. But his mother never answered that one.

Flame met Peanut only five times in his life, the last when he was fourteen and already two inches taller than his father. That time, Flame didn't even want to see him. Flame had been reading, and learning. And rejecting.

"I know what you are," he'd said that last time. He walked out of the house, ignoring his mother's protests. Peanut hadn't said a word.

Four years later, Flame bogarted money out of a trust fund he wasn't supposed to touch until he turned twenty-one. He changed his name and became an orphan. He absorbed the lessons of Malcolm, Stokely, and Rap, and set vicarious fires in Watts and Detroit. He became the conflagration that would reduce his own past to unrecognizable ash.

*Then his enemy Do-Nasty read something in the ashes—
something that hadn't burned away . . .*

And now Peanut was cavorting across the curve of the
windshield. There he was, ear-to-ear grin on his face, chicken
in one hand, watermelon in the other as he hip-hopped and
Bojangled just out of the reach of Will Rogers and Shirley
Temple. There he went, out-steppin' Fetchit. Jersey was gone
from Flame's windshield. There was only one way to bring it
back.

Still doing 85 MPH, Flame reached under the seat and
pulled out the semiautomatic. He eased back on the trigger,
just as the Nam Brothers had shown him. Bullets rocketed into
the windshield; slivers of glass swarmed around his head.

Peanut was still *there*—grinning right at him. Peanut threw
the ol' watermelon to his son. Flame *shot* it. It exploded,
spewing gobbets of red flesh and black seeds. Peanut laughed.

"I don't call you son because you shine," he sang in his
raspy falsetto. "I call you son because—you *mine!*"

Flame jerked the trigger again. Peanut danced on his toes;
nothing touched him.

Traffic on Flame's side of the turnpike stopped. Drivers
jumped out of their cars and ran. State troopers came
screaming down the asphalt. They hooked up a bullhorn and
told Flame he had ten seconds to surrender.

Eight seconds later, they blew him away.

Motion Picture and Television Home and Hospital—1988

The orderly stared at his untouched coffee as Henrietta
finished telling him about Flame.

"So you see, sometimes when Peanut see a strange man on
the ward, he think it's Flame comin' to do him in—even
though Flame been dead for nineteen years."

"Damn," said the orderly, stretching it out to three sylla-
bles.

"If Peanut get that way again, you call me or one of the
other nurses." She smiled fondly. "That man still like his
women. He get used to you after a while. You hear what I'm
sayin?"

"Yes'm."

"You got manners. I'll give you that. Now, we got work to
do. Let's get back to it."

Henrietta heaved out of the chair and moved off on her silent crepe soles. The orderly waited until she was gone before he got up.

The orderly stood in Peanut Posey's dark room. His shift had long since ended, yet he hadn't gone home. But he knew Henrietta had.

Peanut was deep in sedated sleep. The old man didn't stir when the orderly eased the pillow out from under his wrinkled head. Holding the pillow in both hands, the orderly gazed down on the dancer who had long since ceased to dance.

Peanut Posey had gone through a lot of women.

And he had more than one son.

Somebody Like You

Dennis Etchison

One morning they were lying together in his bed.

"Hi," she said.

Then her lids closed, all but a quarter of an inch, and her eyes were rolling and her lips were twitching again.

Later, when her pupils drifted back into position, he saw that she was looking at him.

"What time is it?"

He kept looking at her.

She kept looking at him.

"I was watching you sleep," he said.

"Mm?"

With some difficulty she turned onto her back. He saw her wince.

Finally she said, "How long?"

"A couple of hours," he guessed.

They waited. Within and without the room there was the sound of the ocean. It was like breathing.

"Sometimes I talk in my sleep," she said.

"I know."

"Well?"

"Well what?"

"Aren't you going to tell me?"

She tried to turn her face to him. He watched her long, slender fingers feel for the pillow. She made a frown.

"Hurt?" he said.

"Why won't you tell me what I said?"

"That's it," he said. "You said that it hurts."

"It does," she said.

"What does?"

"The place where they cut us apart."

He said, "Are you sleeping?"

"Mm," she said.

He never knew.

She did not come back.

He tried calling her for several days running, but could not get through.

Then one afternoon she phoned to say that it would be nice if he were there.

He agreed.

When she did not answer his knock, he pried loose the screen and let himself in.

The cat was dozing on the bare boards in the living room, its jowls puffed and its eyes slitting in the heat. The bedroom door was ajar, and as he walked in he saw her curled there on the blue sheets. One of her hands was still on the telephone and the other was wrapped protectively around her body.

He sat down, but she did not see him.

More than once he climbed over her and opened and closed the door to draw air into the room. He ran water, tuned the television so that he could hear it and bunched the pillows behind him on the bed, but she did not want to wake up.

When the sun fell low, he drew the thin curtains so that it would not glare on her and leaned forward and fanned her face for a long time with the folded TV log. Her hair was pasted to the side of her head in damp whorls, and her ears contained the most delicate convolutions.

It was dark when she finally roused. Her eyes were glazed over, so that they appeared to be covered with fine, transparent membranes.

She smiled.

"How are you?" she asked.

"What was it this time?" he asked. "You were breathing hard and your mouth was going a mile a minute, but I couldn't understand anything." He waited. "Do you remember?"

She seemed to founder, feeling for the thread that would lead her back into it before it dissolved away.

"I thought we were at *his* place," she said, "and I kept trying to tell you that you had to get out of there before he came home. I couldn't wake up."

She lay there smiling.

"Isn't that funny?" she said.

"Who?" he said. But already it was too late.

He spent the next morning rearranging his place.

Perhaps that would work.

He tied back the frayed blue curtains, cleaned the glass all the way to the low ceiling, spread an animal skin over the divan and moved it close to the bay window; she had liked to sit, sometimes for hours, staring out into the haze that came to settle over the water this time of year. He plumped up the cushions on the long couch and positioned it against the opposite wall, so that they would be able to be together later as they watched the glow.

He washed dishes, piled newspapers in the closet, hid his socks, and even found a small notions table and placed it next to the window so that she would not have to get up so often. Then he got out the plywood he had bought and slipped it between the mattress and box springs. She was right; it was too soft a bed in which to sleep comfortably, though he had not realized that until she mentioned it.

He found himself padding from room to room, trying to see, to feel as she would. *Yes*, he thought, *it will be better this way, much better, and nothing will hurt*.

And yet there was something that was not quite right, something somewhere that was still off-center, vaguely out of place or missing altogether. But the morning passed and, whatever it was, he did not spot it.

The afternoon came and went, but she did not show.

He tried calling. Each time the girl at the answering service screened his ring. She had strict instructions, she admitted at last, to let only one person through, and did not even wait to take his message.

It was twilight when he got there. There were the sounds of unseen people within their separate houses, and he seemed to hear music playing nearby.

I sing this song of you, he thought.

He knocked, but there was no answer.

He shook his head, trying to remember her.

When he began to pry his way in, he discovered that it was not locked.

The living room was warm and the air stale, as though the door and windows had not been opened in a long time. He was nearly to the bedroom when he noticed her stretched out on the old pillows, almost hidden behind the front door.

He saw that her eyes were only partly closed, her corneas glistening between her lids. Her hands and arms were wrapped around herself, her head and neck this time, in the manner of a child in a disaster drill.

"Didn't you hear me knocking?" he said to her.

Her eyes popped open and she looked up, startled, almost as if she expected to see herself. Then she sank back again.

He went to her.

He moved his hand up to her face, ran his finger along her cheek. She made a sleepy sound.

"Hm?" he asked again.

"What?" she said. "Oh, I thought the sound was coming from the other place."

"What other place?" he said.

When she did not answer, he bent to kiss her.

I sing this song of you.

The receiver had time to warm in his hand before he tried again.

The girl at the answering service cut in.

He muffled his voice this time, trying to disguise it. "Let it ring through," he said forcefully.

"Who's calling, please?"

"Who do you think?" he said. "I'm sure she told you to expect my call."

A surprised pause, a rustling of papers. "Let me see, this must be . . ."

She mentioned a name he had never heard before.

"Of course it is. Are you new there?"

She hesitated. In the background he heard buzzes, voices interrupting other calls and messages being taken and posted.

"I'm going to dial again now, and I want you to let it ring through," he said. "Do you understand?"

"Yes, of course," the girl said quickly. "Um, wait a sec," she added, reading from a paper. "I—I'm afraid she's not in this afternoon. I'm sorry."

He darkened. Then, "She did leave a reference number, didn't she?"

"I'll check. Yes, here it is. Well, not exactly. She said to tell you she'll be at 'the other place.' She said you'll know."

He almost gave up. Then he said, "Right. But which one? It could be either of two. Now don't tell me she's going to hang me up with one of her guessing games again."

It was hopeless, but he waited.

"Look," he said, "this is an emergency, for God's sake, and I really don't have time for her to get back to me."

"Um, I'll see. I'm not the one who took the call. Hold, please, and I'll see if I can locate the girl who worked that shift."

The phone went dead for a moment.

I don't believe it, he thought. *It's working.*

She came back on the line.

"It was someone on the late shift," she announced. "I guess she's left messages for you several times in the last week or so. It looks like it was always in the middle of the night, and since you didn't call they're all still on the board. The first one I have here—I'll just read it to you. It says, 'Tell him to meet me at the studio on Ocean Front.' Okay? That might be the place, do you suppose?"

"All right," he said.

"I'm sorry. We aren't usually so confused around here. It's just that—well, she's left so many messages for you, and when you never called, I guess the other girl stuck them in with last week's."

"Thanks," he said.

"Thank you for calling. We were beginning to wonder if you'd ever—"

He hung up.

She was having a hard time waking up.

Her lips were parted very slightly, and a narrow, opaque crack of whiteness shone between her eyelids. She resisted the hand on her shoulder, her neck, her head with faint, inarticulate protest until she could stand it no longer.

Her face twisted and she tried to rise, struggling to focus her vision.

"What's the matter?" she managed to say.

"You were asleep a long time," he told her, his voice more gentle and tender than it had ever been before. "I've been waiting a couple of hours. It's starting to get pretty late."

He caressed the back of her head, his thumb behind her ear.

"The way your eyes were jerking around, you must have been dreaming."

She shook her head, trying to clear it.

"It seemed like someone was outside, trying to get in," she said.

"That was me, I'm afraid."

"Oh. Then that part was true, after all." Her eyes swam, then held on him. "But why would it be you? This is your place. Didn't you have your key?"

"I—forgot it."

"Oh." She stretched. "Never mind. It was just so strange. So real. I thought someone else was here with me. And you know what? He looked a lot like you."

"So where is he, in the closet?"

"Don't worry—he wasn't as good-looking. Only he wouldn't leave, even though he knew you were going to get here any minute. Isn't that funny?"

"Like an open grave," he said uneasily.

"I know," she said, as if it really mattered.

She looked at him, unblinking, in that way she had, until he said something.

"So?"

"So that's all, I guess. I don't know why, but I think I'd like to remember it." And, quite suddenly, tears sprang from her eyes. "All of it."

"Take it easy, will you?"

He moved to her.

"He was trying to be so good to me. Except that it was you, all the time it was you."

"I love you," he said.

"And you know I need you, too, don't you? So much. I don't know what's wrong with me, I really don't. I promise I'll try—"

He stood and quieted her by pressing her head to his body. Her arms went around his waist and they held each other.

"I know you will," he said. "Don't worry about anything. I'm here with you now, and I wouldn't want you any other way."

He went down the stairs from the loft bedroom.

The thick blue drapes, the richest blue he had ever seen, were set off perfectly by the white walls and ceiling, and as he passed them he considered drawing the cord on the magnificent view of the Pacific he knew they would reveal.

Instead he turned and stood for a moment before the mirror that was mounted below the loft, angled to provide a view of the entire room.

In it he saw the cat arising peacefully from a nap on the deep carpeting. He smiled, his lips curling with satisfaction at the couches, the chairs, the superb appointments.

He stood transfixed, listening to the surf as it washed in around the supports of the house. He almost leaned over to activate the custom stereo system, but could not bring himself to break the spell of the gentle rushing, breathing sound. It almost seemed to be coming from within the house, as well, and it made him remember.

The earliest parts of the dream were already beginning to fade.

Still he recalled tossing in a bed somewhere, a lonely bed to which no one ever came. There had been the sound of waves there, too. He had been dreaming of a girl who would need him as much as he needed her. And when he was finished she did; she needed someone; she needed to be taken care of, and that part had come out right, had been easy enough. . . .

He had forgotten, of course, that she would have dreams of her own.

Soon she needed other things, like more and more time away from the hot little house he had imagined for her. In fact she needed something even better than his own modest beach cottage. It was always the way. Except that this time he had found the street of her dreams, had driven up and down until he saw her car parked here in the shade of the port. . . .

The carport of a house where someone lived. Someone even better suited to her needs.

This time it would take.

He shut his eyes as he dreamed the feel of fine knit against his legs, the designer shoes with the high-rise heels, the hand-tailored shirt of imported silk, the styled hair and the rest of it, all of it, the way she wanted it to be, the look. There would be more details. But they could be arranged, too. Of course they could. Why not? It was worth the effort.

She needed him, didn't she?

She needs somebody, he thought.

Wavering before the mirror as he tossed and turned, he opened his eyes. He smiled.

Somebody like you.

Third Wind

Richard Christian Matheson

Michael chugged up the incline, sweatsuit shadowed with perspiration. His Nikes compressed on the asphalt and the sound of his inhalation was the only noise on the country road.

He glanced at his waist-clipped odometer: Twenty-five, point seven. Not bad. But he could do better.

Had to.

He'd worked hard doing his twenty miles a day for the last two years and knew he was ready to break fifty. His body was up to it, the muscles taut and strong. They'd be going through a lot of changes over the next twenty-five miles. His breathing was loose; comfortable. Just the way he liked it.

Easy. But the strength was there.

There was something quietly spiritual about all this, he told himself. Maybe it was the sublime monotony of stretching every muscle and feeling it constrict. Or it could be feeling his legs telescope out and draw his body forward. Perhaps even the humid expansion of his chest as his lungs bloated with air.

But none of that was really the answer.

It was the competing against himself.

Beating his own distance, his own limits. Running was the time he felt most alive. He knew that as surely as he'd ever known anything.

He loved the ache that shrouded his torso and he even waited for the moment, a few minutes into the run, when a dull voltage would climb his body to his brain like a vine, reviving him. It transported him, taking his mind to another place, very deep within. Like prayer.

He was almost to the crest of the hill.

So far, everything was feeling good. He shagged off some tightness in his shoulders, clenching his fists and punching at the air. The October chill turned to pink steam in his chest, making his body tingle as if a microscopic cloud of needles were passing through, from front to back, leaving pin-prick holes.

He shivered. The crest of the hill was just ahead. And on the down side was a new part of his personal route: a dirt road, carpeted with leaves, which wound through a silent forest at the peak of these mountains.

As he broke the crest, he picked up speed, angling downhill toward the dirt road. His Nikes flexed against the gravel, slipping a little.

It had taken much time to prepare for this. Months of meticulous care of his body. Vitamins. Dieting. The endless training and clocking. Commitment to the body machine. It was as critical as the commitment to the goal itself.

Fifty miles.

As he picked up momentum, jogging easily downhill, the mathematical breakdown of that figure filled his head with tumbling digits. Zeroes unglued from his thought tissues and linked with cardinal numbers to form combinations which added to fifty. It was suddenly all he could think about. Twenty-five plus twenty-five. Five times ten. Forty-nine plus one. Shit. It was driving him crazy. One hundred minus—

The dirt road.

He noticed the air cooling. The big trees that shaded the forest road were lowering the temperature. Night was close. Another hour. Thirty minutes plus thirty minutes. This math thing was getting irritating. Michael tried to remember some of his favorite Beatle songs as he gently padded through the dense forest.

Eight Days A Week. Great song. Weird damn title but who cared? If John and Paul said a week had eight days, everybody else just added a day and said . . . yeah, cool. Actually, maybe it wasn't their fault to begin with. Maybe George was supposed to bring a calendar to the recording session and forgot. He was always the spacey one. Should've had Ringo do it, thought Michael, Ringo you could count on. Guys with gonzo noses always compensated by being dependable.

Michael continued to run at a comfortable pace over the powdery dirt. Every few steps he could hear a leaf or small branch break under his shoes. What was that old thing? Something like, don't ever move even a small rock when you're at the beach or in the mountains. It upsets the critical balances. Nature can't ever be right again if you do. The repercussions can start wars if you extrapolate it out far enough.

Didn't ever really make much sense to Michael. His brother Eric had always told him these things and he should have known better than to listen. Eric was a self-appointed fount of advice on how to keep the cosmos in alignment. But he always got "D's" on his cards in high school, unlike Michael's "A's," and maybe he didn't really know all that much after all.

Michael's foot suddenly caught on a rock and he fell forward. On the ground, the dirt coated his face and lips and a spoonful got into his mouth. He also scraped his knee; a little blood. It was one of those lousy scrapes that claws a layer off and stings like it's a lot worse.

He was up again in a second and heading down the road, slightly disgusted with himself. He knew better than to lose his footing. He was too good an athlete for that.

His mouth was getting dry and he worked up some saliva by rubbing his tongue against the roof of his mouth. Strange how he never got hungry on these marathons of his. The body just seemed to live off itself for the period of time it took. Next day he usually put away a supermarket, but in running, all appetite faded. The body fed itself. It was weird.

The other funny thing was the way he couldn't imagine himself ever walking again. It became automatic to run. Everything went by so much faster. When he did stop, to walk, it was like being a snail. Everything just . . . took . . . so . . . damn . . . looooonnnngggg.

The sun was nearly gone now. Fewer and fewer animals. Their sounds faded all around. Birds stopped singing. The frenetic scrambling of squirrels halted as they prepared to bed down for the night. Far below, at the foot of these mountains, the ocean was turning to ink. The sun was lowering and the sea rose to meet it like a dark blue comforter.

Ahead, Michael could see an approaching corner.

How long had he been moving through the forest path? Fifteen minutes? Was it possible he'd gone the ten or so mile length of the path already?

That was one of the insane anomalies of running these marathons of his. Time got all out of whack. He'd think he was running ten miles and find he'd actually covered considerably more ground. Sometimes as much as double his estimate. He couldn't ever figure that one out. But it always happened and he always just sort of anticipated it.

Welcome to the time warp, Jack.

He checked his odometer: Twenty-nine, point eight.

Half there and some loose change.

The dirt path would be coming to an end in a few hundred yards. Then it was straight along the highway which ran atop the ridge of this mountain far above the Malibu coastline. The highway was bordered with towering streetlamps which lit the way like some forgotten runway of ancient astronauts. They stared down from fifty-foot poles and bleached the asphalt and roadside talcum white.

The path had ended now and he was on the deserted mountaintop road with its broken center line that stretched to forever. As Michael wiped his glistening face with a sleeve, he heard someone hitting a crystal glass with tiny mallets, far away. It wasn't a pinging sound. More like a high-pitched thud that was chain reacting. He looked up and saw insects of the night swarming dementedly around a kleig's glow. Hundreds of them in hypnotic self-destruction dive-bombed again and again at the huge bulb.

Eerie, seeing that kind of thing way the hell out here. But nice country to run in just the same. Gentle hills. The distant sea, far below. Nothing but heavy silence. Nobody ever drove this road anymore. It was as deserted as any Michael could remember. The perfect place to run.

What could be better? The smell was clean and healthy, the air sweet. Great decision, building his house up here last year. This was definitely the place to live. Pastureland is what his father used to call this kind of country when Michael was growing up in Wisconsin.

He laughed. Glad to be out of *that* place. People never did anything with their lives. Born there, schooled there, married there and died there was the usual, banal legacy. They all missed out on life. Missed out on new ideas and ambitions.

The doctor slapped them and from that point on their lives just curled up like dead spiders.

It was just as well.

How many of them could take the heat of competition in Los Angeles? Especially a job like Michael's? None of the old friends he'd gladly left behind in his hometown would ever have a chance going up against a guy like himself. He was going to be the head of his law firm in a few more years. Most of those yokels back home couldn't even *spell* success much less achieve it.

But to each his own. Regardless of how pointless some lives really were. But *he* was going to be the head of his own firm and wouldn't even be thirty-five by the time it happened.

Okay, yeah, they were all married and had their families worked out. But what a fucking bore. Last thing Michael needed right now was that noose around his neck. Maybe the family guys figured they had something valuable. But for Michael it was a waste of time. Only thing a wife and kids would do is drag him down; hold him back. Priorities. First things first. *Career*. Then everything else. But put that relationship stuff off until last.

Besides, with all the inevitable success coming his way, meeting ladies would be a cinch. And hell, anyone could have a kid. Just nature. No big thing.

But *success*. That was something else, again. Took a very special animal to grab onto that golden ring and never let go. Families were for losers when a guy was really climbing. And he, of all the people he'd ever known, was definitely climbing.

Running had helped him get in the right frame of mind to do it. With each mileage barrier he broke, he was able to break greater barriers in life itself, especially his career. It made him more mentally fit to compete when he ran. It strengthened his will; his inner discipline.

Everything felt right when he was running regularly. And it wasn't just the meditative effect; not at all. He knew what it gave him was an *edge*. An edge on his fellow attorneys at the firm and an edge on life.

It was unthinkable to him how the other guys at the firm didn't take advantage of it. Getting ahead was what it was all about. A guy didn't make it in L.A. or anywhere else in the world unless he kept one step ahead of the competition. Keep moving and never let anything stand in the way or slow you down. That was the magic.

And Michael knew the first place to start that trend was with himself.

He got a chill. Thinking this way always made him feel special. Like he had the formula; the secret. Contemplating success was a very intoxicating thing. And with his running now approaching the hour and a half mark, hyperventilation was heightening the effect.

He glanced at his odometer: Forty-three, point six.

He was feeling like a champion. His calves were burning a little and his back was a bit tender but at this rate, with his breathing effortless and body strong, he could do sixty. But fifty was the goal. After that he had to go back and get his briefs in order for tomorrow's meeting. Had to get some sleep. Keep the machine in good shape and you rise to the top. None of that smoking or drinking or whatever else those morons were messing with out there. Stuff like that was for losers.

He opened his mouth a little wider to catch more air. The night had gone to a deep black and all he could hear now was the adhesive squishing of his Nikes. Overhead, the hanging branches of pepper trees canopied the desolate road and cut the moonlight into a million beams.

The odometer: Forty-six, point two. His head was feeling hot but running at night always made that easier. The breezes would swathe like cool silk, blowing his hair back and combing through his scalp. Then he'd hit a hot pocket that hovered above the road and his hair would flop downward, the feeling of heat returning like a blanket. He coughed and spit.

Almost there.

He was suddenly hit by a stray drop of moisture, then another. A drizzle began. Great. Just what he didn't need. Okay, it wasn't raining hard; just that misty stuff that atomizes over you like a lawn sprinkler shifted by a light wind. Still, it would have been nice to finish the fifty dry.

The road was going into a left hairpin now and Michael leaned into it, Nikes gripping octopus-tight. Ahead, as the curve broke, the road went straight, as far as the eye could see. Just a two-lane blacktop laying in state across these mountains. Now that it was wet, the surface went mirror shiny, like a ribbon on the side of tuxedo pants. Far below, the sea reflected a fuzzy moon, and fog began to ease up the mountainside, coming closer toward the road.

Michael checked the odometer, rubbing his hands together for warmth. Forty-nine, point eight. Almost there and other than being a little cold, he was feeling like a million bucks. He punched happily at the air and cleared his throat. God, he was feeling great! Tomorrow, at the office, was going to be a victory from start to finish.

He could feel himself smiling, his face hot against the vaporing rain. His jogging suit was soaked with sweat and drizzle made him shiver as it touched his skin. He breathed in gulps of the chilled air and as it left his mouth it turned white, puffing loosely away. His eyes were stinging from the cold and he closed them, continuing to run, the effect of total blackness fascinating him.

Another stride. Another.

He opened his eyes and rubbed them with red fingers. All around, the fog breathed closer, snaking between the limbs of trees and creeping silently across the asphalt. The overhead lights made it glow like a wall of colorless neon.

The odometer.

Another hundred feet and he had it!

The strides came in a smooth flow, like a turning wheel. He spread his fingers wide and shook some of the excess energy that was concentrating and making him feel buzzy. It took the edge off but he still felt as though he was zapped on a hundred cups of coffee. He ran faster, his arms like swinging scythes, tugging him forward.

Twenty more steps.

Ten plus ten. Five times . . . Christ, the math thing back. He started laughing out loud as he went puffing down the road, sweat pants drooping.

The sky was suddenly zippered open by lightning and Michael gasped. In an instant, blackness turned to hot white and there was that visual echo of the light as it trembled in the distance, then fluttered off like a dying bulb.

Michael checked his odometer.

Five more feet! He counted it: Five/breath/four/breath/three/breath/two/one and there it was, yelling and singing and patting him on the back and tossing streamers!

Fifty miles! Fifty goddamn miles!

It was fucking incredible! To know he could really, actually *do* it suddenly hit him and he began laughing.

Okay, now to get that incredible sensation of almost standing still while walking it off. Have to keep those muscles warm. If not he'd get a chill and cramps and feel like someone was going over his calves with a carpet knife.

Hot breath gushed visibly from his mouth. The rain was coming faster in a diagonal descent, back-lit by lightning, and the fog bundled tighter. Michael took three or four deep breaths and began trying to slow. It was incredible to have this feeling of edge. The sense of being on *top* of everything! It was an awareness he could surpass limitations. Make breakthroughs. It was what separated the winners from the losers when taken right down to a basic level. The winners knew how much harder they could push to go farther. Break those patterns. Create new levels of ability and confidence.

Win.

He tried again to slow down. His legs weren't slowing to a walk yet and he sent the message down again. He smiled. Run too far and the body just doesn't want to stop.

The legs continued to pull him forward. Rain was drenching down from the sky; he was soaked to the bone. Hair strung over his eyes and mouth and he coughed to get out what he could as it needled coldly into his face.

"Slow down," he told his legs: "*Stop,* goddamit!"

But his feet continued on, splashing through puddles which laked here and there along the foggy road.

Michael began to breathe harder, unable to get the air he needed. It was too wet; half air, half water. Suddenly, more lightning scribbled across the thundering clouds and Michael reached down to stop one leg.

It did no *good*. He kept running, even faster, pounding harder against the wet pavement. He could feel the bottoms of his Nikes getting wet, starting to wear through. He'd worn the old ones; they were the most comfortable.

Jesus fucking God, he really *couldn't stop!*

The wetness got colder on his cramping feet. He tried to fall but kept running. Terrified, he began to cough fitfully, his legs continuing forward, racing over the pavement.

His throat was raw from the cold and his muscles ached. He was starting to feel like his body had been beaten with hammers.

There was no point in trying to stop. He knew that, now. He'd trained too long. Too precisely.

It had been his single obsession.

And as he continued to pound against the fog-shrouded pavement all he could hear was a cold, lonely night.

Until the sound of his own pleading screams began to echo through the mountains, and fade across the endless gray road.

The Boy Who Came Back from the Dead

Alan Rodgers

Walt Fulton came back from the grave Sunday evening, after supper but before his mom had cleared the table.

He was filthy, covered from head to toe with graveyard dirt, but all the things the car had crushed and broken when it hit him (things the mortician hadn't quite been able to make look right) were fixed.

"Mom," Walt called, throwing open the kitchen door, "I'm home!" His mother screamed, but she didn't drop and break the porcelain casserole dish she was holding.

There's something in an eight-year-old boy that lets him understand his mother, though he could never know that he had it or put words to what it told him. Walt couldn't have told anyone how when his mother saw him she first wanted not to believe that it was him—the boy was dead and buried, by God, and let the dead rest—but because she was his mother and mothers *know,* she knew that it was him returned from the grave.

Then Walt saw the shock setting in, saw her begin to paralyze. But she was stronger than that; she set her teeth, shook off the numbness. She was a strong woman. His return brought her joy beyond words, for she loved him. But she wanted him to go away and never come back, because seeing him again meant remembering the moment at the highway rest stop when she'd looked up to see him running out into traffic after his ball—and then suddenly splattered like a fly across the front bumper of a late model Buick. And she couldn't bear to have that dream again.

Walt didn't resent any of it, not even knowing that she felt that way about him. The same thing that let him know what she was thinking (despite the fact that it was impossible) made sure that he would always love her.

After a minute and a half she composed herself. "Walt," she said, "you're late for dinner and you're filthy. Wash your hands and face and sit down at the table." His father and sister smiled; Dad had tears in his eyes, but he didn't say anything. Mom got up and set him a place at the table.

And Walt was home.

The morning after he came back Walt sat at the kitchen table for hours, coloring in coloring books, while his mother fussed about the house. There was a certain moodiness and elegance in his crayon-work; he wondered at the strangeness that grew on the pages as he colored.

"Walt," his mother said, peeking over his shoulder and humming in surprise, "you can't imagine how much trouble it's going to be to get you back in school." She walked into the kitchen and bent down to look into the cabinet underneath the sink. "They're all certain that you're dead. People don't come back from the dead. No one's going to believe that it's you. They'll think we're both crazy."

Walt nodded. She was right, of course. It was going to be a lot of trouble. He looked down at the floor and scuffed his feet against the finish.

"I ought to tell someone," he said.

"What's that, Walt?" His mother's head was buried deep inside the cabinet under the sink, among the cleansers and the steel wool and the old rusty cans.

"About being dead," he told her. "I remember it."

Walt knew his mother wasn't listening. "That's nice. You all ready for school this afternoon? We have an appointment with the principal for one o'clock, right after lunch."

"Yeah," he said, "school's okay." He scratched his cheek. "I know people need to know what it's like, about being dead, I mean. It's one of those things that everybody has needed to know forever."

Walt's mother pulled her head out of the cabinet slowly. She turned to stare at him, her mouth agape.

"*Walt!* You'll do nothing of the sort. I won't have that." Her voice was frantic.

"But *why?* They need to know."

But she only clamped her lips and turned beet red. She wouldn't talk to him again until after lunch.

The principal, Mr. Hodges, was a man with dry red skin and gray-black hair who wore a navy blue suit and a red silk cloth in his breast pocket. Walt didn't like him and he never had. He never acted friendly, and Walt thought the man would do him harm if he only could.

"He's Walt all right," Mom told the man. "Never mind what I *know;* Sam and I went out to check the grave this morning as soon as the sun was up. All the dirt is broken, and you can see where he crawled up out of it."

"But it can't be done. We don't even have the files any more. They've been sent away to the fireproof vault downtown." He stopped for a moment to catch his breath. "Look, I know it's horrible to lose a child. Even worse to see him die while you're watching. Walt's not the first kid I've had die in an accident. But you can't delude yourself like this. Walt's dead and buried. I don't know who this young man is, much less why he's preying on this weakness of yours . . ."

Walt's mother looked outraged, so angry that she couldn't speak. He wanted to settle things, to quiet them: "What kind of proof do you want?" he asked the man. "What would make you certain that I'm me?"

Neither his mother nor the principal could respond to that at first. After a moment Mr. Hodges excused himself and left the room.

For twenty minutes Walt sat staring out the window of the principal's office, watching the other kids at recess. His mother never got out of the seat by the principal's desk. She stared at the wall with her eyes unfocused while her fingers twisted scraps of paper into tiny, hard-packed balls.

Finally, Mr. Hodges opened the door and came back into the room. He looked tired now, and even shell-shocked, but he didn't look mean anymore. He set two thick file folders onto his desk.

"Any proof I'd want could be manufactured, Walt. But it isn't right for me to try to stop you this way. If nothing else, you've got a right to call yourself anything you want." He opened one of the files. "I can't connect you to these files without moving heaven and earth. But I don't think you need them. There's nothing here that would make us treat you any differently than we'd treat a new student." He began to read. "You're in the third grade. The class you were in has gone on now, but your teacher, Miss Allison, still works for us. You haven't been gone quite a year; you've already been through this part of the third grade, but I don't think the review will do you any harm."

Later, before Walt and his mother finished filling out the forms, the principal called Miss Allison in to see them. Walt looked up when she opened the door to Mr. Hodges's office, and he felt her recognize him when she saw him.

Miss Allison screamed, and her legs went limp underneath her. She didn't faint—she was never unconscious—but when she fell to the floor it looked as though she had.

She screamed again when he went over to help her up.

"*Wal—ter!*" long and eerie, just like something out of an old horror movie.

"It's all right," Walt said. "I'm not a ghost."

"What are you?" Her voice was still shrill with terror.

"I'm just . . . just Walt. I'm Walt."

Miss Allison glared at him impatiently.

"Really. I'm Walt. Besides, Mom said I couldn't tell."

Walt heard his mother snap the pencil she was chewing on. "Tell her," she said. Her voice was furious. "Tell me."

Walt shrugged. "It was the aliens. They were walking all around the graveyard, looking into people's dirt."

"What aliens?"

"A whole bunch of them, all different kinds. They landed in a spaceship over in the woods. A couple of them looked kind of like fish—or snakes, maybe—one of them kind of like a bear, a couple looked like mole crickets when you see them in a magnifying glass. Others, too.

"But the one I paid attention to—he was the one telling all the rest what do to—that one was really gross. It had this big lumpy head—shaped like the head on that retarded kid Mrs. Anderson had—"

"Walt! Billy Anderson is a mongoloid idiot. You mustn't speak ill of those less fortunate than you."

Walt nodded. "Sorry. Anyway, the thing had this big, lumpy,

spongy head, and this face that looked kind of like an ant's—
with those big pincer things instead of a mouth—and kind of
looked like something you dropped on the floor in the kitchen.
It drooled all over the place—"

"*Walt!*

"—and it kept making this gross sound like someone
hawking up a great big clam.

"But it wasn't what it looked like that bothered me so much.
What scared me was when it got to my grave, and it looked
down like it could see me right through the dirt. And its pincers
clacked and rubbed against each other just exactly like the way
a cat licks its lips when it sees a mouse, and its elbows flexed
backward like it wanted to pounce. It made this whining
sound, like a dog when it begs, and I thought it was going to
reach right through the dirt and eat my putrid body. And even
though I knew I was dead and I couldn't get any deader, it
scared me. It was bad enough being something trees couldn't
tell from mulch, without being dinner for a ghoul. But then the
thing turned away and went back to looking at other people's
dirt. After they'd looked at everyone, they came back to me
and broke up my dirt and shined their ray down on me. It didn't
hurt—but nothing does when you're dead. After five minutes I
was alive again, and I felt things but I couldn't just know them
anymore, and I pushed my way out of the dirt.

"But when I got up to the ground the aliens had already
gone. So I went home."

It was Miss Allison who finally said it.

"Walt, that can't be. How could you know all that when
you're dead, buried in the ground? Even if your eyes were
open, how could you see through all the dirt?"

Walt shrugged. "That's what I need to tell them. About what
it's like to be dead. They've all been needing to know forever,
because they're all afraid. It's like the feeling of your
fingernails on a dusty chalkboard, like being awake so long
you get dizzy and start hearing things. And you can't feel
anything, and you know everything that's going on around
you, and some things far away. It's bad, and it's scary, but not
so terrible that you can't get used to it."

Neither Miss Allison nor his mother spoke to Walt again that
afternoon.

No one saw any sense in disrupting things by bringing him

into class in the middle of the day. Tomorrow morning was soon enough. (Maybe too soon, the look on Miss Allison's face said, but everyone did his best to ignore that.) When they got home Anne, his sister, had a hug for him, and they played cards until supper time. After dinner Dad and Walt and Anne roughhoused and threw pillows at each other in the playroom.

It was fun.

Before bed Walt wanted Dad to tell him a story—he'd missed Dad's ghost stories—but Dad wouldn't. After a while, Walt stopped asking. He wasn't dumb; he knew why it scared his father.

But what could he do? He sure didn't want to go away, go back to being dead. He liked being alive. He liked having people see him, hear him, know he was there. The dead made poor companions. Almost all of them were quiet and tired, waiting for the resurrection, not so much world-weary as exhausted by its absence.

Tuesday and Wednesday were quiet days in school. Almost no one in his new class had known Walt before the accident. Those few who did took a while to reason out that Walt was something they'd only seen on Saturdays on the afternoon horror movie.

But by Thursday word had got around, and the boldest of the boys from his class the year before—four of them—looked for him and found him in an empty corner of the school yard during recess.

"Hey Zombie," Frankie Munsen called at him from behind, throwing a dirt clod that caught Walt in the soft part of his shoulder, just below his neck.

"Count Dricula, I *pri*sume . . . ?" Donny James taunted him, stepping out from behind a tree on Walt's left. He draped his blue Windbreaker over his forearm and shielded his chin with it, the way vampires do with their capes in the movies. "You got bats in your belfry, Walt? What's it like to be *un*dead?"

Walt flinched when a dirt clod hit him in the belly from the right. He looked over to see John Taylor and Rick Mitchell standing in the knot of pine trees throwing dirt clods. As he saw them a clod hit him on the forehead and the dust splattered in his eyes.

When he could finally open them again he saw four boys standing over him, surrounding him.

"What's the matter, Zom-boy? Smoke get in your eyes?" Donny jeered, shoving Walt by the shoulders so that he fell on his back. Donny straddled Walt's chest and pinned him by digging his knees into the muscles of his upper arms. "Ain'tcha gonna fight back, Zom-boy?" He snickered. "Too late now, sucker."

Walt's voice wasn't frightened, wasn't scared at all, just a little angry: "What's the matter with you? I haven't done anything to you."

"Don't like to see dead people walking around our school, Zom-boy." Donny drooled spit into Walt's eyes. "Want you to leave, sucker."

Walt rolled over, surprising Donny, throwing him off. As he stood up he wiped the spit from his eyes with one arm and grabbed Donny's collar with the other. Walt hauled the older boy to his feet.

"I'm not dead," he said. His voice was furious now, trembling. He threw Donny against a tree where his head made a liquid cracking sound.

None of the other boys said or did anything. They didn't run yet, either. Donny sat up, drooling bloody spit into the dirt.

"I bit my tongue," he said. He swayed back and forth unevenly.

Walt turned away. "Don't do anything like this again," he said. And he went home.

Someone should have done something about that—called his house, sent someone after him, marked him truant at least. But no one did. It was not as though no one noticed him gone. And certainly no one missed seeing what he'd done to Donny James. But Miss Allison couldn't bring herself to report him, and no one would contradict her.

When his mom got home, he was sitting by the TV with a coloring book spread out over the coffee table. He had the sound turned almost all the way down.

"You're home early, dear. Why's that?" she asked. Walt mumbled without using any real words, just low enough that she'd think his answer got lost in the sound of her walking.

"Sorry, dear, I didn't hear you. Why was it?"

Walt's hand pressed too hard, and his crayon left a dark, flaky wax mark on the paper. It looked like a scar to Walt.

"I got into a fight," he said. "I think I hurt Donny James pretty bad. He looked like he was going to have to go see a doctor. I didn't want to have to talk to them anymore. So I went home."

"You just left school? Just like that?"

"Mom, they think I'm a monster. They think I'm some sort of vampire or something." Walt wanted to cry, mostly from frustration, but he didn't. He set his head down onto his arms so that his nose rubbed against the coloring book.

Mom sat down beside him and lifted him up so that she could put her arms around him. In front of them, on the television with the sound turned down, the characters in a soap opera worried at each other silently, the way a dog worries a bone.

"You aren't a monster, Walt," she said as she held him, hugging him tighter to her. "Don't let them tell you that." But her voice was so uncertain that even though he wanted to more than anything else in the world, Walt couldn't make himself believe her.

Walt went out an hour before dinner time, looking for something to do. He walked a long way, blocks and blocks into the neighborhood, trying to find someone he knew, or a sandlot game to watch or even play in, or *something,* but all he found was some floating waterbugs (the ones his mother told him never to bring home because they were really *roaches*) in the creek down on Dumas Street. It wasn't much fun. Walking home, the stars were gloriously bright, even though it wasn't very dark out yet. Walt tried to find Betelgeuse—he loved the star's name, so he got his father to show him how to find it— but the star was nowhere Walt could see. Three stars turned to meteors as he watched. At first he just stared, marveling at the pencil-marks of light that the shooting stars left behind them— but then they all began to spiral down and each in turn to head toward him. Three blocks away there was a big woods, fifteen or twenty square blocks' worth of land where no one had ever got around to putting in streets or building houses. Walt ran there, as hard and fast as he could. He ran deeper into the woods than he'd ever been before, until he couldn't see any houses or landmarks that he knew, and he wasn't sure where he was. When he heard the sound of people running toward him he climbed into the biggest, tallest, leafiest tree he could find. He hid there.

The aliens should have found him. Walt knew that.

There were seven of them, each one strange and different from every other. The only one he really saw was the one who held the gadget that looked like a geiger counter, the one with the giant ant pincers for a mouth—it was a maw, really, not a mouth. (Walt knew that. He'd gone to the library on Tuesday and spent hours reading about bugs.)

That was the same one that'd stared at him right through the graveyard dirt when he was still dead. The thing came right up to the tree Walt had hidden in, where the widget in its hands beeped and whirred maniacally. He stared at the thing from above, chewing on his lower lip. So close, it was even uglier than when it'd looked into his grave. The things at the ends of its arms weren't hands or fingers, really. They didn't have palms or fingers, just muscley, wormy flaps of skin dangling and fluttering at the ends of its wrists. Its skin was just exactly the color a roach is when you squish it. It smelled kind of like rotten eggs and kind of like the mouse that nested in the TV one summer and chewed on the wrong wire and got itself electrocuted. Its arms looked ordinary at first (or something in Walt's eyes wanted to make them look ordinary) but then the thing reached out to lean on the tree trunk, and its arm wasn't just bent double, it was *bending* in an arc under the weight. The legs were like that, too, and they bent ass-backward in a half-crouch when it walked. It had a tunic on, so Walt couldn't see its torso, but then it bent sideways and the cloth (or was it some stretchy, rubbery plastic?) stretched thin enough to see through, and Walt could see that it was twisted off like a sausage in the middle, two big, bulbous pieces connected only by a touch.

Its eyes were the worst thing, though. They were big, bigger than the saucers in Mom's good china, and they were sort of like what they say a spider's eyes look like when you see them up close. But not quite. More like a bowl full of eggs, broken and ready to scramble, but with the yolks still intact. Around each eye's half dozen yellow pupils, through the clear matter, Walt could see veins and nerve endings pulse against the eye socket. Phlegm dripped down steadily from the eyes, into the maw. That was why the thing kept making that sound like somebody hawking up a big wad of snot.

The thing spent a long time prowling around the base of Walt's tree, sifting through every log and bush and leaf pile, while the other aliens combed through the rest of the woods.

But it never looked up. None of the aliens, not one of them, ever looked up.

They searched for him carefully, methodically, sticking electronic probes into the ground, turning every stone and rotted log, sifting every drift of mulch.

But not once did any of them check the branches of a tree.

Stupid aliens, Walt thought. Later, reflecting on it, he decided he was right.

After they'd prowled around him for three quarters of an hour they gave up and left. Walt stayed in the tree for twenty minutes longer, against the possibility that they were hiding, waiting for him. He'd meant to wait longer but he couldn't make himself be still.

That was just as well. No one came to get him when he climbed out of the tree.

The aliens are more impatient than me, Walt thought. The idea of jittery aliens made him want to laugh, but he didn't.

It was night now, and Walt didn't know this part of the woods at all. The moon at least was already up and nearly full, so there was light enough to see by, to see the trail (not a very well used one at all; thick clumps of grass grew out of it in places) that led in both directions, ways he didn't recognize.

He wasn't worried so much for himself—after all, he was lost not far from home, almost a silly thing to be—but he knew that his mother would be concerned. By the time he got home she'd be angry at him. He hurried as best he could.

After about fifteen paces the trail opened up into Walt's cemetery.

The one he'd spent eleven months and seven days buried in. The tree he stood by was the tree whose roots would almost tickle him on sunny mornings. In front of him was his headstone, desecrated with graffiti.

Even by the dim moonlight he could see it; bold strokes of spray paint crowding out the letters carved in the granite.

It had to be new. He'd looked back to see the stone the night he'd crawled out of the grave, and it was clean then.

And someone had packed the dirt back into his grave and tucked the sod grass back in above it.

Walt stood on the grave, kicking the toe of his shoe into the roots of the grass, staring at the gravestone, reading it over and over again. He tried to read the graffiti, too, but it wasn't made up of words or even letters, but of strange squiggles like the graffiti that covered the subways Walt had seen when Dad took him to New York. (Dad said the graffiti in the city was that way because the kids who painted it could never learn to read or write, that they were too dumb to ever even learn the alphabet. That seemed too incredible to believe, but Walt couldn't imagine any other reason why they didn't know how to use letters.) He thought maybe the aliens had left the graffiti, but then he thought, *Why would the aliens use bright red spray paint?* and he knew it couldn't be them.

Looking at the grave made him feel sleepy and comfortable. It was getting late, and he knew he should go home. But he couldn't stop himself, not really. He lay down on his grave, rested his head on the headstone (the paint was still fresh enough that Walt could smell it), and for an hour he stared into the sky, watching the stars. Not to search for alien starships, but because nothing in the world could be more comfortable.

His mom wasn't in when Walt got home. Just Dad and Anne, watching TV in the den.

"Hiya, Walt," Dad called when he walked in. "Late night with the Cub Scouts?"

Walt chuckled. "Yeah," he said. It wasn't *really* a lie; Dad was just being facetious. Walt sat down at the card table behind Dad's recliner. Anne, sitting in the love seat against the wall, didn't turn away from the TV until the commercial was on.

"Cards?" she asked him.

"No, I'm going to bed early, I think."

"There's dinner left over for you in the refrigerator, Walt," Dad said. "Stuffed pork chops and green beans."

Walt nodded. "Thanks." He got up and started toward the kitchen.

"Oh, and Walt," Dad said, "I forgot. The man from that newspaper called. *The Interlocutor.* He wants to come by and talk to you tomorrow morning. Before school."

"Huh." Walt wasn't certain what he thought.

"Yeah," Dad said. "It should be interesting. I wonder how they found out so soon."

Walt shrugged, then realized his father couldn't see that. "I don't know. Someone at school, I guess."

"Yes." His father nodded at the television set. "I guess that would have to be it."

In the kitchen he took the plate from the refrigerator and

tried to eat what his mom had left him. Walt loved stuffed pork chops. Even cold. But he couldn't find the appetite to eat them or the green beans, and after twenty minutes he left the plate virtually untouched on the kitchen table, and went to bed.

His mom came in through the backdoor while he was on the stairs up to his room. He turned to say good night to her, and she was already on the stairway just below him, charging up to God knew what, not seeing him at all in the dark.

"Mom," Walt said, trying to get her attention before she collided into him.

"Oh my God!" His mother screamed. In the darkness she swung her arm out and her fist hit Walt hard just below the right eye. That knocked him down; he would have rolled down the stairs if his left ankle hadn't jammed against her feet.

For five minutes, trembling and breathing deeply, she leaned into the banister that was screwed into the wall. Walt didn't move—it didn't seem safe to—he just lay on the stairs at her feet. In a moment his father and sister got to the foot of the stairs, and they could see. They stood there, watching. They didn't say anything.

"Walt," his mother finally said (her voice was colder and more inhuman than it would ever seem to any stranger). "A hundred times I've told you to turn the lights on when you use the stairs and hallways."

"Sorry," he said, afraid she'd get angrier if he said anything else.

"Don't do it again."

He nodded. "I was going to bed. I meant to say good night."

"Good night," she said, her voice harder and lonelier than his grave had ever been.

In bed, drifting off to sleep, he realized that he'd hardly eaten all week, and that he hadn't been hungry since he came back from the dead.

Dad woke him up real early in the morning, shaking him by the shoulder with his big soft hand. Walt took a shower and got dressed before he'd really woke up; later he discovered that he'd put his shirt on backward.

When he got to the kitchen his mom was already cooking breakfast—scrambled eggs and bacon—and the man from *The Interlocutor* was sitting at the kitchen table. He stared at Walt the way Walt remembered staring at the lizards in the House of Reptiles at the zoo when he was six. But the lizard couldn't see him, or it acted like it couldn't.

"Hi, Walt." The man held out his hand to shake, but he still stared. "I'm Harvey Adler from *The National Interlocutor*. I'm here to take your story." He smiled, but it reminded Walt of the lizards' smiles: more a fault in their anatomy than a true expression.

"Are you going to eat with us?" Walt asked. He wasn't sure why he did.

"Ahh—" Adler began uncomfortably, but then Walt's mom set a plate in front of him and another in front of Walt. "Well. It looks like I am." Walt felt somehow betrayed.

"Coffee, Mr. Adler?" Walt's mom asked. That was even worse; Walt didn't know why.

"No, thank you, Mrs. Fulton. I've already had two this morning." He turned back to Walt. "Did you really die, Walt? And come back from the dead? What was it like to die?"

Walt picked at his food with his fork. "I started to run across the highway, and I forgot to look. There was a screaming sound. I guess it was the car trying to stop. But I didn't see. I never even turned my head. It happened too fast. Then everything was black for a while."

Adler had his tape recorder on, and he scribbled notes furiously. "Then what, Walt?"

Walt shrugged. "Then I was dead. I could see and hear everything around me. Just like the other dead people. But I couldn't move."

"You were like that for a year? It must have been pretty lonely."

"Well. You know. You don't care that much when you're dead. And the dead people can hear you. And can talk to you. But they don't much. They just don't ever want to."

They went on like that for an hour. He told the man everything—about the aliens, about climbing out of his grave, about his friends and school and all. Finally, Walt was late for school. It probably wasn't a good day for that; when he finally got to class Miss Allison still wasn't talking to him from the day before.

At morning recess, Donny James (black and blue but not really hurt) found Walt and asked him to come to the Risk game they always had on Friday afternoons. He acted like nothing had happened, maybe even a little bit embarrassed. Walt could never understand that, and though later in life he knew that people could do such things, he could never expect or believe it.

It came to trouble with Miss Allison about an hour after recess. She asked the class a question ("Where is the Malagasy Republic?") that she meant no one to answer. But Walt raised his hand and answered it quite thoroughly ("The Malagasy Republic *is* the island of Madagascar off the southeast coast of Africa. The people are black, but they speak a language related to Polynesian"), which made her look awfully silly, and the class giggled. Walt didn't mean to do it. But as soon as he opened his mouth he knew that he'd made her look silly. Answering questions was a compulsion for him, and he knew the answer because the old man in the grave next to his had been a sailor in the Indian Ocean for thirty years, and when he did talk (which was almost never) it was always about Africa or India or the Maldives or some such.

Miss Allison didn't take it well at all. She hadn't taken anything well since Walt got back. And it didn't help any when Walt (feeling bold since he'd explained everything to the man from *The Interlocutor* at breakfast) tried to explain how it was he knew such an odd fact and why, after all, it really wasn't so important. For the third time this week Miss Allison's expression grew violent, and she pulled her hand back to strike him, and for the third time Walt glared at her as though if she did it might be the last thing she ever did. (Not that he meant it or even was able to carry out the threat. It was a bluff. But he knew her well enough to know that it would make her stop.) Miss Allison didn't go back to her desk, shaking, the way she did the times before though. She ran out of the classroom and slammed the door behind her. She didn't come back for twenty minutes, and when she finally did Mr. Hodges, the principal, was with her.

He took Walt away from Miss Allison's class and moved him ahead a year—into the class he'd shared with Donny James, Rick Mitchell, and all the rest.

He liked it better there. Even if the fourth-grade teacher was a battle-axe, at least she wasn't hysterical.

In the afternoon he walked home with Donny and helped him set up the Risk game. Six boys showed up, all together—Walt, Donny, Rick, Frankie, John, and Donny's little brother

Jessie—and the game went well enough. Walt didn't win, but he didn't lose, either. Nobody lost, really. It got to be dinner time before anyone got around to conquering the world, so they left it at that.

When he got to the house, his father and sister weren't home yet. His mom was sitting at the kitchen table drinking coffee with the aliens.

He knew the things were there before he even banged into the kitchen; when he opened the front door he could smell electrocuted flesh and sulphury-rotten eggs, and he knew they were there for him. His first thought was that they'd taken his mother hostage, kidnapped her to make him go with them. He rushed into the kitchen (where the smell came from) on the tide of one of those brave reflexes a boy can have when there isn't time to think.

But there was no need for him to save her.

As soon as he opened the kitchen door he knew that he should turn around and run right then, but he didn't. Shock paralyzed him. He backed up against the wall by the door he'd just come through and stared at them with his eyes open wide and his mouth agape.

His mom sat at the kitchen table drinking coffee with the aliens. The ugly one, the one with skin the color of roach guts and eyes like a spider's corpse, he sat right there at the table with her. Behind them, in the hall that led from the garage, the rest of the aliens crowded together at the doorway to stare at him.

"Walt," his mom said, "this is Mr. Krant. He's going to take you with him."

Walt wanted to scream, but his throat cramped, jammed, and he couldn't make any sound. Something in his knees wanted to spring loose and let him fall into the ground, so he leaned his body into the wall enough for it to take his weight.

"That's why they woke you up, dear. They wanted you. They're here for you. They're here to help you."

Walt didn't believe a word of it, not for a minute. His mother's tone was saccharine and *too*-sincere; she'd lied to him just like that just after he had died.

"No!" he shouted. His voice was shrill. He still wanted to scream, but now he wanted to cry, too. *God,* why his mom? Why did *she* have to be with them?

"It's okay, Walt." She was still lying. "You don't have to go with them, if *you* don't want. But listen. Talk to them. Hear them out."

Right away he knew that was the last thing he should do. The alien reached into the purse he carried and took out a gadget that Walt got dizzy looking at.

A hypnotizer, Walt thought, and he turned his head away as fast as he could.

"Relax, Walt." The thing's voice sounded like the air that bubbles up in a toilet when the pipes are doing funny things. Walt could hear it tinkering with the gadget. "You can call me Captain Krant. We've come a long way to find you. From galaxies and galaxies away." Walt couldn't help himself; he turned to see it talking. The pincers didn't move much, but the maw jumped and squirmed crazily. That made booger-clotted mucous drool down the thing's chinless jaw. Walt watched it ooze down the cloth of the alien's tunic and feed into the stain-ring below the neck—

—and he had to puke, even though he hadn't eaten in days, and his legs propelled him through the aliens toward the bathroom—

—and he realized he could move again, could run—

—so where the hall split he went straight, through the garage and out the side door, to run and run and run without looking back at his mother's house.

Which, maybe, he should have done, because he never saw it again.

He didn't pay much attention where he ran to, so it didn't surprise him much when he found himself, moments later, panting and crying and leaning over his own headstone. The grave was his home, probably the best one he'd ever had— though there was an element of bias, of bitterness, in that thought. Walt didn't mind it. There was nothing wrong with bitterness when your mom turned against you like she was a rabid dog—maybe there was even something right about it. Mothers were supposed to be the ones who *protected* you, not the ones who sold you into slavery (worse: gave you away) when the aliens came for you.

"Walt?" And a hand on his shoulder. He jumped and nearly screamed, but stopped himself. He hadn't heard it coming. Not at all.

"Walt, are you okay?" His sister. No one else. No one with her. His heart stomped up and down like a lunatic inside his chest.

"Yeah." He took a deep breath, let it out real slow. "Okay. I ought to say good-bye, though. Got to run away."

"Huh? What's that?"

"Mom—" He stopped. "You wouldn't believe me."

Anne shook her head.

"It's hard to believe you're alive. What could be worse?"

Walt tried to think about that for a moment, then decided he didn't want to. He shrugged. "The aliens, the ones who made me alive again. They came back for me. Mom wants me to go with them."

She shrugged. "Maybe she's right. Something is wrong. Hasn't been right since you came back."

"*God!* Not you, too. If you saw them, if *you* had to go with them . . . ! They're *scarey!*" Walt was trying not to cry, but it wasn't doing much good. "I don't want to go. I don't want Mom to try to get rid of me."

Anne stood there, empty-faced, not saying anything. Walt didn't really know why or how, but he knew there was no way she could respond to what he'd said.

And there was nothing left for him to say. "Yeah," he said, finally, because he needed to fill the space with something—he didn't really mean anything when he said it. "Well. I guess good-bye, then."

She nodded, and she hugged him and she wished him luck. She turned around and before she'd gone five paces he was in the woods, quietly skulking his way into the darkest place he could find. He didn't see her again for a long time.

He sat in the woods for hours, trying to figure out what he was supposed to do next.

He still didn't know at midnight, when he heard his dad's footsteps. Dad didn't have to say anything for Walt to know who it was; he knew his walk by the sound of it.

"Son," Dad called, almost as though he could hear him breathing. "Walt . . . ? Are you still out there, son?"

Walt tucked himself deeper into the niche between the two big rocks where he was resting.

"It's okay, son," Dad called. In the sound of his voice Walt heard everything he wanted to believe: that his dad loved him,

wanted him, needed him. That his mom was just having a bad
time, and that soon she'd be loving him just like she always
had. Real soon—next week, maybe the week after at the latest.

"It's all right, Walt," Dad called again. "Nobody's going to
make you do anything you don't want to do. Really, son. Your
mom's a little upset, sure, but it'll work out okay. Maybe you
and me and Anne can take a week or two and rent a cabin up by
the lake." Lake Hortonia, in Vermont, where they went every
year for vacation since Walt was three. "And let your mom
have a little time to herself, time to get used to things."

Dad was real close now, but Walt wasn't really trying to hide
anymore. He wasn't getting up and letting his dad know where
he was, either, though. He'd gotten cautious. Reflex wouldn't
let him just stand up. Then his leg twitched and made some dirt
clods fall.

That gave him away.

"Walt?" His dad's voice was tense now, sharper. The
flashlight spun around, and there he was, trapped in it.

Walt wanted to scream in terror, in frustration at being
caught. But what happened was a lot more like crying even
though he tried hard as he could for it not to be, and then he
was running to his dad with his arms stretched out, and calling,
"Daddy," and hugging his dad with his arms around his waist
and his face buried in Dad's big soft belly. And crying into his
soft flannel shirt, and smelling clean laundry because his dad
never sweated.

"Daddy," Walt said again, and he hugged him harder.

"Oh God, Walt, oh God, Walt, I love you son, you know
that."

And Walt nodded into his dad's stomach even though it
wasn't really a question.

"And I hope to God that some day you'll forgive me what
I'm doing. God, your mother *made* me, she *made* me . . . !"
And then his father's hands wrapped around his wrists, tight
and hard as iron neck bands, and he shouted back in the
direction of the cemetery, "I've got him," and . . .

Something down inside Walt busted and without his even
thinking, without his even knowing what he did, a scream
bubbled up from some black, fireless pit at the base of him.

A scream so horrible and true that it shook the woods and,
for weeks, the dreams of everyone who heard it.

His father's hands fell loose from Walt's hands.
And Walt *ran*.

Walt ran all night. He wasn't going anywhere. Not yet. He hadn't thought that far yet.

So he kept moving, because he knew they were looking for him. More than once he heard their walking just behind him— his mother's, his father's, the weird rhythms of the aliens. Others, later.

It was after moonset but before even the beginning of dawn when he heard the shrill, grating stage whisper of a hiss.

"Hssit. Walt."

He thought at first it came from Donny James's house—he was in the woods behind it—but then he realized it came from Mr. Hodges's next door.

Walt couldn't imagine why the school's principal would call him. He went to the back window—it was open but it had a screen—to find out.

"What's happened, Walt? Your parents have been here, and then the police, looking for you. They must've gone to every house in the neighborhood, to watch them. What did you do?"

Walt shrugged. "I ran away, I guess. The aliens that made me alive again came back for me. Mom wants to give me to them."

Mr. Hodges didn't believe a word of it. "Even if that is what happened—I suppose it's no more preposterous than anything else about you these days—why would your mother call the police? They'd just complicate matters for her later."

Walt shrugged again. "Mom's tricky."

Mr. Hodges shook his head. "I don't know what you are, Walt, but you're strange." He looked out into the woods, back and forth. "You want to come in for cocoa?"

Walt knew he shouldn't trust the man; he knew from experience that he shouldn't trust anyone tonight. But he was tired of being scared and bored of running, so he nodded and said, "Yes."

"Come around to the side door," Mr. Hodges told him, and he did.

Inside, it was still dark. They sat at the kitchen table while the principal made cocoa (he brewed coffee for himself) with only the light that came in through the windows from the streetlamp out front.

"Best to leave the lights out," he said, "the way they're searching out there, they're sure to see you if we turn them on."

"Yeah." Walt nodded.

There was nothing, really, for them to talk about. Walt had already said more about himself and about the aliens than he ever meant to say to anyone. Besides, he didn't know much, really. There was school, but Walt felt uneasy telling the principal anything interesting; he might get someone in trouble.

"Miss Allison is in the hospital," Mr. Hodges said. "She had a breakdown yesterday afternoon. Right in her own classroom. The janitor came in at four o'clock to sweep and mop, and there she was, looking off into the distance just like she was waiting for something. And nothing anyone did would even make her blink—though if you watched long enough you might see her do that on her own."

Walt nodded and stirred his cocoa with his finger. "She was acting strange in the morning."

Mr. Hodges lit his pipe, sucking in fire from a butane lighter three times with a hissing-sucking sound. Smoke billowed up to freeze in the street light. The smell was rich, but bitter and powdery.

Walt knew the sun would rise soon. He felt himself slipping away just like a fade out on a television set; felt his muscles let go bit by bit, felt his head sinking down to the cushion of his arm on the table beside the cocoa. He tried to make himself be taut, awake, but it didn't do any good.

"Walt? Are you going to be okay?"

Mr. Hodges's asking woke him up. He shook his head. "Sorry. I'm all right."

"Do you want to camp out on the couch here? Do you need to sleep?"

"Could I?" Walt was tired, but he was scared, too. He pictured his mother finding him while he slept, and giving him to the aliens without even waking him to let him know. He could see himself waking on a spaceship, already light-years from home, in the arms of some *thing* that looked and felt like tripe and smelled like rotten eggs. He tried not to shudder, but it didn't do any good.

"Walt? Should I get you a pillow and a blanket? Don't fall asleep there; you might fall off the chair and break your neck."

"Please." He stumbled into the living room, to the couch. He was almost asleep before Mr. Hodges got back.

The clean muslin of the pillowcase felt comfortable and wonderful but somehow alien to Walt. He'd got used to the satin of his coffin, even though he couldn't feel it when he was dead. Muslin seemed too coarse, too absorbent. He lay awake a lot longer than he wanted to, getting used to it.

Walt woke in the early evening. Mr. Hodges wasn't home yet, and he hadn't left a note. Walt went to the bathroom to wash up as best he could without a change of clothes. He didn't know what he would do next; it seemed to him that there was no place to go, no life left for him to gather up the pieces of. He even thought for a moment that he would rather be dead, but he knew that wasn't so.

For the moment, at least, the doorbell decided him. Walt put down the towel he'd used to dry his face and looked around the corner where the hallway ended, into the living room.

Through the window in the alcove he could see three policemen, their hands clasped in front of them just like busboys in some fancy restaurant. His mother stood behind them.

He had to go or they'd get him. He ran to the bedroom in the back, popped the screen out of the window frame, climbed out, and began to run.

"Walt!"

His heart lurched and tried to jump out his throat. He thought they had him, but then he turned and recognized the voice at the same time: Donny James, sitting on a lawn chair in his backyard. The Jameses' house was right next door to Mr. Hodges's.

"Quiet!" Walt stage-whispered. He tried to be quiet, but it didn't work. "They're looking for me. Don't shout."

"Huh . . . ?" Donny was running to catch up to him. Over on the far side of the woods, where the storm drain passed under the interstate highway, there was a big concrete sewer pipe, big enough for a boy to walk through, but too small for an adult. He could hide there, and even if they found him they couldn't get in to catch him. Or even trap him. He could be long gone before they could get around the nearest highway overpass and surrounded him at the far end of the pipe.

"Where're you going, Walt?" Donny asked. Walt didn't answer.

"Just come on," he said.

There still wasn't any sign of his mom or the policemen when they reached the pipe. Walt walked in first—duck-walked, half-squatting, really. In the middle of the pipe he sat down and leaned his back against the curved wall. It was cool and dry and dark. There weren't any bugs around, at least not that Walt could see.

"The police came to school today, looking for you," Donny said. "When they didn't find you they asked everybody questions."

Walt nodded. He'd kind of expected that.

"What happened to you? Why were you running? Why were they looking for you?"

Walt didn't know what to say; he kicked his leg against the far side of the pipe, trying to think.

"The aliens that made me alive again came back for me." He kept expecting people not to believe that, and they kept believing it. Strange. "I didn't want to go 'cause they're real gross. But Mom wanted to make me. So I ran away."

Donny flicked a pebble at the entrance they'd come in through. "Where're you going to go now?"

Walt *still* hadn't thought about that. Not really. He shrugged. "I don't know, I guess."

Donny and Walt sat thinking about that, not talking, for a good five minutes.

"Well," Donny said, "you can't go back home, you know. She'll just pack you away with the aliens. But you got to have some place to stay."

"Yeah." Walt nodded. He hadn't thought that far before. He'd been avoiding it, he guessed.

"And wherever you go, it better be pretty far away. Or your mom'll find you."

"Yeah." It was true. It was why he'd been trying not to think about what he'd do. He didn't *want* to run away. He wanted to go home and stay there and grow up just like any other boy.

But there was just no way in hell. He felt like he needed to cry—more out of frustration than anything else—but he didn't want to do that where anybody could see it. Especially Donny.

"I guess I better go," Walt said.

Donny nodded. "Where're you going to go?"

"I don't know. I'll be back sooner or later, though. I'll see you again."

But he never did. By the time Walt got back to town Donny had been gone a long time.

In the window of the Seven-Eleven by the on ramp to the interstate, Walt saw himself on the cover of the *National Interlocutor*.

BOY CRAWLS OUT OF GRAVE

Walter Fulton, age eight, dug his way out of his grave last week, after being buried for more than a year. Walt died last year when a car hit him as he crossed a street.

"Dying wasn't so bad," says Walt. "Two angels took my arms, lifted me from the car wreck, and brought me up to heaven.

"Heaven's a great place, and everybody's happy there," Walt continues, "but it's no place for an eight-year-old boy. There isn't any mud, no baseball bats, and nobody ever gets hurt in the football games."

Dr. Ralph Richards of the Institute for Psychical Research in Tuskegee, Alabama, speculated that Walt's experience may not have been mystical in nature at all. "It's possible that young Fulton wasn't dead at all when he was buried, but suffering from a Thanatesque condition, from which he later recovered."

(continued on page 9)

Walt marveled at the newspaper, reading it again and again, staring at the photos. There were two of them: one a photo of the cemetery, focused on his tombstone. There was no graffiti on it yet, and the ground before it was still crumbled and spilling out from Walt's crawling out. Policemen—fifteen or twenty of them—milled about the cemetery. Walt had never seen the photo, but he knew it must have been taken not long after the caretaker found Walt's grave abandoned. That would be the Monday after his resurrection. The other photo was a head shot of Walt. He recognized it; it had to have been cut from his first-grade class picture, the group photo where the whole class had stood in three parallel lines and posed for the camera together.

Walt went into the Seven-Eleven and bought a copy of the paper with some of the lunch money he'd hoarded this week. He hadn't been hungry at all at lunch.

The paper amazed him; it was as though they'd written the article before they'd sent the man to talk to him. He took the paper off the counter, paid the woman, walked out of the store, and wandered out to the street, still reading the article over and over again. He felt awed; the paper had the aura of The Mysteries—even things mystical—about it.

Out on the street, Walt set his teeth and pointed himself at the ramp to the interstate highway. He walked for thirty minutes, thumb out, hitchhiking along the grassy strip to the right of the southbound lane.

It was almost dark when the station wagon stopped for him.

"Where're you going?" the guy in the front passenger seat asked him. There were four people in the car already. The smell of burning marijuana drifted out from the window. Walt could see beer cans littering the floor, and at least one of the four men was drinking.

"South," Walt said. "A long way."

"You want to ride on the back shelf?"

It was mostly empty.

"Sure."

"Open the door and let him in, huh, Jack?"

Jack opened the door and leaned away from it enough for Walt to climb over him; Walt settled in among the duffel bags and piles of etcetera. He rode for hours lying on his back with his head on a pillow made of what felt like clothes. He stared up into the sky as he lay there, watching the stars.

Meteors whizzed back and forth over the highway in the sky above them. And three times police cars screamed by them, lights flashing, sirens wailing.

Once Jack asked him if he wanted a hit off a joint, but he didn't. Jack and everybody else in the car laughed uproariously.

At four in the morning they stopped at a rest area to use the men's room. When they stopped moving the odor in the car became unbearable.

"We're going to get off the highway at the next exit," Jack told him. He got back before the others did. "If you're still going south, this is probably a better place to get a ride than that is."

Walt nodded. "Yeah," he said. He started to climb out, relieved at the chance to get away from the stink. As he got up, he saw what it came from: the pile he'd been using for a pillow. Dirty socks and underwear. His stomach turned, he retched a little, but nothing came out. It'd been too long since he'd eaten, and thank God for that.

"Take it easy, kid," Jack said. He was awfully close when Walt's body was trying to puke. "You okay? You going to be all right?"

Walt got out of the car. He stood bent over with his hands on his knees. "I'll be all right," he said. The smell was horrible, and it was in his hair and clothes, and he was so *tired*. "Thanks for the ride."

He went to the water fountain by the picnic tables, and he drank water for ten minutes, hardly even pausing to breathe. When he looked up, the station wagon was gone.

Home was miles and miles away, and he was tired and he stank. He went into the men's room and tried to clean himself, but it didn't help. The smell had ground its way into his pores.

He needed someplace to sleep. He was sure his mom or someone would find him if he fell asleep on one of the benches in the little roadside park. If nothing else he'd be so conspicuous that some highway patrolman who had nothing to do with any of this would find him. But he couldn't stand the thought of trying to get another ride. He looked past the fence that wrapped itself around the rest stop and thought about the great thick woods that surrounded the highway. It was deep and dark and big; silent and endless. It extended as far as he could see.

The fence was three strands of barbed wire strung through rough wood posts. This far from any city there was no need for anything more elaborate. Walt pressed down the lowest wire and slipped between it and the wire above. His shirt snagged and tore on one of the barbs; another barb gave him a long bloody scratch on his upper arm. But he didn't care. He was too tired. He just wanted to find a dry, soft, comfortable bed of pine needles and sleep for a million years.

But he went much deeper into the forest than he meant to.

He needed the hike, he guessed; at the same time he wanted to collapse something like a nervous tic in his legs kept pushing him deeper and deeper into the woods. Maybe it was his body trying to bleed off excess adrenaline, or maybe it was a need to get as far away from the highway as he could, just to be safe.

Not long before dawn, his right foot caught on a gnarled, twisty root he hadn't seen, and he came down chest-first into an enormous heap of soft, wet, acid-smelling dung. It splattered all over the front of his shirt, onto his upper arms (even into the fresh cut), and under his chin. He started sobbing, then; it wasn't so bad to cry since no one was looking. He took his shirt off and used the back of it to wipe off his arms and neck. It didn't do any good. It took some of the clumps off him, but the shitty edges smeared him where he was clean. He threw the shirt onto a pile of rocks and crawled away from the bearshit, over to the base of a pine tree.

He sat there with his back to the tree until the sun came up, paralyzed with frustration and hopelessness. He thought about dying again, but he didn't think that would do any good either.

Late in the morning he fell asleep, still filthy, his skin beginning to burn and itch where the shit was. He hadn't moved since he'd crawled over to the tree. He barely noticed the transition between wakefulness and sleep.

The touch of something cool and clean and wet woke him. Before he opened his eyes, while he was still waking up, he thought it was rain.

But it wasn't.

When his eyes finally focused he saw it was the alien, wiping Walt's body clean with a white cloth that smelled like lemons or something citrus. Its hand brushed him, and it felt just exactly like tripe in the refrigerator case in the grocery. Behind the citrus was the alien's smell of sulphur and . . . preserved meat. Walt's first impulse was to scream in stark raving bloody terror—was it cleaning him the way you clean an animal before you slaughter it?—but all the heart for screaming had worn out of him. If this was the end, then that was that: whether he'd meant to or not he'd already come to terms with it. He stared calm and cool into its drooling eyes.

"You are hurt?" the alien asked him, its voice bubbles in a fish tank, its breath rotten eggs. Walt turned his face away from it.

"No," Walt said. He sighed. "I'm okay."

The alien nodded its head back and forth slowly like a rocking chair. It finished wiping off Walt's right shoulder and reached over to clean the left. Walt could feel that under his chin was already clean. "Stop that," he said.

The alien looked startled, but it pulled its hand back. "It burns your skin," the thing said.

"Just don't."

The alien sat there staring at him for a long minute. "You can't go back home," it told him. "Your mother would be unhappy with you. She would hurt you."

"I know," Walt said. He'd known it for a while now.

"Where will you go? Where will you have a life?"

Walt shrugged.

"You were unhappy being dead. That's strange for your people; almost all of them rest content. We needed an assistant, so we woke you." The alien looked down into the dirt. "You don't have to come."

Walt could feel the bearshit, deep in his pores even where the creature had cleaned him. He could feel the filth matted into his hair in the station wagon. His clothes were filthy, kind of greasy; he'd been wearing them for three days now. And the alien—hands like tripe, smelling like something dead and something rotten—didn't seem gross or disgusting at all. Not in comparison.

He went with the aliens. Whether that was the right choice or not, he never regretted it.

And he had fun.

And when he grew up, he lived a great and full life out among the galaxies, a life full of stars and adventures and wonders. When he was forty he came home to the world to make his peace.

His father and he and his sister and her family spent a week of reunion and celebration. It was a good week, joyful as thirty Christmastimes at once.

But his mother was already dead when he came back. She hadn't lived a long life; she died not long after Walt left. He went to her grave to say good-bye to her.

She didn't answer. She did her best to ignore him.

Popsy

Stephen King

Sheridan was cruising slowly down the long blank length of the shopping mall when he saw the little kid push out through the main doors under the lighted sign which read COUSINTOWN. It was a boy-child, perhaps a big three and surely no more than five. On his face was an expression to which Sheridan had become exquisitely attuned. He was trying not to cry but soon would.

Sheridan paused for a moment, feeling the familiar soft wave of self-disgust . . . but every time he took a child, that feeling grew a little less urgent. The first time he hadn't slept for a week. He kept thinking about that big greasy Turk who called himself Mr. Wizard, kept wondering what he did with the children.

"They go on a boat-ride, Mr. Sheridan," the Turk told him, only it came out *Dey goo on a bot-rahd, Meestair Shurdone.* The Turk smiled. *And if you know what's good for you, you won't ask anymore about it,* that smile said, and it said it loud and clear, without an accent.

Sheridan *hadn't* asked anymore, but that didn't mean he hadn't kept wondering. Tossing and turning, wishing he had the whole thing to do over again so he could turn it around, walk away from the temptation. The second time had been almost as bad . . . the third time not quite . . . and by the fourth time he had stopped wondering so much about the bot-rahd, and what might be at the end of it for the little kids.

Sheridan pulled his van into one of the parking spaces right in front of the mall, spaces that were almost always empty because they were for crips. Sheridan had one of the special license plates on the back of his van the state gave to crips; that kept any mall security cop from getting suspicious, and those spaces were so convenient.

You always pretend you're not going out looking, but you always lift a crip plate a day or two before.

Never mind all that bullshit; he was in a jam and that kid over there could bail him out of it.

He got out and walked toward the kid, who was looking around with more and more bewildered panic in his face. Yes, he thought, he was five all right, maybe even six—just very frail. In the harsh fluorescent glare thrown through the glass doors the boy looked white and ill. Maybe he really was sick, but Sheridan reckoned he was just scared.

He looked up hopefully at the people passing around him, people going into the mall eager to buy, coming out laden with packages, their faces dazed, almost drugged, with something they probably thought was satisfaction.

The kid, dressed in Tuffskin jeans and a Pittsburgh Penguins t-shirt, looked for help, looked for somebody to look at him and see something was wrong, looked for someone to ask the right question—*You get separated from your dad, son?* would do—looking for a friend.

Here I am, Sheridan thought, approaching. *Here I am, sonny—I'll be your friend.*

He had almost reached the kid when he saw a mall rent-a-cop walking slowly up the concourse toward the doors. He was reaching in his pocket, probably for a pack of cigarettes. He would come out, see the boy, and there would go Sheridan's sure thing.

Shit, he thought, but at least he wouldn't be seen talking to the kid when the cop came out. That would have been worse.

Sheridan drew back a little and made a business of feeling in his own pockets, as if to make sure he still had his keys. His glance flicked from the boy to the security cop and back to the boy. The boy had started to cry. Not all-out bawling, not yet, but great big tears that looked reddish in the reflected glow of the COUSINTOWN MALL sign as they tracked down his smooth cheeks.

The girl in the information booth waved at the cop and said something to him. She was pretty, dark-haired, about twenty-five; he was sandy-blonde with a moustache. As he leaned on his elbows, smiling at her, Sheridan thought they looked like the cigarette ads you saw on the backs of magazines. Salem Spirit. Light My Lucky. He was dying out here and they were in there making chit-chat. Now she was batting eyes at him. How cute.

Sheridan abruptly decided to take the chance. The kid's chest was hitching, and as soon as he started to bawl out loud, someone would notice him. He didn't like moving in with a cop less than sixty feet away, but if he didn't cover his markers at Mr. Reggie's within the next twenty-four hours or so, he thought a couple of very large men would pay him a visit and perform impromptu surgery on his arms, adding several elbow-bends to each.

He walked up to the kid, a big man dressed in an ordinary Van Heusen shirt and khaki pants, a man with a broad, ordinary face that looked kind at first glance. He bent over the little boy, hands on his legs just above the knees, and the boy turned his pale, scared face up to Sheridan's. His eyes were as green as emeralds, their color accentuated by the tears that washed them.

"You get separated from your dad, son?" Sheridan asked kindly.

"My Popsy," the kid said, wiping his eyes. "My dad's not here and I . . . I can't find my P-P-Popsy!"

Now the kid *did* begin to sob, and a woman headed in glanced around with some vague concern.

"It's all right," Sheridan said to her, and she went on. Sheridan put a comforting arm around the boy's shoulders and drew him a little to the right . . . in the direction of the van. Then he looked back inside.

The rent-a-cop had his face right down next to the information girl's now. Looked like there was something pretty hot going on between them . . . and if there wasn't, there soon would be. Sheridan relaxed. At this point there could be a stick-up going on at the bank just up the concourse and the cop wouldn't notice a thing. This was starting to look like a cinch.

"I want my Popsy!" the boy wept.

"Sure you do, of course you do," Sheridan said. "And we're going to find him. Don't you worry."

He drew him a little more to the right.

The boy looked up at him, suddenly hopeful.

"Can you? Can you, mister?"

"Sure!" Sheridan said, and grinned. "Finding lost Popsies . . . well, you might say it's kind of a specialty of mine."

"It is?" The kid actually smiled a little, although his eyes were still leaking.

"It sure is," Sheridan said, glancing inside again to make sure the cop, whom he could now barely see (and who would barely be able to see Sheridan and the boy, should he happen to look up), was still enthralled. He was. "What was your Popsy wearing, son?"

"He was wearing his suit," the boy said. "He almost always wears his suit. I only saw him once in jeans." He spoke as if Sheridan should know all these things about his Popsy.

"I bet it was a black suit," Sheridan said.

The boy's eyes lit up, flashing red in the light of the mall sign, as if his tears had turned to blood.

"You *saw* him! Where?" The boy started eagerly back toward the doors, tears forgotten, and Sheridan had to restrain himself from grabbing the boy right then. No good. Couldn't cause a scene. Couldn't do anything people would remember later. Had to get him in the van. The van had sun-filter glass everywhere except in the windshield; it was almost impossible to see inside even from six inches away.

Had to get him in the van first.

He touched the boy on the arm. "I didn't see him inside, son. I saw him right over there."

He pointed across the huge parking lot with its endless platoons of cars. There was an access road at the far end of it, and beyond that were the double yellow arches of McDonald's.

"Why would Popsy go over *there?*" the boy asked, as if either Sheridan or Popsy—or maybe both of them—had gone utterly mad.

"I don't know," Sheridan said. His mind was working fast, clicking along like an express train as it always did when it got right down to the point where you had to stop shitting and either do it up right or fuck it up righteously. Popsy. Not Dad or Daddy but Popsy. The kid had corrected him on it. Popsy meant granddad, Sheridan decided. "But I'm pretty sure that was him. Older guy in a black suit. White hair . . . green tie . . ."

"Popsy had his blue tie on," the boy said. "He knows I like it the best."

"Yeah, it could have been blue," Sheridan said. "Under these lights, who can tell? Come on, hop in the van, I'll run you over there to him."

"Are you *sure* it was Popsy? Because I don't know why he'd go to a place where they—"

Sheridan shrugged. "Look, kid, if you're sure that wasn't him, maybe you better look for him on your own. You might even find him." And he started brusquely away, heading back toward the van.

The kid wasn't biting. He thought about going back, trying again, but it had already gone on too long—you either kept observable contact to a minimum or you were asking for twenty years in Hammerton Bay. It would be better to go on to another mall. Scoterville, maybe. Or—

"Wait, mister!" It was the kid, with panic in his voice. There was the light thud of running sneakers. "Wait up! I told im I was thirsty, he must have thought he had to go way over there to get me a drink. Wait!"

Sheridan turned around, smiling. "I wasn't really going to leave you anyway, son."

He led the boy to the van, which was four years old and painted a nondescript blue. He opened the door and smiled at the kid, who looked up at him doubtfully, his green eyes swimming in that pallid little face.

"Step into my parlor," Sheridan said.

The kid did, and, although he didn't know it, his ass belonged to Briggs Sheridan the minute the passenger door swung shut.

He had no problem with broads, and he could take booze or leave it alone. His problem was cards—any kind of cards, as long as it was the kind of cards where you started off by changing your greenbacks into chips. He had lost jobs, credit cards, the home his mother had left him. He had never, at least so far, been in jail, but the first time he got in trouble with Mr. Reggie, he thought jail would be a rest-cure by comparison.

He had gone a little crazy that night. It was better, he had found, when you lost right away. When you lost right away you got discouraged, went home, watched a little Carson on the tube, went to sleep. When you won a little bit at first, you chased. Sheridan had chased that night and had ended up owing $17,000. He could hardly believe it; he went home dazed, almost elated by the enormity of it. He kept telling himself in the car on the way home that he owed Mr. Reggie not seven hundred, not seven *thousand*, but *seventeen thousand* iron men. Every time he tried to think about it he giggled and turned the volume up on the radio.

But he wasn't giggling the next night when the two gorillas—the ones who would make sure his arms bent in all sorts of new and interesting ways if he didn't pay up—brought him into Mr. Reggie's office.

"I'll pay," Sheridan began babbling at once. "I'll pay, listen, it's no problem, couple of days, a week at the most, two weeks at the outside—"

"You bore me, Sheridan," Mr. Reggie said.

"I—"

"Shut up. If I give you a week, don't you think I know what you'll do? You'll tap a friend for a couple of hundred if you've got a friend left to tap. If you can't find a friend, you'll hit a liquor store . . . if you've got the guts. I doubt if you do, but anything is possible." Mr. Reggie leaned forward, propped his chin on his hands, and smiled. He smelled of Ted Lapidus cologne. "And if you do come up with two hundred dollars, what will you do with it?"

"Give it to you," Sheridan had babbled. By then he was very close to wetting his pants. "I'll give it to you, right away!"

"No you won't," Mr. Reggie said. "You'll take it to the track and try to make it grow. What you'll give me is a bunch of shitty excuses. You're in over your head this time, my friend. Way over your head."

Sheridan began to blubber.

"These guys could put you in the hospital for a long time," Mr. Reggie said reflectively. "You would have a tube in each arm and another one coming out of your nose."

Sheridan began to blubber louder.

"I'll give you this much," Mr. Reggie said, and pushed a folded sheet of paper across his desk to Sheridan. "You might get along with this guy. He calls himself Mr. Wizard, but he's a shitbag just like you. Now get out of here. I'm gonna have you back in here in a week, though, and I'll have your markers on this desk. You either buy them back or I'm going to have my friends tool up on you. And like Booker T. says, once they start, they do it until they're satisfied.''

The Turk's real name was written on the folded sheet of paper. Sheridan went to see him, and heard about the kids and the bot-rahds. Mr. Wizard also named a figure which was a fairish bit larger than the markers Mr. Reggie was holding. That was when Sheridan started cruising the malls.

He pulled out of the Cousintown Mall's main parking lot, looked for traffic, and then pulled across into the McDonald's in-lane. The kid was sitting all the way forward on the passenger seat, hands on the knees of his Tuffskins, eyes agonizingly alert. Sheridan drove toward the building, swung wide to avoid the drive-thru lane, and kept on going.

"Why are you going around the back?" the kid asked.

"You have to go around to the other doors," Sheridan said. "Keep your shirt on, kid. I think I saw him in there."

"You did? You really did?"

"I'm pretty sure, yeah."

Sublime relief washed over the kid's face, and for a moment Sheridan felt sorry for him—hell, he wasn't a monster or a maniac, for Christ's sake. But his markers had gotten a little deeper each time, and that bastard Mr. Reggie had no compunctions at all about letting him hang himself. It wasn't $17,000 this time, or $20,000, or even $25,000. This time it was thirty-five thousand big ones if he didn't want a few new sets of elbows by next Saturday.

He stopped in the back by the trash-compacter. Nobody parked back here. Good. There was an elasticized pouch on the side of the door for maps and things. Sheridan reached into it with his left hand and brought out a pair of blued steel Koch handcuffs. The loop-jaws were open.

"Why are we stopping here, mister?" the kid asked, and the quality of fear in his voice had changed; his voice said that maybe getting separated from Popsy in the busy mall wasn't the worst thing that could happen to him.

"We're not, not really," Sheridan said easily. He had learned the second time he'd done this that you didn't want to underestimate even a six-year-old once he had his wind up.

The second kid had kicked him in the balls and had damn near gotten away. "I just remembered I forgot to put my glasses on when I started driving. I could lose my license. They're in that glasses case on the floor there. They slid over to your side. Hand 'em to me, would you?"

The kid bent over to get the glasses case, which was empty. Sheridan leaned over and snapped one of the cuffs on the other hand as neat as you please. And then the trouble started. Hadn't he just been thinking it was a bad mistake to underestimate even a six-year-old? The kid fought like a wildcat, twisting with an eely muscularity Sheridan never would have believed in a skinny little package like him. He bucked and fought and lunged for the door, panting and uttering weird birdlike little cries. He got the handle. The door swung open, but no domelight came on—Sheridan had broken it after that second outing.

He got the kid by the round collar of his Penguins t-shirt and hauled him back in. He tried to clamp the other cuff on the special strut beside the passenger seat and missed. The kid bit his hand, twice, bringing blood. God, his teeth were like razors. The pain went deep and sent a steely ache all the way up his arm. He punched the kid in the mouth. He fell back into the seat, dazed, Sheridan's blood on his mouth and chin and dripping onto the ribbed neck of the t-shirt. Sheridan clamped the other cuff on the arm of the seat and then fell back into his own, sucking the back of his right hand.

The pain was really bad. He pulled his hand away from his mouth and looked at it in the weak glow of the dashlights. Two shallow, ragged tears, each maybe two inches long, ran up toward his wrist from just above the knuckles. Blood pulsed in weak little rills. Still, he felt no urge to pop the kid again, and that had nothing to do with damaging the Turk's merchandise, in spite of the almost fussy way the Turk had warned him against that—*demmage the goots end you demmage the velue*, the Turk had said in his fluting accent.

No, he didn't blame the kid for fighting—he would have done the same. He would have to disinfect the wound as soon as he could, might even have to have a shot—he had read somewhere that human bites were the worst kind—but he sort of admired the kid's guts.

He dropped the transmission into drive and pulled around the brick building, past the empty drive-thru window, and back onto the access road. He turned left. The Turk had a big ranch-style house in Taluda Heights, on the edge of the city. Sheridan would go there by secondary roads, just in case. Thirty miles. Maybe forty-five minutes, maybe an hour.

He passed a sign which read THANK YOU FOR SHOP-PING THE BEAUTIFUL COUSINTOWN MALL, turned left, and let the van creep up to a perfectly legal forty miles an hour. He fished a handkerchief out of his back pocket, folded it over the back of his right hand, and concentrated on following his headlights to the forty grand the Turk had promised.

"You'll be sorry," the kid said.

Sheridan looked impatiently around at him, pulled from a dream in which he had just made twenty straight points and had Mr. Reggie groveling at his feet, sweating bullets and begging him to stop, what did he want to do, break him?

The kid was crying again, and his tears still had that odd reddish cast. Sheridan wondered for the first time if the kid might be sick . . . might have some disease. Was nothing to him as long as he himself didn't catch it and as long as Mr. Wizard paid him before finding out.

"When my *Popsy* finds you you'll be sorry," the kid elaborated.

"Yeah," Sheridan said, and lit a cigarette. He turned off State Road 28 onto an unmarked stretch of two-lane blacktop. There was a long marshy area on the left, unbroken woods on the right.

The kid pulled at the handcuffs and made a sobbing sound.

"Quit it. Won't do you any good."

Nevertheless, the kid pulled again. And this time there was a groaning, protesting sound Sheridan didn't like at *all*. He looked around and was amazed to see that the metal strut on the side of the seat—a strut he had welded in place himself—was twisted out of shape. *Shit!* he thought. *He's got teeth like razors and now I find out he's also strong as a fucking ox.*

He pulled over onto the soft shoulder and said, "Stop it!"

"I *won't!*"

The kid yanked at the handcuff again and Sheridan saw the metal strut bend a little more. Christ, how could *any* kid do that?

It's panic, he answered himself. *That's how he can do it.*

But none of the others had been able to do it, and many of them had been in worse shape than this kid by now.

He opened the glove compartment in the center of the dash. He brought out a hypodermic needle. The Turk had given it to him, and cautioned him not to use it unless he absolutely had to. Drugs, the Turk said (pronouncing it *drucks*) could demmege the merchandise.

"See this?"

The kid nodded.

"You want me to use it?"

The kid shook his head, eyes big and terrified.

"That's smart. Very smart. It would put out your lights." He paused. He didn't want to say it—hell, he was a nice guy, really, when he didn't have his ass in a sling—but he had to. "Might even kill you."

The kid stared at him, lips trembling, face as white as newspaper ashes.

"You stop yanking the cuff, I won't use the needle. Okay?"

"Okay," the kid whispered.

"You promise?"

"Yes." The kid lifted his lip, showing white teeth. One of them was spotted with Sheridan's blood.

"You promise on your mother's name?"

"I never had a mother."

"Shit," Sheridan said, disgusted, and got the van rolling again. He moved a little faster now, and not only because he was finally off the main road. The kid was a spook. Sheridan wanted to turn him over to the Turk, get his money, and split.

"My Popsy's really strong, mister."

"Yeah?" Sheridan asked, and thought: *I bet he is, kid. Only guy in the old folks' home who can bench-press his own truss, right?*

"He'll find me."

"Uh-huh."

"He can smell me."

Sheridan believed it. *He* could sure smell the kid. That fear had an odor was something he had learned on his previous expeditions, but this was unreal—the kid smelled like a mixture of sweat, mud, and slowly cooking battery acid.

Sheridan cracked his window. On the left, the marsh went on and on. Broken slivers of moonlight glimmered in the stagnant water.

"Popsy can fly."

"Yeah," Sheridan said, "and I bet he flies even better after a couple of bottles of Night Train."

"Popsy—"

"Shut up, kid, okay?"

The kid shut up.

Four miles further on, the marsh broadened into a wide empty pond. Here Sheridan made a left turn onto a stretch of hardpan dirt. Five miles west of here he would turn right onto Highway 41, and from there it would be a straight shot into Taluda Heights.

He glanced toward the pond, a flat silver sheet in the moonlight . . . and then the moonlight was gone. Blotted out.

Overhead there was a flapping sound like big sheets on a clothesline.

"Popsy!" the kid cried.

"Shut up. It was only a bird."

But suddenly he was spooked, very spooked. He looked at the kid. The kid's lip was drawn back from his teeth again. His teeth were very white, very big.

No . . . not big. Big wasn't the right word. *Long* was the right word. Especially the two on the top at each side. The . . . what did you call them? The canines.

His mind suddenly started to fly again, clicking along as if he were on speed.

I told im I was thirsty.

Why would Popsy go to a place where they (?*eat was he going to say eat?*)

He'll find me. He can smell me. My Popsy can fly.

Thirsty I told him I was thirsty he went to get me something to drink he went to get me SOMEONE to drink he went—

Something landed on the roof of the van with a heavy clumsy thump.

"Popsy!" the kid screamed again, almost delirious with delight, and suddenly Sheridan could not see the road anymore—a huge membranous wing, pulsing with veins, covered the windshield from side to side.

My Popsy can fly.

Sheridan screamed and jumped on the brake, hoping to tumble the thing on the roof off the front. There was that groaning, protesting sound of metal under stress from his right again, this time followed by a short bitter snap. A moment later the kid's fingers were clawing into his face, pulling open his cheek.

"*He stole me, Popsy!*" the kid was screeching at the roof of the van in that birdlike voice. "*He stole me, he stole me, the bad man stole me!*"

You don't understand, kid, Sheridan thought. He groped for the hypo and found it. *I'm not a bad guy, I just got in a jam, hell, under the right circumstances I could be your grandfather—*

But as Popsy's hand, more like a talon than a real hand, smashed through the side window and ripped the hypo from Sheridan's hand—along with two of his fingers—he understood that wasn't true.

A moment later Popsy peeled the entire driver's side door out of its frame, the hinges now bright twists of meaningless metal. He saw a billowing cape, some kind of pendant, and the tie—yes, it was blue.

Popsy yanked him out of the car, talons sinking through Sheridan's jacket and shirt and deep into the meat of his shoulders. Popsy's green eyes suddenly turned as red as blood-roses.

"We only came to the mall because my grandson wanted some Transformer figures," Popsy whispered, and his breath was like flyblown meat. "The ones they show on TV. All the children want them. You should have left him alone. You should have left *us* alone."

Sheridan was shaken like a rag doll. He shrieked and was shaken again. He heard Popsy asking solicitously if the kid was still thirsty; heard the kid saying yes, very, the bad man had scared him and his throat was *so* dry. He saw Popsy's thumbnail for just a second before it disappeared under the shelf of his chin, the nail ragged and thick and brutal. His throat was cut with that nail before he realized what was happening, and the last things he saw before his sight dimmed to black were the kid, cupping his hands to catch the flow the way Sheridan himself had cupped his hands under the backyard faucet for a drink on a hot summer day when he was a kid, and Popsy, stroking the boy's hair gently, with great love.

Behind the *Masques*

Alphabetically

ROBERT BLOCH
The creator of Lefty Freep, Norman Bates and countless other
characters continues to work a regular work schedule and
divides it from his time at home, but he also says, "research is
what I do all the time I'm not writing." In his introduction to
How to Write Tales of Horror, Fantasy and Science Fiction,
Bloch said he'd "misspent" his life "writing fantasy, horror,
mystery-suspense, and science fiction in books, magazines,
radio, television, films, and the insides of matchbook covers,"
and stressed originality in fiction. "If the theme is old, the
twist or payoff should be new." Consider *The Scarf*, "Yours
Truly, Jack the Ripper," *American Gothic* or *Psycho*. Robert
Bloch has always been true to his word.

RAY BRADBURY
Professionals in any field can be measured by what their peers
think of them. Orson Scott Card, Ardath Mayhar, Ramsey
Campbell, Jane Yolen, Stephen King, Roger Zelazny and I
were among those to place works by Ray Bradbury on their top
ten favorites lists in a 1987 survey. In that poll, 238 pros placed
Bradbury first in fantasy novels, second in fantasy short
fiction, eighth in horror short stories, ninth in best-remembered
horror novels, and fourth in favorite science fiction novels. He
tied for seventh in science fiction short stories. In fact, a total

of thirty-one Bradbury short stories made that book's recommended reading lists, and nobody else came close. The same survey mentioned nine writers whom their fellow professionals cited for twelve or more works of fiction; six of the authors are included in this book, and one is Ray Bradbury.

RAMSEY CAMPBELL
The Merseyside master of fictional frights is one of the anointed few who receives warm welcomes from horror readers throughout the world. Ramsey Campbell has also managed to become almost equally well-known as novelist, short story writer, and lecturer, and is a generous supporter of the small press. Among his many successful books are *The Doll Who Ate His Mother*, *Scared Stiff*, *The Face That Must Die*, *Incarnate*, and *The Nameless*.

DENNIS ETCHISON
The dynamic Dennis, author of such admired story collections as *The Dark Country* and *Red Dreams*, was called "The best short story writer in the field today, bar none" (by Charles L. Grant). But this native of Stockton, California, born March 30, 1943, has also become a novelist and anthologist since crafting the exquisite tale you find here with the publication of *The Darkside*, and the anthology *The Cutting Edge*.

CHARLES L. GRANT
The New Jersey–based, second president of Horror Writers of America is equally established as the editor of such award-winning anthologies as *Shadows* and the author of many subtly scary novels, including several placed in the mythical town of Oxrun Station. Husband of top-notch writer/editor Katherine Ptacek, Charles L. Grant is credited, with Karl Edward Wagner, with creating that familiar alternate term, "dark fantasy." Among his other honors, Grant won a World Fantasy Award for his story collection entitled *Nightmare Seasons*.

JAMES HERBERT
British novelist Herbert (born April 8, 1943) is an overseas success story. In such international best sellers as *The Dark* and *The Rats*, he has used his boyhood terrors to craft tales guaranteed to scare adults of all ages. The stand-alone story included herein was originally part of the U. K. edition of

Domain, a post-nuclear holocaust novel that has shocked readers throughout the world. It may be considered Jim Herbert's first short fiction.

STEPHEN KING
Introducing this writer, I've noted elsewhere, is like "introducing Abe Lincoln." Saying something fresh about Stephen King is next to impossible without personal asides such as this: King informed me at a World Fantasy Convention he'd be sending along a new story for *Masques II*. It came in due time, proving that the Maine man does not merely write a lot of interesting words. He keeps them. King is a working writer and a far better one than critics care to admit. He also seems taller, in person.

JOE R. LANSDALE
Regarded for years as a sort of American Clive Barker, Texas's own J.R. actually predated the Englishman with a remarkable chain of powerfully original stories which appeared in horror magazines and anthologies, commercial as well as small press. These stories include "Fish Night," "The Pit," "Dog, Cat, and Baby" and, from the critically-acclaimed limited anthology *Nukes*, Joe's genre-crossing "Tight Little Stitches in a Dead Man's Back," which received a World Fantasy Award nomination. In 1987, his hard-hitting *Act of Love* was joined by other novels, *Dead in The West* and *The Nightrunners*, and an anthology about the American Old West edited for Doubleday. Lansdale was the acting treasurer for Horror Writers of America during the second half of the organization's first year.

ROBERT R. McCAMMON
McCammon, whom *Masques* publisher John Maclay called (in *2AM*) "a young genius," is the Alabama author of such resoundingly successful novels as *Swan Song*, *Bethany's Sin*, *Usher's Passing* and *Mystery Walk*. Yet it was his present story, "Nightcrawlers" (a runner-up for the 1985 World Fantasy Award), which may have boosted Rick toward lasting fame. In a survey taken for *How to Write Tales of Horror, Fantasy and Science Fiction* in 1987, this yarn was the favorite horror tale since 1940. It was also dramatized (and received raves) on the revived "Twilight Zone" television series. The personable man who conceived the idea of Horror Writers of America often

writes for *Rod Serling's Twilight Zone*, *The Horror Show*, and recently contributed to an anthology published by Dark Harvest, *Night Visions #4*.

RICHARD MATHESON

With the exception of Rod Serling himself, Richard Matheson supplied more stories for the original "Twilight Zone" TV show than any other writer. For that program's devotees, such an achievement would have been sufficient. But the New Jersey–born (February 20, 1926), soft-spoken, tall and handsome Matheson also wrote *The Shrinking Man*, *What Dreams May Come*, and *Hell House*. In a recent poll of writers, reviewers, editors, etc., RM's *I Am Legend* was the seventh favorite horror novel since 1940, his "Born of Man and Woman" was the fourth favorite horror short story; and he was one of the nine writers cited for twelve or more works of fiction. Presently, Richard Matheson is writing a new novel and screenplays; he has already written for such feature or televised productions as "Night Stalker," "The Martian Chronicles," "The Morning After," "Dracula," and the quite probably immortal "Duel."

RICHARD CHRISTIAN MATHESON

Few thoughtful people would wish to be—apart from monetary considerations—Walt Disney, Jr., Oscar Robertson II or Willie Mays's kid, the namesake of Ursula K. Le Guin, Sugar Ray Leonard, Dean R. Koontz, Ella Fitzgerald or, say, William Shakespeare, Jr. Fewer still make their achievements on their own, in the same or similar fields. Then there's the witty, charming, polite R. C., with a story collection (*Scars and Other Distinguishing Marks*), screenplays for Steven Spielberg, feature films for United Artists, story editorships of "Quincy" and "The A-Team," and such short fiction as "Red," "Deathbed" and "The Dark Ones" behind him—five years before he's forty! Who knows? It may be a shame his by-line isn't William Christian Shakespeare!

THOMAS F. MONTELEONE

The Baltimore-based Monteleone is one of those versatile writers who just keeps getting better. The editor of two anthologies, writer of two screenplays and two produced plays,

Tom has published a dozen or more novels, including *Night Train*, *Lyrica*, and the recent *Magnificent Gallery*. Scarcely forty, Thomas Monteleone has already been a secretary for Science Fiction Writers of America and a successful candidate for office in Horror Writers of America.

WILLIAM F. NOLAN

A smiling, strapping huggy-bear of a man, arguably the best-liked guy standing under the fantasy "umbrella," Bill Nolan was co-author with George Clayton Johnson of everyone's favorite, *Logan's Run*. Coming from K. C. originally, Nolan, whose remarkably wide-ranging collection *Things Beyond Midnight* was published in 1984, has also written screenplays or screen treatments for Robert Marasco's *Burnt Offerings*, his own *Bridge Across Time*, and my own *The Longest Night*. He has submitted over ninety stories since 1953 and written seven novels, all of which sold, many of which won awards. He figures he must be doing something right.

ALAN RODGERS

Associate editor of *Twilight Zone* magazine since the time of T.E.D. Klein, editor of the late, lamented *Night Cry*, Rodgers's first work of fiction appears in this volume. Still on the sunnier side of thirty, Alan, who attended college in Florida, is married to an editor at a leading publisher. While he is planning an anthology, affable Alan Rodgers has another new story in Graham Masterton's international *Scare Care* anthology and has just sold his first novel to Bantam Books. His article entitled "Putting It On the Editor's Desk" was an essential part of *How to Write Tales of Horror, Fantasy & Science Fiction*.

RAY RUSSELL

Unclassifiable but ever classy, the executive editor of *Playboy* during its formative, first seven years, Russell is a writer's writer whose story, "Sardonicus," and novel, *Incubus*, were made into memorable motion pictures—the latter involving a six-figure sale. Among his other books are *The Case Against Satan*, *Haunted Castles*, and what Ray calls his "comédies noires": *The Colony*, *Princess Pamela*, *The Book of Hell* and *The Bishop's Daughter*. Short stories of his that have been or soon will be endlessly reprinted include such classics as "Xong of Xuxan," "Comet Wine," "The Charm," and "The Secret of Rowena." His work is virtually the definition of "originality" and "professional."

JESSICA AMANDA SALMONSON
Currently editing a sequel to her Stephen King–introduced anthology, *Tales by Moonlight*, Jessica Salmonson is a shrewdly witty, editorially demanding, extraordinarily well-read, versatile Washingtonian whose work has appeared all over the commercial and small press. Her story in the limited anthology *Nukes*—"The View from Mt. Futaba"—combined her intelligent interests in the nature of war, Japan, and women's roles. Jessica's story collections include *Innocent of Evil*, her novels *Ou Lu Khen and the Beautiful Madwoman* and *Tomoe Gozen*.

CHARLES R. SAUNDERS
The creator of Imaro, the fascinating "black Tarzan" of the DAW series, Saunders is a pointedly witty, jovial, Canadian-based giant who happens to be one of the finest fantasists alive today. Writer of the screenplay for Roger Corman's *Amazon*, Saunders also has recently written the novelization of the major motion picture, *Erzulie*. Versatile writer, teacher, basketball enthusiast and small press supporter, Charles R. Saunders is fully expected to have a career ahead of him as big as he is.

STEVE RASNIC TEM
Although Tem has quickly sprung to the top ranks of America's admired writers of horror, until Avon published *Excavation* in 1987, he'd done it with short fiction. Only a handful of weirdworkers, since the heyday of Charles Beaumont, have become well-known principally because of their short stories. Steve Tem managed it by writing well enough to appear in *Twilight Zone*, the *Shadows* and *Whispers* series, *Weirdbook*, *Asimov's*, and the *Night Visions* anthologies. He is also an award-winning poet. His novel-in-progress is titled *New Blood*.

F. PAUL WILSON
Horror *and* science fiction writer, full-time physician, composer and musician, father, Paul Wilson is a laid-back, likable man barely into his forties—and one of the most respected writers

alive in both his genres of choice. Consistently nominated for Nebula awards from Science Fiction Writers of America, Paul—at the moment this is written—is also in the running for Horror Writers of America's first Bram Stoker short story awards (for "Traps" in *Night Cry*, "Dat-Tay-Vao" in *Amazing*). His novel *The Keep* will be read as long as any horror novel written in the last quarter of this century.

GAHAN WILSON
The writer of the column "Screen" for *Twilight Zone*; arguably the wittiest and most macabre cartoonist ever to grace *Playboy*'s pages (repeatedly); and the writer of the famous story entitled "The Manuscript of Dr. Arness"—they're all the same guy, it's that simple. How he's done it and also written one of this anthology's freshest and most line-blurring tales when he seems relaxed, pleasant, unhurried, and enviably young, no one is quite sure. We must remain satisfied just to know that Gahan plans to write *more* fiction—and we'll fight to be first in line to read it!

DOUGLAS E. WINTER
The creator of a series of splendid short stories he's called "legal gothics," the impeccable, sociable and witty Winter is a man for all seasons. His critical writings have run in the *Washington Post, Cleveland Plain-Dealer, Philadelphia Inquirer* and magazines as diverse as *Saturday Review, Harper's Bazaar,* and *Rod Serling's Twilight Zone.* Doug's "Darkness Absolute: The Standards of Excellence" was a vital feature of *How to Write Tales of Horror, Fantasy & Science Fiction,* and he may best be known as the perspicacious author of *Stephen King: The Art of Darkness* and *Faces of Fear.* At present, Doug is working on his first novel, a collaboration with Charlie Grant.

J. N. WILLIAMSON (EDITOR)
At age nineteen, I was made a titular-investitured member of the Baker Street Irregulars; quite a bit, after that, was anti-climax. Being a singing recording artist, astrologer, detective, and combined father and stepfather of six wasn't. My novels include *Noonspell, Ghost,* and *The Evil One*; my roughly one-hundred short pieces have been written for publications

including *Tales From Ellery Queen's, Rod Serling's Twilight Zone*, Underwood-Miller's *Reign of Terror, Nukes, Scare Care, Night Cry, The Best of The Horror Show, 14 Vicious Valentines*, and *Whispers VI*. My first novel appeared in 1979; number thirty will be *The Black School* from Dell Books.